2ND ANNEX

The Gambler

Also by Olle Högstrand

ON THE PRIME MINISTER'S ACCOUNT

The Gambler

OLLE HÖGSTRAND

Translated from the Swedish by Alan Blair

PANTHEON BOOKS

A Division of Random House, New York

Library of Congress Cataloging in Publication Data
Högstrand, Olle E. 1933–
The Gambler.

Translation of Spelarna.
   I. Title.
PZ4. H693Gam3   [PT9876.18.0327]   839.7′3′74   73-7028
ISBN 0-394-48506-8

Manufactured in the United States of America by
The Colonial Press Inc., Clinton, Mass.

First American Edition

To my Barbro

The Gambler

The Trainer

JAN LINDGREN WAS standing at the stable door. He was twenty-eight, with ginger hair and a slim figure. He was dressed in gray pants and a red nylon jacket with a yellow cross on the back. Around his neck hung a stop watch in a rubber case.

There are many different kinds of trainers. Some—quite a lot in fact—drink and neglect the horses. Others simply don't know their job. They have never learned it properly and can't handle their precious charges. A number are skillful trainers but bad sulky drivers. Their horses are the picture of health but are never given a chance to show what they can do, since they are never really put through their paces.

Then there are good trainers who are also excellent drivers. Jan Lindgren was one of them. He was all the rage in Värmland. He had dozens of horses in training; one of them was the three-year-old stallion Stylist. In the program the horse was down as being owned by Stable Stylist, which was a pseudonym for the journalist Karl Berger.

"Hi, Kalle," Lindgren greeted me. "So you've found your way home to Årjäng. Stylist has the stall right at the end on the left."

"How does he seem?" I asked.

"He's shaping up pretty well," he replied. "Nice easy gait around 1.26. I think he'll win this evening."

That sounded all right. I had bought Stylist after a very unexpected win at Solvalla. The horse had been hideously expensive and now it was high time he started paying off the debt.

"How many horses do you have here this year?"

"I brought twenty. My brother's here giving me a hand. There he is, by the way."

3

Håkan Lindgren was not unlike his brother. He had the same ginger hair but was more stocky. He was two years older but had never had his brother's success. Håkan was a good hand with horses and had once had a trainer's license, but didn't do very well. When Jan became successful Håkan started working for him, and now acted as a kind of assistant trainer.

Håkan held out a strong weather-beaten hand in greeting.

"Well, well, a visitor from Stockholm," he said. "Are you on vacation?"

"Yes," I replied. "I'm staying here for a month."

"Is Sam Boy ready?" Jan asked.

"Sure," Håkan said. "Bring out Sammy!"

A girl of seventeen or eighteen led Sam Boy out, he was one of Jan's publicity horses, one of Prince Sam's old offspring, and at the age of eight had taken a new lease on life with Lindgren, having won seventy-five thousand kronor in less than two years.

The girl was holding the bay firmly. Despite his age Sam Boy was a ruffian. He was bursting with surplus energy, which he tried to work off by knocking the girl down with his forelegs. She spoke soothingly to her bad-tempered charge and he gradually calmed down.

"Try him out on a proper heat," Jan told his brother.

It was part of Jan Lindgren's method never to drive when he was training the horses. He generally left this to the stablemen.

Håkan climbed into the sulky and Sam Boy set off toward the track as if shot from a gun.

Jan laughed.

"There's a rascal if you like," he said with' warmth in his voice. "When I first got him for training I couldn't do a thing with him. Scared out of his wits at the mere sight of a sulky."

"How did you win him over?" I asked.

"With food and coaxing" was the answer. "Let's go over to the rail and see how Sammy performs when Håkan puts him through a heat. Coming, Anette?"

Anette was evidently the girl who looked after Sam Boy. She was pretty. She was wearing blue jeans and a large overblouse.

"You've met Håkan's wife, haven't you?" Jan asked.

"No, actually, I haven't. I didn't know he had such a young wife."

She opened her mouth for the first time.

"I'm older than I look," she said. "Most people think I'm only about eighteen, but in fact I'm twenty-three."

I muttered a suitable answer.

"Don't you believe me?" she asked.

"Of course I believe you. Why shouldn't I?"

"I don't know."

We had reached the rail and stood just by the exit from the stable. There was a pungent but not unpleasant smell from a heap of manure immediately behind us. A couple of kittens were scampering about, quite unconcerned by all that was going on around them.

At first Sam Boy was made to do a couple of laps to limber up. He was still inclined to act up and was trotting with a kicking strap. It was stretched across his hindquarters and was to prevent him from kicking the driver behind him.

Jan Lindgren checked against the stop watch that Sam Boy wasn't going too fast. After another lap Jan shouted to his brother.

"Give him two thousand at thirty tempo and let him speed the last five."

Håkan drove the back way to the straight. There he volted with the horse a couple of turns and then he started. Sam Boy "lay" down and trotted. He was dashing along and the driver was evidently having difficulty in keeping the speed down.

After one and a half laps he gave Sammy his head. The stallion became still lower and now you could see that he was really going fast. When horse and driver passed the judges' tower Jan Lindgren pressed his stop watch. He looked at it and didn't seem able to believe what he saw.

"Did he move fast?" I asked.

Without answering he held onto the watch and let me look. The hand showed 37 seconds. That meant that Sam Boy had trotted the last five hundred at the rate of 1.14.

"Are you sure you pressed it at the right post?"

5

"I don't usually make a mistake. Did you take the time, Anette?"

The girl was standing with one hand in her pocket. She pulled out a stop watch and checked.

"Mine says a good 1.14 the last five," she said. "He's fine now."

Jan Lindgren still looked incredulous but submitted to the evidence. At that moment Sam Boy came storming into the stableyard at full speed. Håkan was dragging desperately at the reins but the bay was stronger. He passed us a couple of yards off and his eyes were white and wild. A second later he crashed headlong into the stable door. Håkan, still clutching the reins tightly, was flung out of the sulky.

Sam Boy staggered back from the door. For a moment he stood there, stiff-legged, then collapsed on the ground. He kicked once or twice with his hind legs, reminding me of a newsreel I had seen of Ingemar Johansson after his defeat by Floyd Patterson.

Jan had stood the whole time as though paralyzed. Now he rushed over to the horse and lifted its head. Then he looked over at his brother lying a couple of yards away with the reins wound around his powerful hands.

"He's stone dead," Jan said. "What the hell do you mean, driving like that?"

Håkan had picked himself up and was sitting on the gravel. One arm was badly scraped. He looked utterly blank and seemed unable to grasp what had happened.

"It was impossible to hold him," he muttered at last. "He was wild."

A crowd had collected around the horse's carcass. A tall, hefty man in a light blue summer suit was the focus of all eyes. I recognized him. He was a porno publisher named Bengt Ring. He was also Sam Boy's owner.

The Owner

"CHRIST, what a bit of goddam luck he was insured," Ring said, flipping a cigarette butt over his shoulder.

Ring must have been about thirty. He was said to be very rich.

I must say I was rather surprised at Ring's reaction. He was known to be difficult to please. Many trainers had found that out to their cost. He quite often moved his horses from the stable after some dispute. Sometimes it had been over mere trifles, yet Sam Boy's death didn't seem to upset him very much.

"It wasn't your fault," he said to Håkan Lindgren, who was still sitting on the gravel but got up when the horse owner addressed him.

"I saw that you did what you could," Ring went on. "What on earth was the matter with him?"

"I don't know," Håkan replied. "Once I started driving fast, Sammy neither heard nor saw a thing."

Jan Lindgren was still squatting by the dead horse's head. He stroked the muzzle, which still looked moist; white froth hung from the corners of Sam Boy's mouth.

"I think I'll ask for an autopsy," Jan said.

The journalist in me came to life.

"Do you think he was doped?" I asked.

"What else could it be? No healthy horse behaves like that."

Murmurs of agreement were heard from the many spectators of the drama. But not from Ring.

"Why should he have been doped? It's not the first time a horse has gone crazy and rushed at a door. Anyway, it's still my horse, and I don't want an autopsy."

"Are you afraid of the findings?"

It was Anette Lindgren who asked the question. It was insolent in itself, but her tone was even worse.

"What the hell have I to be afraid of? The stables are not my goddam responsibility."

"No, they're mine," Jan snapped. "And if I want an autopsy of a horse that dies suddenly, I'll damn well get it. I'll see to that. Then you can whistle for your insurance money. Anette! Try and get hold of the vet, will you?"

"How many horses have I with you?" Ring asked.

"Six," Lindgren replied. "And if you want to move them, that's okay by me."

But miraculously, Ring didn't rise to the bait. Instead, he looked about him sheepishly.

"You must do as you like, of course," Ring said. "I just thought it was unnecessary to make such a fuss because an old horse goes and breaks its neck."

"You've earned seventy-five thousand kronor on it in less than two years."

Again it was Anette who spoke and her voice was still full of dislike. Ring stared at her but said nothing. He left the circle around the horse and walked to his car.

"I'm going down to have something to eat," he said. "I'll be back for the races this evening."

Jan Lindgren nodded in answer and turned to Anette.

"I told you to call the vet."

"He's on the way," one of the spectators informed him. "There's a truck coming, too, so we can get the horse away."

After a while the vet arrived. He was a small, corpulent, shortsighted man. He made a cursory examination of Sam Boy, lifting the head and staring into the glazed eyes.

"I want an autopsy on the horse," Jan Lindgren said.

"Yes, I think it would be best, too," the vet replied. "We'd better get in touch with the judge first."

The judge at the course was one of the local dentists. He had held the leading office as far back as anyone could remember. He was reputed to know nothing whatever about the sport to which he had devoted himself for so many years. On the other hand, he was a good mixer and was, no doubt, valuable to the trotting association in a social way.

"Do you think he has turned up at the track yet?" Jan asked.

"No, I don't suppose he has. At any rate, we must get the horse out of the way before we do anything else. It must be sent to the Veterinary College if there's to be an autopsy. I think I've space on the farm where the carcass can lie for the time being."

The vet lived some distance out of Årjäng on a farm where he bred dogs.

Meanwhile a truck had driven up. With the aid of a crane the horse was heaved onto the truck and it drove off.

The crowd outside Lindgren's stable door slowly dispersed. The trainer, his brother, and his sister-in-law went into the stable and I went with them. We were all feeling depressed. It was the worst for Håkan Lindgren. He was walking in a daze. His wife tried to take his hand but he snatched it away.

"It wasn't your fault," she said. "Was it, Janne?"

"No, it could have happened to anybody."

"That's what I think," Håkan said. "All the same, I can't help feeling I'm to blame. Sam Boy always did pull, but this time it was worse than ever. It was like trying to hold back a car. And of course it would have to be one of Ring's horses."

"Never mind about Ring," Anette snapped. "He didn't give a damn about the horse. He's only scared there might be a hitch over the insurance."

"Do you think he doped Sam Boy?"

She looked surprised at my question. That possibility had evidently not occurred to her.

"Why should he? It was his horse."

"If so, it wouldn't be the first time. Maybe he wanted Sam Boy to show up badly this evening; maybe he'd back some other horse."

"No, it doesn't add up," Jan Lindgren said. "I know he's a bastard, but I don't think he'd go as far as that."

No one said anything more for a while. Håkan dressed his lacerated arm with Anette's help and Jan sat down on a chair without a word and closed his eyes. I left them and went to have a look at my Stylist. He seemed in fine fettle and gobbled up his oats. I slipped him a lump of sugar, which he accepted after careful inspection.

I heard someone come into the stall. It was Anette.

9

"He looks fine," she said. "If all goes as it should, he'll win easily this evening. But there won't be any odds. He's a favorite in all the papers after his last showing."

Stylist shoved me with his muzzle, demanding more sugar. I gave him another lump. The girl was still there.

"You don't seem to think much of Bengt Ring," I said.

"No. I loathe him."

"Why?"

She hesitated.

"I dislike that type of person," she said at last. "All he thinks of is money."

"He's not the only one, surely?"

"No, but he's capable of anything at all to get his own way. Utterly ruthless."

"Anyway, he let his horses stay with Jan, though he did have cause to move them."

"Oh, I expect he had good reasons," Anette retorted.

She was very attractive in her anger. Very attractive indeed.

I noted her outbreak of temperament and went out to Jan and Håkan. They sat talking but broke off when they saw me. Håkan now had a large bandage on his underarm.

"I was just saying to Håkan that he's to drive this evening. He has a couple of races that he'd rather skip. But I think he'd better drive."

"I think so too," I agreed.

Håkan heaved a sigh.

"I'm damned if I ever want to see another horse," he growled, going out into the alley between the stalls, where he began to wind a bandage around the legs of the horse that was tied there. Jan smiled.

"Håkan's crazy about horses. He'll stick to this job as long as he lives."

I decided to pump Jan a little. I was interested in Anette's background.

"Where does Anette come from?"

He looked at me.

"From Karlstad," he said. "She's a great girl. She passed her university entrance exam and shouldn't go messing around trotting stables. But she's as gone on horses as Håkan is."

"How did he get hold of her?" I asked.

"She's been haunting my stables for years and, well, that was that. Maybe you don't know that she was once engaged to Bengt Ring."

"Was she now!" Perhaps this explained her angry dislike of Ring.

"Why was it broken off?"

"I don't really know. I suppose she got tired of him. I got fed up with him myself long ago. He buys one wreck after the other and expects me to make them trot."

"You succeeded with Sam Boy."

"Yes, I did. But that doesn't mean I can repeat the trick with every nag he buys all over Sweden."

"But he has plenty of money?"

"Well, he did have. I don't really know how things are now. Sometimes he gets behind with the training fees. That's not usually a good sign. Besides, he bets heavily and stupidly."

"Is he married?"

"Sure. She's quite a dish. Her name's Mia. Well, we can talk more this evening, I must see to the horses now. Take it easy and back Stylist. He'll win by a mile."

That sounded reassuring. I left the Lindgrens and went to the new stable café and had some food. The place was crowded and all around me everyone was talking of Sam Boy's sudden death.

"If that horse wasn't pumped full of drugs I'll give up racing," said a Gothenburg trainer with a florid face.

I was inclined to agree with him. But it would be a week or so before the result of the autopsy was known. I'd find out soon enough.

So I thought.

The Gambler

By DEGREES my slumbering professional ambitions came to life and I made my way to the press tower. I called up my newspaper and improvised a bit about Sam Boy's death, hinting quite openly that the horse was drugged.

Then I went down to the track, where people were starting to gather, although it was a good hour yet until the first race. I went on toward the stables, past the natural grandstands on the rise.

"Any tips, Kalle?"

I was deep in thought and didn't grasp at first that the question was addressed to me. But I recognized the voice. It belonged to an almost morbidly corpulent man who was sitting on a white bench with a stop watch in his hand.

"Hi, Bjarne," I greeted him. "How are things?"

"Oh, might be worse."

Bjarne Svensson was an old schoolmate of mine. Now and then we ran across each other at some harness track or other. He was never called anything but the Railroader; at one time he had had a job with the State Railroad. Nowadays he was a full-time gambler. Horses and poker.

"How's business?" I asked.

"So-so. I thought you might give me a couple of winners."

"Back Stylist," I said.

"I might just as well go to the bank and exchange the money," he retorted. "He'll hardly give you your money back. I've heard he already does twenty-five and nothing can beat that. If you want to win, of course."

The Railroader was one of those gamblers who never take anything for granted. Over the years he had mastered the art of muscling in on nearly every big job. With his unerring intuition, and by snooping about and keeping his ears open, he usually

12

managed to ferret out when some driver was out to make quick money.

"I don't think you need be afraid that Janne Lindgren doesn't want to win," I replied.

He sighed heavily.

"I never trust trotting drivers," he said. "If I did, I'd never get a cent back. But you don't bet any more, so you've nothing to worry about."

He was right. It hadn't always been so. A few years ago the gambling demon had very nearly caught me in his clutches, but I escaped in time.

"Do you remember when the guys from Dalsland took their nags down to Åby and settled who was to win on the way down? Those were the days! I was well in with one of them and he tipped me off in return for a promise that I wouldn't put more than five hundred on each winner."

"Did you stick to the bargain?"

"Yes, except once. I put three thousand on a horse that was dead certain. The trouble was that Alf Dahlroth had a dark one that went still faster."

"Your sins will find you out," I moralized.

"They did that time, at any rate."

"But you surely agree that the sport is cleaner now?"

"I doubt it. I think it's just that the methods have become more subtle."

Svensson stood up with an effort. It was hard to imagine that he had once been a promising sprinter who had run a hundred meters in 11.2 without training. He pocketed his stop watch.

"Were you on your way to the stables?" he asked.

I nodded. Together we went through the barrier, the guard waving us past without asking to see our stable cards. As horseowner and journalist I had the right of admission, but it was doubtful if the Railroader had. This is one of the big drawbacks in Swedish trotting. The stables swarm with people who have no business being there.

We went into the stable café and elbowed our way to the counter.

13

"Would you like a beer?" I asked the Railroader.

He shook his head.

"No, coffee for me."

I remembered then that he was a teetotaler. I got myself a beer, for which the place charged an exorbitant price.

Svensson bought coffee and three cream cakes. He had a sweet tooth and was evidently a gormandizer.

It was barely an hour now to the first race and the horse transports were beginning to arrive. Mammoth trucks from Karlstad and Örebro, ramshackle vehicles from near and far, and countless private cars with the horse van as a trailer.

Svensson put away his revolting cream cakes and I downed my beer. We went on to Lindgren's stable. The trainer didn't look too pleased when we turned up.

"Would you mind marking my program?" Svensson asked.

Lindgren seemed annoyed.

"I really only give tips to my horse owners," he said.

"They're not the only ones who back your horses, are they?" the Railroader retorted in his peculiar treble voice.

"No, you're right there," Lindgren admitted.

He took Svensson's program and began marking in his tips. It's a nuisance for trainers everywhere, having to oblige all the punters in quest of tips. The horse owners of course come first, but who knows when a heavy gambler like the Railroader might take it into his head to buy a horse.

A trainer is nothing but a small businessman and can't afford to get on the wrong side of a future customer.

It took Jan Lindgren a couple of minutes to tip the eight races. He seldom hesitated, quickly checking the names of the horses he thought would be the evening's winners.

He handed the program back to Svensson, who glanced through it with the same inscrutable expression he put on when he was playing poker. If anyone had a poker face, he had. He was a phenomenal card player. I knew that to my cost. He was born with the gift of being able to remember hands that had been dealt years before.

He stuck the program into the hip pocket of his enormous,

14

tailor-made pants. With his huge body, he could never buy clothes off the rack; nothing fitted him.

"No outsiders exactly," he said rather crossly.

Lindgren smiled. His white teeth gleamed in the semidarkness of the harness room.

"No, I tip the ones I think are going to win."

Svensson looked very disbelieving, but did thank Lindgren as he left the stable to continue to the next trainer. After that he was sure to ask some horse owners, a couple of apprentices, and possibly an official.

For the Railroader, betting was not a pastime but a profession. He was an expert at his job and left nothing to chance. He covered himself against all eventualities.

"Do you know him well?" I asked Lindgren.

"No, not very, but he has been poking about the stables here for as long as I can remember."

"He didn't seem too confident about your tips."

"No, he never is. He came take them or leave them."

"Don't you ever get mad at all the people who want tips?"

"Sure, but what can I do? If they don't get their way, they begin to smell a rat and rumors start flying around. I can't afford that."

"Don't you think that sometimes they may have good reasons for their suspicions?"

Lindgren didn't answer at once.

"Of course they may have," he said at last.

He shot me a glance.

"Remember, I'm talking to you now as a horse owner and not as a journalist," he added. "But you know as well as I do that certain things happen now and then."

"Why, do you imagine?"

Lindgren jerked his thumb at the wall to the next stable, where the trainer Sven Nilsson hung out.

"Don't get me wrong, but let's take Svenne as an example. He has ten horses in training. None of them is a star. In a year they bring in perhaps fifty thousand. He gets ten percent and the training fees. Now I made over six hundred thousand last year, and after deducting all expenses I cleared a good fifty thousand.

15

Make the same calculation with Svenne's figures and maybe you'll see what I mean."

"That temptation may be too great for some people."

"Something of the kind."

"But isn't it possible to squeeze some money out of the actual training fee?"

"Only at the expense of the horses. Hungry and lame horses don't win any money, I can tell you that."

I left the harness room as Jan took out a thermos and poured a mug of coffee. He asked if I'd like some but I said no.

Out in the alley Anette was already at work on Stylist, who was to run in the very first race. He stood there twitching his ears but was otherwise very calm.

Anette glanced up at me and smiled.

"His laziness is misleading," she said. "But rather that than a fiery horse."

"Seen anything more of Ring?" I asked, patting the stallion's neck.

"No, but I expect he'll turn up before long. If I were Jan I wouldn't take on Ring's horses. You know, don't you, that I was once engaged to him?"

I was rather surprised that she herself brought up the subject.

"I did hear someone say it," I answered.

"Jan?"

"Yes, I think so."

"I was young and silly and impressed by his money and cars."

"You needn't confess to me," I said. "Why did you call it off, by the way?"

"I met Håkan. He's a good guy."

She lapsed into a defensive attitude when she said that.

"I don't doubt it for a moment. Where is Håkan?"

"Having a bite to eat. I saw you with the Railroader. Do you know him?"

"Sure. He's from Årjäng. We're old schoolmates."

"He's a full-time gambler, isn't he?"

"Yes. Why do you ask?"

"I just wondered. I've seen him together with Ring once or twice."

16

"That's not so strange. They both bet heavily."

"I didn't say it was strange."

She fastened the sulky on, deftly and with a practiced hand. Anette was a capable stable girl.

"Have you never thought of driving yourself? Girls are allowed to nowadays."

"I don't want to."

She turned and shouted to Jan.

"He's ready now," she said. "They'll soon be ringing for the first race. Try for once to be in time for the post parade."

Anette used an almost motherly tone to Jan. It happened fairly often that he was fined fifty kronor for "late arrival at the post parade," as it said in the judges' reports.

A minute later Lindgren came out into the alley. He looked, as usual, very smart. Anette handed him the reins and he drove out with Stylist.

Jan Lindgren looked the very picture of life itself as he swung himself expertly up into the sulky. The hair sticking out under the driving helmet caught the evening sun.

For some reason the image engraved itself on my memory. Many times later I was to recall that particular situation.

As Stylist trotted indolently onto the track I caught sight of the Railroader. He was standing by the rail.

Together with Ring.

The Syringe

I LEFT THE STABLES and returned to the press tower. Only one colleague had come.

If he could be called a colleague. Erik Olsson wasn't really a journalist at all but a sales clerk at the Cooperative Stores. He had a job on the side, however, with a Värmland newspaper; he also made a bit extra by phoning in the results to a news agency in Gothenburg and to a couple of Stockholm papers.

Olsson knew almost nothing about trotting. When the races were over he would turn to one of the epxerts, and his words never varied: "What's to be said about this?"

If the expert was kind, Olsson got his information and put together a clumsy report which was published in the paper the next day. Olsson was a very inoffensive man but rather trying.

"Well, well, well," he exclaimed when he caught sight of me.

I muttered some sort of answer, wishing I didn't have to talk to him. He was sure to ask me about my job. No doubt Olsson had once cherished a secret dream of being employed by one of the big national newspapers.

My guess was right. He immediately steered the conversation around to my work. Had I made any long journeys recently? Oh. Hm . . . Yes, he'd read about it in the paper.

"It must be great having a job that allows you to travel," he said.

I agreed. He talked away and I groaned inwardly. I detest dissecting myself and my work. I write for a big morning paper, in the winter concentrating on skating and in the summer on swimming. Like all other sports journalists on big papers I have to travel a lot. I'm considered fairly good at my job. As a journalist I meet a lot of people I have to talk to. In my spare time I keep mostly to myself.

My background is perhaps a little unusual. I started as a general reporter on another paper, specializing in politics and dabbling in sports on the side.

It's almost exotic for a Swedish sports writer to have any interests other than sports, drink, and girls. Many burn themselves out before they're forty, alcoholics and old before their time.

I try to keep aloof. It's not so easy, but I'm sure it's my only chance of surviving as a human being. A man I know has worked for over thirty years as a sports journalist. Nowadays he refuses to go anywhere.

He's an editor on the paper. He writes good poetry, which he never tries to publish. He's a brilliant mathematician but makes no use of his gift. He has a natural aptitude for sculpture. Gustav is always trying to persuade me to quit.

18

"You're an intelligent guy," he says. "Stop this idiocy before it's too late."

"Why do you keep on yourself?" I retort.

He orders another beer and looks mournful.

"It's too late," he replies.

The loudspeakers announced that the start would be called in three minutes. It gave me an excuse to get away from the garrulous Olsson.

"I'll go down and bet ten kronor," I said.

"On which?" Olsson asked, including me in the band of experts.

"I don't know."

I ran downstairs and made my way up toward the start. It was a 2,200 meter race and this meant that the horses started just at the entrance to the straight.

I didn't bother to bet.

Stylist was standing at the start. Jan saw me and saluted me with the whip. The horses began to volt. Stylist seemed just as unconcerned as when he was in the stables. He appeared to regard the whole procedure as a necessary evil that had to be endured.

"Ready!" bawled the voice up in the judges' tower. I glanced at Lindgren. He was concentrating hard as he volted.

"One!"

The horses turned in the direction of the start. Stylist was well there.

"Two!"

The horses rushed toward the starting tape.

"Off!"

The starting tape was released and Stylist at once took the lead without any apparent effort.

After the first lap Stylist was still leading. I pressed my stop watch. He certainly wasn't going very fast: 1.29 the first 1,000 meters.

As the horses swung into the straight the position was the same. The field spread out like a fan. For a moment it looked as if all of them would outflank Stylist.

Lindgren did one thing only. He gave Stylist a smart straight right on the bay rump. The stallion responded by flying ahead of the others by at least three lengths.

It was a very easy win.

Stylist received friendly applause during the victory parade. He still looked just as lazy.

I went to the stables to thank the great lout for repaying the first installment on his purchase price. Anette had already unharnessed him when I got there.

"Look," she said. "He's not even out of breath."

She was quite right. Stylist graciously accepted my sugar lump and looked at me with bright eyes.

Håkan Lindgren came up to me.

"Well, provided his legs hold, you've got the makings of a first-rate horse there," he said. "Hasn't he, Janne?"

"It seems like it. In this game you can never take anything for granted, but he has talent all right."

A number of people came up and congratulated me. One of them was Ring.

"Is he for sale?" he asked.

I did some quick thinking.

"No," I replied.

"Name a price now," he said in a wheedling tone.

I felt anger beginning to smolder inside me. I knew from experience that it could easily blaze up. I tried to keep my temper and managed to make my voice honeyed,—and spiteful.

"Get this into your head, Ring," I said with a smile. "Money won't buy everything. Besides, I've heard that your credit is none too good any more."

There were a lot of people around us and Ring flushed. For a moment I thought he was going to hit me.

But he didn't.

"Go to hell," he snapped.

I was pleased to find that I was no longer angry. I preferred to ignore him.

Ring stood there opening and clenching his fists. Anette looked at him with brilliant eyes.

Then she turned them on me, fixing me for a few seconds. She

20

still seemed almost ecstatic. There was no doubt at all that she disliked Ring.

"If you'd like some coffee, I think there's a drop left," she said, jerking her head toward the back of the stables.

"Thanks, I would."

I managed to jostle my way into the harness room past horses, sulkies, and people. It was empty in there. Jan had already gone out to the next race. I couldn't find the thermos flask.

"I don't see any coffee," I called.

"The thermos is in the cupboard," Anette replied.

She meant the cupboard where Jan kept his silks. They hung there neatly on their hangers. I found the thermos at once. It was standing on a small shelf that was half hidden by the clothes.

I thrust my hand in and took out the thermos. At the same time I knocked down an object that must have been lying on the shelf. It fell on the floor without making any noise other than a slight plop.

The throwaway plastic syringe rolled around a couple of times on the floor and then was still.

I bent down and picked it up carefully. The syringe was blue and a trademark was imprinted on the plastic. Glancing around quickly, I made sure I was not observed. Then I held the syringe up to the light from the single bulb in the harness room.

A few drops of a yellowish liquid flowed sluggishly inside the injection needle.

I took a handkerchief out of my pocket and quickly wrapped the syringe in it. Then I put the little package in my hip pocket.

I poured some coffee into a mug, dropped in two lumps of sugar and stirred them, and took a couple of biscuits out of a packet. I gulped down the coffee and biscuits and left the harness room.

Anette and Håkan were standing in the middle of the alley, talking. Håkan had a pleading look on his face. They didn't even glance at me as I passed them only a foot away.

"Thanks for the coffee," I said.

I left the stables and went back to the press tower, where I kept a small briefcase. I slipped the handkerchief bundle with the blue syringe into it. I was standing inside a call box.

I felt very uneasy. Taking my bottle of whisky out of the briefcase, I had a good swig.

Who had hidden the syringe in Lindgren's stable?

The Official

I SHOULD, of course, have gone to the stewards with my find. But to tell the truth the idea never occurred to me. I don't really know why.

I thought hard and found, to my surprise, that not for one moment did I suspect that it was Jan Lindgren himself who had left the syringe behind in the little stable cupboard.

Only vets are allowed to give horses injections. It is forbidden to give a horse an injection of any kind within ninety-six hours before a race. Not even vitamins are allowed during that period.

I remembered the yellowish drops inside the syringe. They were sure to be enough for an analysis by the doping experts.

Although I had met such experts a couple of times, I could hardly look them up and say, "I've a syringe here that I found in Janne Lindgren's stable. Would you mind having a look at what's in it?"

Anyway, there might be a logical explanation. It was possible that the syringe was quite legitimate. But in that case, why had it been stashed away like that?

I could, of course, ask someone in the stable. Jan, perhaps, or Håkan or Anette. But was that really a good idea? No, I had better keep my discovery to myself and see what happens.

I must admit that I didn't like the atmosphere in Lindgren's stable. There was nothing definite I could put my finger on and say, "There's something amiss here." No, it was a vague feeling in the air that disturbed me.

It might possibly have been my imagination. On the other hand, I usually have a sixth sense for atmosphere. I can feel it when something's wrong.

Intuition? Sure, but I think it's a faculty that should not be belittled. This particular detector of emotional moods has helped me many times in my job.

I am very seldom wrong. But it has happened. Several times, in fact. That's why I couldn't be absolutely sure I was right.

But the uneasiness was there. Gnawing and accusing.

I went out and watched the next race. It was another win for Jan Lindgren, who this time beat his opponents with a daring finish from an almost hopeless position. He certainly knew how to drive.

I decided not to give the matter another thought. Not just then, at any rate. I felt hungry and went down to the restaurant and had something to eat.

An old waitress I recognized eventually brought me a bit of steak as tough as leather and a pile of greasy French fries. It was horrible, but I forced it down and at least it stilled my hunger.

Then I went back to the press room. I fished out my bottle of whisky and took another swig. Erik Olsson glared at me disapprovingly but I didn't give a damn. He was a bigwig in a temperance society and regarded alcohol as the road to ruin, and, of course, he was right.

In any event I was annoyed with him.

"There's a press dinner on Friday, isn't there?"

"Yes," he replied. "But I don't think I'll go."

"Pity. We could have raced you sixty meters again." I said maliciously.

I was alluding to what had happened a couple of years before, when we had succeeded in getting Olsson thoroughly drunk at the trotting association's press dinner. In our alcoholic bullying we had forced him to race us sixty meters.

Olsson was so stoned that we gave him forty meters start, but even so we beat him by at least eighteen.

Poor Olsson went scarlet at the thought of his performance and I regretted having reminded him of his fall. It was a low thing to do.

Feeling rather ashamed, I left the press tower. On the spur of the moment I went straight to the judges' tower. I wanted to ask what the stewards planned to do about investigating Sam Boy's death.

I went to see the secretary, Allan Berggren, who was also an old acquaintance of mine. After leaving school Allan started working at the stewards' office, and through energy and capability he had now advanced to track secretary, which meant in practice that he was managing director.

"Have you a moment to spare?" I asked.

Berggren was red-haired, with a row of freckles right across his large nose. His eyes were intensely blue behind thick glasses.

"Sure," he replied.

"What do you intend to do about this business with Sam Boy?" I asked.

"There must be a post-mortem, of course."

"Do you think he was doped? You had a doping affair some years ago, didn't you?"

"Something went wrong with the analysis. We could never prove anything."

"Never any suspicions up to now that there might be something wrong in Lindgren's stable?"

"No, on the contrary. You know as well as I do that he has the reputation of being honest."

"Never any trouble with Ring?"

Berggren hesitated.

"We-ell, he's no saint."

"What do you mean?"

"You've heard of this regulation, haven't you, which says that horse owners and trainers must not take part in or organize roulette playing."

"Do you suspect Ring of being mixed up in roulette?"

"Please don't write a word about this, but we've been looking into his affairs."

"Any results?"

"No, only rumors."

"Talking of rumors, I heard today that Ring's finances are pretty shaky."

Berggren bared his lovely white teeth in a smile.

"I've also heard rumors to the effect that it was a Stockholm

24

journalist who told Ring to his face that his credit wasn't any too good."

"I see that you have a good intelligence service," I remarked, feeling rather foolish.

He smiled again.

"Oh, one hears a thing or two," he admitted. "But it's true enough that brother Ring's affairs are unsound. Where did you hear it, by the way?"

His question took me by surprise and I answered truthfully, "Janne Lindgren told me that Ring was behind with his training fees."

"Oh," Berggren said, looking thoughtful. "That's bad. That's very bad."

I couldn't quite make him out.

"What do you mean?" I asked.

"Trotting can't afford scandals like that," he said.

Was it merely my imagination or had he hesitated a second before he answered?

There was a knock at the door.

"Come in!" Berggren called.

The door opened. In came a small, dark-haired man of about forty who had a hook nose and walked with a stoop. Sven Karlsson-Gren was part of the fittings at the track. He had gypsy blood. As a child he had had severe meningitis and his brain had possibly been affected. Since then, at any rate, he had been rather dimwitted, but he knew his job.

I said hello to him. For a moment he looked puzzled and then recognized me. He actually seemed quite pleased to see me.

"Well, well, you home, are you?" he said in his broad Värmland dialect. "Remember when we caught that big pike?"

He never forgot that pike. It was several years since we had been fishing together, but whenever we met, which wasn't often, Sven reminded me of it. The event was evidently etched on his mind.

But it *was* a big pike. Over six kilos. That's not so bad for bait casting.

Karlsson-Gren, who was always called Shag—his father had gone under the same name—often talked to himself. Sometimes it

25

was almost impossible to determine when he was carrying on an ordinary conversation and when he was talking to himself.

"I saw the syringe all right," he said as he turned to the door on his way out.

I gave a start, and so did Berggren.

"What syringe?" we said with one voice.

"At Lindgren's. In the harness room. Blue it was."

"Are you telling the truth now?" Berggren asked.

Shag screwed up his little brown eyes.

"Blue it was," he repeated.

"Will you come and show us where it was?" Berggren asked.

"Sure I will."

We set off, with Shag in the lead. We took a short cut and after a couple of minutes we were at Lindgren's stable. Jan was standing in the doorway.

Berggren looked rather embarrassed.

"Er . . . ," he said at last. "Er, the thing is, Shag here says he saw a syringe in your harness room."

"I didn't even know you'd been here today," Jan said to Shag.

"Arr, I went in to get a couple of head numbers that you hadn't returned."

"And you saw a syringe?"

"Arr, that I did."

"May we come in?" Berggren asked.

"Of course you may," Jan replied.

As luck would have it there was no one else but Håkan in the stable. The third race was just about to start and everyone was standing by the rail watching.

Shag led the procession into the harness room. He opened the same cupboard where I had been earlier. He pointed to the shelf.

"It was lying there," he said.

Berggren bent forward and pulled aside a couple of nylon jackets. The thermos flask was still there but, of course, no syringe. It was in safe keeping in my briefcase.

"I don't see anything," Lindgren said.

"It was lying there, and blue it was," Shag maintained.

Berggren rubbed his chin. For a second I thought he looked

disappointed, but I may have been mistaken. He turned to poor Shag.

"Have you told anyone else about this?" he asked.

"No."

"Good. And for Christ's sake, go on keeping your mouth shut."

To his credit, Jan Lindgren kept quite calm throughout. He even appeared rather amused. And above all, sure of himself. Quite convinced that we would find nothing compromising in his well-kept stable.

There was silence for a while. Berggren was the first to speak.

"Well, that's all then. I suppose you'll have to be prepared for an inquiry later."

"Sammy, you mean?"

"Of course."

"Let's see first if the autopsy gives anything. It's by no means certain that he *was* doped."

"What's your own opinion?" I asked.

Lindgren hesitated.

"I don't really know what to think," he replied. "At first I was sure he'd been given something, but . . ."

He shrugged.

Berggren and Shag left the stable. The last I heard was Shag muttering, "Blue it was."

I had a guilty conscience and wished I could have told the poor man that he had not been mistaken. But now it was too late. However remorseful I was, the syringe was in my briefcase.

The Hotel

I STAYED at the course until all eight races were over. I was in and around Lindgren's stable, but nothing startling happened. Jan won yet another race, the last for the day.

As he changed his clothes I asked him whether he was going home to Karlstad that same evening.

27

"No, I'm staying here the whole week," he said. "In any case I'm driving on both Friday and Sunday."

"Where are you staying?" I asked.

"At the Nordmarken."

I too had a room at the old hotel in the market place. I had also managed to wangle a private bath. It wasn't cheap, of course, but not exorbitant either compared with the fancy prices at the new luxury hotels in Stockholm.

And the food was good. I really appreciated that.

"And you're still single?" I asked.

"A guy can't be married when he's never at home. I travel about from one racecourse to the next the whole year. Women won't stand for that."

"What about Anette?"

"She's the exception. You can't expect everyone to be as crazy about trotting as she is."

I decided to change the subject.

"What do you think made Shag get it into his head that he'd seen a syringe in your stable?"

"Darned if I know. He's a bit touched, you know that. I expect he imagined it all."

"Expect?"

"Everything's possible," Lindgren said rather vaguely. "How will you get down to the hotel?"

"Walk."

"Wait a second and I'll give you a lift. I'm almost ready."

Lindgren's expensive-looking sports car was parked in the lot outside the course. I folded myself awkwardly into the front seat beside him. I know nothing whatever about cars—I don't even have a driver's license—but I did realize that Lindgren was a good driver. Smoothly and deftly he guided the small car down the serpentine road to the town center.

He spotted a parking space near the hotel and darted in under the nose of a Gothenburg car that was after the same spot. Lindgren grinned.

"No good being meek and modest," he said.

We got out and went into the hotel. I asked for my key and

went upstairs to my room, carrying my briefcase with its contents; the bottle of whisky, books, and the blue syringe.

I got undressed, had a shower, put on fresh clothes, and gulped down the day's third whisky. This time, out of a glass for a change. I had a headache and my temples were pounding.

To be on the safe side I took a look in the briefcase. Yes, the blue syringe was still there.

I took it out gingerly, dimly aware that I should be careful of fingerprints, but then the whole thing struck me as absurd and I put the syringe into my old blue toilet case that had once been given to me by an airline.

I was thirsty and longed for a beer. Unfortunately I hadn't one handy, so I had to settle for another whisky. I held up the bottle and saw that I had consumed quite a lot during the day. But I was on vacation, after all.

Gradually I pulled myself together and went down to the dining room. I was afraid it would be full. One of the kind waitresses caught sight of me, however.

"Where would you like to sit?" she asked. "I have a table in here and one outside."

I told her I'd rather sit inside. Sidewalk cafés, with gasoline fumes, flies, and noise, have never attracted me.

I was given a window table. I ordered pickled herring, akvavit, and a steak. The beer was nice and cold, the akvavit had been correctly chilled so that mist formed on the glass, and the meat was tender. I felt content with life.

I'm a fast eater as a rule, but now I took my time. It was after eleven o'clock, but I was on vacation and did not need to think of tomorrow. Not much, at any rate.

I had got as far as coffee and brandy when I heard voices I recognized through the half-open window. Jan Lindgren was dining outside with the secretary of the trotting association, Allan Berggren.

I was rather astonished that they were having a meal together. I had never had the impression that they knew each other very well. I must admit that my curiosity was aroused.

Lindgren and Berggren were talking quietly, but by straining

29

my ears I could hear snatches of their conversation, which seemed to be dominated by the trainer. At times it sounded almost like an interrogation with short mumbling answers from Berggren.

"How long will it take before the result of the autopsy is known?" Lindgren asked.

"At least a week."

"What will they examine?"

"I don't know. You'll have to ask the vet."

"That quack! He knows nothing about it."

I was beginning to feel tired and, truth to tell, I was rather stoned. I found it increasingly hard to hear all that was said outside the window.

I did hear, however, that Berggren was drinking pretty heavily. He ordered one grog after the other, which wasn't really like him. Lindgren drank nothing, as usual. He hardly ever touched liquor, and one very rarely saw him with a glass of any kind.

"How's business?" I heard Lindgren ask.

"Oh, so-so."

"I just wondered. As you gather, I'm rather interested."

They were evidently talking about the affairs of the Nordmarken Track. As far as I knew, the trotting association was in a sound financial position, unlike many other tracks around the country which were on the verge of bankruptcy. Årjäng had built and invested in good time before the credit squeeze.

It was a nice warm July evening. The air was as soft as velvet. Out in the street the cars were driving back and forth. It seemed to be the young people's evening pastime. There had been a lot of girls out there to begin with, but now there were only a few left. The rest had been picked up.

For the first time I had a good look around the dining room and saw Bengt Ring at a corner table. He was with two other men and three girls.

I recognized one of the guys. He was a horse owner and gambler from Gothenburg. He nearly always visited Årjäng in the summer. Some years ago I had been in a poker game when, in a single night, he had stripped a wretched farmer of twenty-one thousand kronor. The money was intended for a mortgage and the man had to leave the farm.

30

Just as well, perhaps. He would have been rationalized out of existence in any case. Small holdings don't pay any more. Get the people into the big towns. They'll do well there and be happy in high-rise apartments in some dreary suburb.

I couldn't remember having seen the girls before. Local talent, probably. One of them was no doubt Ring's wife. He was married, Lindgren had said.

Ring must have noticed I was looking at him, for he shot me a glance, and an ugly one at that. Spiteful. I smiled back and bowed with exaggerated courtesy.

At first it looked as if he would get up from the table and come over and hit me. The girl next to him, however, gripped his arm and restrained him.

Yes, it must be his wife, I thought.

I heard Lindgren and Berggren outside getting ready to go. They paid the bill. Berggren was pretty drunk and knocked over the chair as he stood up.

"What the hell am I to do?" he slurred.

"Don't worry," the other man said. "It'll be all right."

What was it that would be all right? The waitress came over to my table. She had been working the hotel for as long as I could remember. Her name was Svea and she treated all guests with the same indulgent, motherly care.

"Do you want anything more to drink before we close?"

I thought it over.

"No, I don't think so," I said at last.

"Quite right, too," Svea said firmly. "Anyway, you've got all you want up in your room."

I paid the bill; it was a stiff one. Luckily I didn't have to worry about money. I drew a good salary from the newspaper and, in addition, had quite a lot left from my big win, even after I had bought Stylist. I must say I enjoyed being, to some extent, financially independent.

Out in the vestibule I bumped into Lindgren. He looked irritatingly perky. My head felt most peculiar, as if it were floating in the air all by itself like some strange kind of satellite.

"Is it quite fitting for a champion trainer to have a tête-à-tête with the track secretary?" I asked.

It was intended as a joke but Lindgren looked embarrassed.

"We had some things to talk over," he said.

"So I heard."

"What did you hear?"

"I heard you talking. I was having dinner inside. You were sitting outside and the window was open."

Lindgren looked hard at me for a moment or two. Then he smoothed his hair and yawned. A few seconds earlier he had been the picture of vitality.

"I'm so damned tired," he said. "I always am after racing. See you tomorrow, eh?"

"Yes, I'll look in at the stables."

He said good night and disappeared up the stairs. I toyed with the idea of taking a walk but changed my mind and went up to my room.

I got undressed and, walking over to the window, opened it wide.

The street was almost deserted. I saw a man get into his car and drive off.

For someone who was tired after a long, hard day of racing, Jan Lindgren drove his car in great style.

A woman, I thought, and went to bed.

The Morning

SMALL ANGRY MEN were hammering busily inside my head when I awoke in the morning. They went away only after I'd eaten a substantial breakfast with a lot of coffee, eggs, and bacon. And a bottle of beer.

I went out to the kiosk and bought the local paper and a couple of other dailies. Perman, a local reporter, wrote quite openly that Sam Boy's death had been caused by dope. Perman has never been afraid to speak his mind.

After I had read the papers, I put a call through to my own

paper in Stockholm and talked to the assistant editor. I was told I could cover the Sam Boy story if I liked. My miserly second self came to life.

"Do I get paid for it?" I asked.

"Same old Kalle," the assistant editor said sorrowfully. "Thinks of nothing but money. Oh, well. I expect we can spare a couple of hundred."

"Thanks, big chief," I said, putting down the phone.

He'd hit me where it hurt. Money does mean quite a lot to me. But I'm not the only one.

It took me a quarter of an hour to walk up to the track. I came past the fairground where the small gray stalls were huddling in the morning sun. I thought back to the days of my boyhood and could once again hear the torrent of words from the barkers and smell the all-pervading cabbage soup, the traditional fair dish.

When I was small, the third Thursday of September was the great day of the fair. We were given a school holiday and perhaps given five kronor to spend.

It was nearly eleven o'clock when I reached the stables. The first person I saw was Shag, who was tidying up after the visitors of last evening.

He was working doggedly and energetically. I saw that he had filled two large jute sacks with empty bottles.

"Do you sell them at the liquor stores?" I asked.

He looked up at me.

"Yes, but I'm allowed to," he said.

I wasn't so sure, but nobody begrudged his earning a little on the side.

I still had a guilty conscience about the syringe.

"I think you were right yesterday," I said. "You did see a syringe in Lindgren's cupboard."

"That I did," he agreed.

"Who do you suppose put it there?"

He smiled slyly but said nothing. I repeated my question.

"I know a lot, I do," he said at last.

Then he retreated into his shell and seemed oblivious of the fact that I was standing beside him. I knew him well enough to realize that it would be impossible to get anything more out of him.

The last I saw of him was when he lifted one of the sacks of bottles onto his back and plodded off to a little room he had in the stable buildings. He looked as if he would collapse under the heavy burden.

After this short conversation with Shag I went to Lindgren's stable. Håkan and Anette were there but I saw no sign of Jan.

"Where's Janne?" I asked.

"He said he'd be here about twelve," Håkan replied.

"How does Stylist seem today?"

"Just fine. Eats everything he can get."

"What about his legs?"

"Splendid," Anette said. "Don't you worry about him. He has four very nice legs."

And you have nice legs, too, I thought.

By nature and habit I'm a true pessimist. So, ever since I've had Stylist I've been convinced that he would go to pieces before he even made a start.

Now he *had* made his first start and had won 950 kronor. Not much, but better than nothing.

"So he can race again on Friday?"

"Easily," Håkan said. "He'll leave the others standing. Then we'll enter him for Solvalla."

"Do you think he has a chance there?"

"I'll say he has," Håkan replied with conviction. "If you want my opinion, you've a horse to be proud of."

Sounds all right, I thought, making my usual inward reservations. After all, he's nothing so very wonderful.

I went into his stall. The rascal regarded me suspiciously with his bright eyes. Then he shoved at my chest with his muzzle. I fished a lump of sugar out of a pocket in my jeans. He nibbled at the sugar with soft, moist lips.

"Good horse," I murmured, feeling ridiculously content with life.

I left the stall and went out to Anette and Håkan. There was another stableman there whose name I couldn't remember.

"Are you going to work Stylist today?" I asked.

"No hard training," Håkan replied. "Just a little gentle exercise."

I felt in need of a cup of coffee and asked Håkan if he'd come with me to the café.

"Haven't time," he said.

For a moment I thought of asking Anette but changed my mind. She certainly attracted me with her shapely legs and her pretty figure, but she was married. There might be complications.

Lacking company, I sauntered alone in the sunshine over to the café. Just as I went in I saw, out of the corner of my eye, Jan Lindgren's car drive up to the stables. He had evidently turned up at work earlier than he had led his brother to expect.

At the counter I bought a large cup of vile coffee and a cheese sandwich. I would have liked a beer too, but had resolved to take it easy.

Quite a number of people were taking a coffee break just now. One of them was my old friend Bengt Ring. He had the same girl with him as last evening. She was slim and fair. Ring didn't even look at me, though he must have noticed me.

I balanced my tray and made my way over to a vacant table where I sipped the horrible liquid that was supposed to be coffee. No, it was impossible to drink. Despite all my good intentions I went back to the counter and bought a beer.

When I returned to my table I saw that Ring had left the café. But his female companion had not. She was still sitting at the table, smoking a cigarette with studied boredom. Her movements were almost like a parody. Had it not been for the modern clothes she would have been the perfect vamp of the 1920s.

I chewed at my sandwich. The cheese was rubbery and damp. The lettuce leaf was very tired. I removed it and crumpled it into the ash tray.

I was just about to leave when a shadow fell across the table. At the same moment I was almost anaesthetized by cheap perfume. To my astonishment, I saw Ring's girl standing there.

The charms on her heavy gold bracelet clinked as she put out a slender hand with its nails painted green. Her handshake was like lukewarm water. I hardly felt it.

"My name's Mia Ring," she said, and I distinctly heard the Karlstad dialect.

"Mine's Kalle Berger."

35

"I know," she went on. "May I sit down?"

"Why, of course."

She sat down opposite me. She had the same color on her eyelids as on her nails.

There was silence for a few seconds. I felt embarrassed. What the devil did she want?

"Can I get you anything?" I asked, merely for something to say.

"I wouldn't say no to a beer," she twittered. "It's so hot today."

I agreed that it was indeed a hot day. I got another beer and poured it out for her. She sipped it genteelly as if it were a liqueur.

"I suppose you're wondering what I want," she said.

I said nothing.

"It was Bengt who wanted me to speak to you," she continued.

"Oh?"

"Yes, he wanted to clear up the misunderstandings between you."

"Why couldn't he do it himself, then?"

"He feels so awkward about it. Would you care to come to a little party this evening?"

My astonishment grew. This was crazy. But it wasn't only my astonishment that grew; my curiosity did too. This might be rather fun. I decided to accept the Rings' invitation.

"Thank you. I'd like to."

"Oh, I'm so glad! Shall we say eight o'clock at the hotel?"

"The Nordmarken?"

"Yes. And if you'd like to bring someone, please do."

"Thanks, but I'll come alone. Am I to be the only guest?"

"I'm not sure, but I think Bengt said that Janne was coming. I hope we'll all have a nice time."

Silence again.

"Well, I must be going," she said. "Bengt will be so happy when I tell him you're coming."

"Where is he now?"

"I don't know. I think he was going to drive down to the liquor stores."

She stood up in her cloud of scent and teetered out through the door like a mannequin. Her beer was almost untouched. I drained my own glass.

I stayed for a while, trying to puzzle out what Ring really wanted with me, but I gave up. Perhaps it was as simple as his wife said. That he wanted to be on good terms with me. Possibly he had found out that I was a journalist. Many people are frightened of getting on the wrong side of the press. Maybe Ring was one of them.

But to hell with it. Time would soon show what lay behind his eagerness to make my closer acquaintance.

I sat there idly for another few minutes. I was tired and my temples were throbbing rather alarmingly. I had been wise enough to suspect that the morning's headache would return. I took a couple of aspirins and washed them down with a mouthful of beer from Mia Ring's glass.

It was hot outside now. I mopped my brow and went out into the blazing sun. A persistent fly was buzzing around my head. I swiped at it but missed. Its blue-green body glittered in the hard light.

There weren't many people about. Shag's second sack of empty bottles was still standing by the stable wall. Even he was taking it easy in the heat.

I made my way, dawdling, to Lindgren's stable. Jan was bent double, shoeing a horse. He was alone. I couldn't help admiring his deftness. He drove the nail in with absolute precision.

He straightened up as I came in.

"Hi," he said. "How are things?"

"Oh, so-so. Bit of a hangover."

"Late?"

"No, not particularly. I went to bed soon after you."

Lindgren made no reply. He finished the shoeing.

"There, that's that," he said. "Has Ring invited you this evening?"

"Yes. I wonder what he wants?"

"So do I. I can't make that guy out."

"Where are Håkan and Anette?" I asked.

"Out on the track working a couple of horses."

It was rather dark in the stable. I saw a switch and turned it on. Nothing happened.

"The bulb is broken," Jan said. "I've asked Shag to fix it, but he always takes his time."

"I saw him not long ago. I think he went to his room. Anyway, I've nothing to do so I can go and get you a bulb."

"That's nice of you," Jan said.

Coming out of the darkness of the stable I was blinded by the glare. My eyes had just gotten used to the light by the time I reached Shag's room. I knocked.

No answer. I knocked again.

Still silence.

I pressed the handle down, opened the door and looked in.

It took a couple of seconds for my eyes to adjust themselves again. But when they did, I saw the scene inside in crystal clear focus.

The first thing I saw clearly was two wall hangings in peasant style. Brown horses, green meadows, white daisies.

But quite another color dominated the horrible picture in the room. Blood was everywhere.

Shag was lying on his back on the floor. He had an ugly wound on the right side of his head. But the murderer had wanted to make quite sure that Shag would not wake up again. He had taken one of the new pitchforks standing in a corner of the room and run the sharp prongs several times through his victim's body.

Swarms of flies were buzzing around in the room. I imagined they looked heavy and bloated.

I began to feel very ill. I tried to restrain the nausea but it was no use.

The Afternoon

I FELT HORRIBLY SICK. It was the flies that upset me most. I just got out of the door and around the corner before my stomach turned itself inside out.

Not until I began to feel better after a minute or so did I realize that I had gotten myself into a nasty fix. But at the same time I was journalist enough to know that I had a scoop.

I looked about cautiously. Not a soul. No one had seen me standing there vomiting.

Steeling myself, I went back into the room. The flies were still there with all the rest. I looked around and tried to make a mental note of everything in the room.

But in fact, there was very little to remember. Only the distorted body, a table, and two stools. A drawer in the table was pulled out and, as far as I could see, empty.

I would like to have taken a closer look but was afraid of getting blood on my shoes.

It had taken three minutes from the time I discovered Shag until I left him. I closed the door behind me.

I returned to the café and asked to use the phone. It was on the counter so I couldn't talk privately. But I'm used to that in my job. After all, it's pretty noisy when you phone a report in from an icy hockey game or a football stadium.

The first call I made was to the police. I had hoped it would be someone I knew, but it wasn't. I told Constable Johansson, who answered, what had happened.

"You mean he's dead?" he asked skeptically. "Shag?"

"Stone dead," I replied.

"We'll come then," he informed me.

"Fantastic," I said, trying to sound sarcastic, but it was wasted.

"We'll be there in five minutes," he promised. "Don't touch anything."

"I've seen whodunits on TV," I mumbled.

"What was that?"

"Nothing."

My next call was to the paper. I got hold of an assistant editor in the general editorial office. He didn't sound too enthusiastic.

"Hadn't we better send someone from the Criminal Investigations Division?" he suggested.

"Can't you hear what I say?" I nagged. "I know people here. I'm right in the thick of the whole thing."

"All right," he said at last.

"Then I'm on expenses from now on," I said.

"Everyone fleeces this poor paper," he sighed, sounding the complete bureaucrat. "Of course you're on expenses if you're working for us."

For a moment I thought of asking him what would happen now about the money the sports editor had promised me for the doping story. I stopped myself in time.

"Well, so long," I said. "I've a date with the cops."

I paid for my calls, went out, and took up my stand at the gate. I was surprised to see Jan Lindgren come out with a horse that he was evidently taking out to drive. Jan was wearing gray coveralls.

He caught sight of me.

"Did you get the bulb?" he said.

"He wasn't there," I lied.

"Oh, he'll be back soon," Lindgren said.

"Where are you off to?" I asked.

"This one is a bit tenderfooted so I usually drive him on the forest roads near here."

Should I, after all, tell him what had happened? I decided against it. What was the point? Lindgren settled down in the training sulky and drove out through the gate.

Out on the track I saw Håkan and Anette coming, each with a horse. They drove neatly between a water truck and some other sulkies. Anette only just managed to swerve as the water truck backed into a small pocket on the straight to refill from a large tap.

I walked over and waited by the gate. It was a good five minutes before the police car came sweeping up from the main road. Two men were in the front seat, one in uniform and one in plain clothes.

I stopped the car.

"Was it you who called up about a death?" asked the plainclothesman.

He was tall and fair. He regarded me with large, Swedish blue eyes. I couldn't help noticing his hands. They were enormous, with tufts of ginger hair. His uniformed colleague looked like every other cop nowadays: lean, gloomy, and, of course, with the inevitable side whiskers.

"Yes, it was," I replied.

"My name's Bodén. I'm the inspector here in the village," said the plainclothesman. "This is Constable Johansson. May I ask who you are?"

I told him. From his expression I gathered that he knew my name.

"Let's look at the body, then," he said.

We went to Shag's room. I led the other two. Bodén, who looked about fifty, moved with the gait of an outdoorsman. The much younger Johansson, on the other hand, was puffing a little in the heat.

I stopped at the door.

"It's in there," I said.

Johansson took a step forward, stretching out his hand with a large signet ring on his littte finger.

"Are you crazy!" Bodén exclaimed. "There might be finger-prints on the door."

Taking an ingeniously folded handkerchief out of the breast pocket of his gray suit, he cautiously opened the door.

He stood for some seconds gazing at the ghastly scene inside. Then he turned slowly toward me. He was pale under his sun tan. Johansson, on the other hand, seemed to be fascinated by what he saw.

"Well I'll be damned," he said. "I never knew there was so much blood in a human being."

Bodén threw him a disapproving glance.

"You're a journalist, aren't you?" he asked me.

"Yes," I admitted.

"Then, of course, you've already phoned your paper?"

"Yes."

"I was afraid so," he sighed. "You didn't touch anything in there, I hope?"

"No."

"What are you doing here in Årjäng?"

"I'm on vacation," I replied. "I was born here."

"I see. Johansson, call up the head of police at Säffle immediately and tell him what happened. Say that we need every man he can get hold of. Christ, this would happen in the middle of vacation time."

He took a notebook out of his pocket and scribbled something. Then he made a rapid sketch of the room. When he had finished he closed the door carefully.

Rumors of the murder had evidently begun to spread around the stables. About a dozen people had gathered outside. Johansson returned sweating and with a limp shirt.

"I got hold of him," he said. "He's coming himself and promised to get extra men from Karlstad."

"Good," Bodén said. "Stand outside this door and don't let anyone in. Come on, get moving."

He said this to the inquisitive crowd, who reluctantly moved away. I saw that Berggren, the secretary, was among them. He came up to me and drew me aside.

"Is it true that Shag has been murdered?"

I informed him that it was quite true.

"How?"

"Someone stuck a pitchfork into him. He's had a blow on the head too, I think."

"Jesus," Berggren murmured with feeling.

He said nothing more for a while. Then he looked at me with his large eyes.

"What did you tell the police?" he asked.

"How do you mean, tell?"

"You know, about the syringe yesterday."

"No, I didn't tell them anything."

My answer seemed to be a great relief to him.

"I don't think it has anything to do with the murder either," he said.

"You've got me wrong," I retorted. "I didn't say anything about the syringe for the simple reason that I never thought of it. But now that you mention it . . ."

"Do me a favor, Kalle," he implored. "You know quite well that Shag was always going around with his cock-and-bull stories. There'd be one hell of a row if anything leaked out."

"Put the track in a bad light, you mean?"

Bodén came toward us.

"Hi," he said to Berggren. "Can you let me have a room so that I can get going with the questioning?"

"You can use the owners' room," Berggren replied. "There's a phone in there too. I'll come with you and unlock it."

"Fine. Let's go."

They started to move off. I gave no sign of following. Bodén turned around.

"Why don't you come?" he asked.

"No one asked me."

"Well, I'm asking you now," he said, with a note of irritation in his voice. "You must realize that you're the very first one I want to talk to."

"I'm not in charge of the investigation," I retorted.

"Nor am I."

He was right, of course. I had answered back from force of habit.

We reached the restaurant. The owners' room was on the second floor of the same building. Berggren took out a bunch of keys and searched methodically through them until he found the right one. He unlocked the door and we went in.

"Yes, this looks all right," Bodén admitted. "I might want you later. How can I get hold of you?"

"I'll still be here at the track. I'm in the judges' tower. You've only to call me up there."

"The number?" Bodén asked.

"You'll find a list on the phone over there," Berggren said.

"Good," Bodén replied.

As Berggren left, I somehow got the impression that he wanted to stay on as long as possible. I looked at him and he gazed back at me with a look of appeal.

Aha, I thought. The syringe.

Making sure that Bodén's attention was elsewhere, I nodded to Berggren as stealthily as possible. He closed his eyes for a fraction of a second.

He seemed enormously relieved. Almost as if he had been facing a firing squad and been reprieved at the last second. I wondered why.

Berggren went out and I was left alone with Inspector Bodén.

The Interrogation

WITH HIS SPRINGY GAIT Bodén glided across the room to a table. He drew up a chair and sat down. Then he took out his notebook again from an inside pocket.

The pad was of a type that I hadn't seen in years. It even had "Memorandum Book" printed on the outside cover. He then fished two ball-point pens out of his breast pocket.

I was still standing.

"Do sit down," he said politely, pointing to a chair.

I did so.

After the pens, Bodén took out a pack of cigarettes and offered me one. I declined. I had expected him to take a cigarette himself but he didn't.

I must say I was pleased. I don't smoke myself and I always feel ill if I have to spend any length of time with people who systematically pollute the air. On the way to the Olympic Games in Mexico, for instance, I sat beside two guys who chain-smoked all the way from Copenhagen to New York. It took me several weeks to recover from that experience.

"How did you discover him?" Bodén asked abruptly.

"I was going to get a bulb for Jan Lindgren's stable."

"Why?"

"Well, you see, an electric bulb in the stable was broken. I offered to go and get a new one, since I had nothing particular to do at the time."

"How did you come to be in Lindgren's stable?"

"He's training a horse of mine."

There was a flicker of interest in the blue gray eyes.

"Oh," he murmured. "I didn't know that."

"Know what?"

"That you're a horse owner, of course. So you went to Karlsson-Gren's room?"

"Yes."

"And everything looked just as it did when we were there just now?"

I thought back rapidly.

"Yes, exactly," I said.

"And after you made the discovery, what did you do?"

"Went out and threw up."

He looked disappointed. I couldn't help asking why.

"I saw that someone had been sick outside. I hoped it would be the murderer. It might have yielded something."

An idea struck me.

"Have you sent for the doctor?" I asked.

He looked decidedly amused.

"You don't seem to think much of our efficiency in the provincial police," he said. "But I did ask Johansson to call up the district medical officer or, if he was out on a sick call, to get a doctor from the hospital. Are you satisfied?"

I felt foolish and said nothing.

"Did you know Karlsson-Gren?"

"Slightly," I replied.

"Tell me more."

"We lived next door when we were little. We used to go fishing together and that sort of thing."

"What was he like?"

"What was he like? . . . I think he was very ill with meningitis when he was little. After that he was never quite right in the head. 'Daffy' we call it here in Nordmarken. I think that just about covers what Shag was."

"I see," Bodén said, and I think he really did.

He rubbed his nose and wrote down a few words in the old-fashioned notebook.

"You said you went out and threw up," he went on. "What did you do then?"

"I went in again."

"Why?"

"Because I'm a journalist. You've got to do things like that. You've got to have the right vulture instincts."

The next question was unexpected.

"Why were you sick?"

"The flies," I answered. "They were big, fat, and bloated."

A suspicion began to gnaw at me.

"Do you think I killed him?" I asked rather indignantly.

"No, I don't," he replied. "I just want to know as much as possible."

"And I'm to believe that?"

"You have every right to believe what you like," he said in the smoothest imaginable voice.

I persuaded myself to keep calm. It wasn't easy, but I managed it after a short struggle. My respect for Bodén had grown during our conversation. The man was no fool.

"You know more about this environment than I do," he went on. "My contact with trotting is limited to the drunks we have to take charge of. Have you a theory?"

"The most likely one is that Shag found out or saw something he shouldn't have."

"Have you any reason to think that this is really so?"

"No, I merely answered your question. You wanted to know if I had a theory, and I do have one."

"Let us assume you're right. What, in that case, could he have found out?"

Now he had me cornered. What was I to answer? I decided to take the bull by the horns.

"He might have seen someone fiddling with a horse."

"Fiddling with a horse? Is that a euphemism for doping?"

"For example. It's also possible that he stumbled onto something else."

"Such as?"

I shrugged as I tried desperately to hit on a plausible answer.

"Well, he might have seen someone trying to injure a horse. There are other explanations too. A love affair, for instance, which the person in question didn't want to leak out."

"Was Karlsson-Gren in the habit of gossiping?"

"I don't know about gossiping. But he used to go around talking to himself."

"What did he say then?"

"How should I know?"

46

"Excuse me a moment," he said, picking up the phone.

I noticed that he dialed an area code first. From the following conversation I inferred that he was calling police headquarters at Säffle. He asked someone if there were any experts on the way from Karlstad, and the answer was evidently yes.

"These goddam Stockholmers," he exclaimed feelingly.

"Hell, I'm no Stockholmer," I protested indignantly.

"I didn't mean it like that. But everything was much better when the head of police had his office here. Then he'd have been here ages ago and taken over the investigation."

"I think you're managing pretty well on your own," I said.

He shot me a glance to make sure I meant what I said. I did mean it and he seemed to realize this.

"I've never had a murder case before," he said.

"Has the head of police had any?"

"Oh yes, several. He did very well, but I've an idea this is not going to be so easy."

Bodén took a large handkerchief out of his pants pocket and blew his nose with the incredibly piercing sound that some people are able to produce. During this procedure he tilted his head in a curious way and glared about him.

"Excuse me," he said. "I've just caught a cold. In this heat, too."

"Summer colds are hard to shake off."

"So are certain people," he said. "Have you any idea why Berggren hung about here for so long?"

"No, I haven't. Come to think of it, it didn't strike me that he stayed very long."

"Well, *I* thought so," Bodén persisted. "I saw you two talking over by the stables. May I ask what about?"

"Ask, by all means, but don't be sure of an answer. He was simply curious and wanted to know what had happened."

"Seems reasonable," Bodén said.

Then he asked me for some personal data. I told him that I was thirty-five, single, etc., etc.

"So you have a horse in training with Jan Lindgren?"

"Yes."

"Didn't a horse drop dead there yesterday?"

47

"Yes."

"Do you think it might have anything to do with Karlsson-Gren's murder?"

"What's your opinion?"

"I'm the one asking the questions."

His voice had an edge to it now.

"It's possible, I suppose," I said slowly. "He might have known too much."

"Too much about what?"

"How should I know? After all, this is mere speculation."

"I've heard that this horse—what was its name again?"

"Sam Boy."

"Ah yes. Well, it's rumored that he was doped. One of the big Stockholm dailies even hints it openly today."

Now it was my turn to stare at him. Did he know that I was the one who had written that article?

"I wrote that," I said. "Lindgren, at any rate, thought it was doping."

"Both brothers?"

"I thought you said you didn't know anything about trotting."

"Enough to know that there are two Lindgren brothers."

"Jan said straight out that Sam Boy was doped. I don't remember whether Håkan said anything, but I certainly got the impression that he too thought it was fishy."

"It was Bengt Ring who owned the horse, wasn't it? What do you know about him?"

"That he was making a lot of money out of his publishing business. He's not doing so well now, so it's said. Perhaps there's a glut in the porno market."

"I see. Nothing else."

"I don't know whether it has anything to do with the matter, but Ring was once engaged to Håkan Lindgren's wife. Her name's Anette."

"Indeed."

He made rapid notes on his pad. Only now did I notice that he could take shorthand. People like that are a menace.

"Come to think of it, I once met that guy Ring," Bodén said without explaining himself.

48

"In what connection?" I asked.

"In connection with my work," he said with a cagey look, and that was all I got out of him.

Bodén turned back a few pages, evidently checking what he had written. Then he closed the notebook and put it in his pocket.

"Well, that's all for now," he said. "How long are you going to stay here at Årjäng?"

"I had thought of returning to Stockholm on Monday," I replied, "but it depends what happens."

He asked where I was staying and how he could reach me. We parted with mutual courtesies.

The Evening

I REMAINED at the track until the investigators from Karlstad had done their job.

I was still the only Stockholm journalist at Årjäng and I made the most of the situation.

In due course I got a lift back to the hotel and knocked out a pretty dreadful story. I felt rather ashamed, but then I often am. Self-respect is never a predominant quality with journalists.

I phoned the editorial desk and was told, somewhat grudgingly, that my story would make the front page.

The whisky bottle was empty, but I was in luck and got to the liquor store on the main street just before it closed.

Then I went back to the hotel, had a shower and a couple of drinks, and listened to the radio.

At last I dozed off on the bed. I woke up with a start and looked at the time. A quarter to eight. Hell. I was to meet Ring and his pin-up of a wife at eight o'clock.

I got up and dressed, feeling gloomy. I took another quick drink before going downstairs.

Ring and his wife stood waiting outside the dining room. The porno publisher was exuding good will. His wife greeted me with the same lukewarm handshake as she had earlier in the day.

Mia Ring's outfit left little or nothing to the imagination, the little being a pair of binkini panties discernible under the crocheted dress.

"We're just waiting for Janne," she said in her Karlstad dialect. "He promised to be here in a couple of minutes. He just called up."

"From where?" I asked.

"I don't know, but I bet he was with a girl. He usually is."

"Well, you ought to know," her husband remarked.

"Why, Bengt!" she exclaimed. "Kalle—you don't mind if I call you Kalle, do you?—will think you're jealous."

Ring beamed. He seemed to take his wife's remark as a good joke.

"I'm not in the least jealous," he said.

He turned to me.

"You see," he went on, "Mia and I are always having a bit of fun on the side. We've given each other that liberty."

She gave an embarrassed laugh.

"Bengt will make those jokes. Part of his business, I suppose. It's not at all the way he says."

Her husband still looked pleased with himself. He took a step toward me and held out his hand. He was the very picture of sincerity.

"We've had our differences of opinion, but it's all forgotten now, eh?"

"Sure, sure," I lied.

"Let's go in and sit down," Ring suggested. "I hope you're as hungry as I am."

"I mumbled a suitable reply. I've never been a very sociable person. One of my nightmares has been that I was placed on the left of the hostess and had to make a speech. It would be the death of me.

"Aren't we going to wait for Jan?" Mia Ring asked.

"Oh, he'll turn up when he feels like it. Let's have some food."

Mia led the way to a reserved table placed away from the other tables. There were not many people in the restaurant. A couple of stray tourists, a man who was obviously a commercial traveler, and one of the town's more well-to-do alcoholics. That was all. A very ordinary evening.

The Rings had evidently ordered the dinner. A waitress hurried over.

"Would you like anything to drink with the first course?" she asked.

"It depends what it is," I said.

"Prawns," Ring said curtly.

"In that case, I'll have an akvavit and a beer, please."

The other two followed my example.

"But we'd like a drink before dinner too," Ring said. "What will you have, Kalle?"

"A dry martini, please."

"Ooh, lovely." Mia Ring twittered. "Three dry martinis."

The waitress quickly returned with three glasses. I sipped the drink. Apparently the American dry martini with a gin base had not yet reached Årjäng.

"Christ, this isn't a dry martini," Ring growled.

"Yes it is," the girl affirmed. "It said so on the bottle."

I realized that she had given us the vermouth without the gin. Ring muttered something about going over to the other hotel.

"I don't think they know much about it there either," I said. "Hang on a minute."

I asked the waitress if I might go into the kitchen and lend a hand. Once, long ago, I had been forced by cruel circumstance to learn how to mix dry martinis.

Under the suspicious eye of the liquor cashier I mixed three drinks—"really dry," any American would have said. I set the three glasses on a tray and carried them out to the others. Lindgren had still not appeared.

"Here we are!" I said, serving the drinks.

"Ooh, aren't you clever." Mia Ring said.

Her husband glared at her and then put on his jovial face in the same way an actor puts on his when the cameras start to roll.

We finished our drinks and had just begun on the prawns when Lindgren appeared, looking spruce and fit as usual.

He was openly discourteous to Ring. If the latter noticed, however, he ignored it.

We ate our prawns. They were not very good and tasted of ammonia. Ring and his wife made small talk with us. I was beginning to wonder what Ring had meant when he called this a party.

With the main dish we had a tolerably good red wine. Coffee was served, then Lindgren made his excuses and got up to leave.

"Is your girlfriend waiting?" Ring asked.

"That's right," Lindgren replied.

"Good luck," Ring said.

I looked at his wife. Her face had gone dark. Perhaps the insinuation of an affair with Lindgren had a genuine background. It was not impossible, of course.

Ring gulped at his brandy. His wife was drinking a greenish liqueur, the very sight of which made me want to retch.

"I suppose you're wondering why I invited you," Ring said.

"No," I answered ingenuously. "You said it was to let bygones be bygones."

"Yes, that of course, but there is, in fact, another reason."

"Well, well."

"I wanted to hear your opinion about Sam Boy."

I reflected that my opinion on that matter hardly justified the evening's party. But presumably everything went down on his expense account, so it didn't cost him so much.

"Do you think he was doped?" he asked.

"Yes."

"Why?"

"Everything points to it, surely?"

"Aren't there other methods of making horses crazy?"

"Such as?"

"I've heard that a burr under the tail is effective. Another possibility is a painful bite."

"Some kind of mechanical influence, you mean."

"Exactly. Do you really think it's out of the question?"

I thought hard for a moment and came to the conclusion that he might be right. But it didn't sound likely.

My career as a journalist has taught me always to suspect

people's motives. I take nothing for granted. If, for instance, a club owner calls me up and says he's damned satisfied with his new acquisition, I assume automatically that it's just the reverse and that he's out to sell the dud to another club. I reacted much the same now.

"Do you want me to write about this?"

"Well, I just thought you might be interested in the idea as such."

"As I see it, a theory like that means that suspicion falls on someone in the stables."

"It does with doping, too."

He was right, of course. But I wasn't going to give in so easily.

"Surely it's much easier for an outsider to give a horse a shot than to put something under his tail."

Ring looked skeptical.

"I don't agree. Suppose I wanted to fiddle with a horse. I come into the stables and have a perfectly legitimate excuse, as you and I would, for instance. The horse is standing harnessed and ready in the paddock. When no one's looking, I slip something under the tail."

I shook my head.

"It doesn't fit. Sam Boy was trotting the whole time. If it had been anything like you suggest he would have bolted."

"Not necessarily," he protested. "Sammy was a trotting machine. He hardly ever galloped."

"At least not since Janne began to train him," I admitted. "All the same, I still think he was doped. You or I can go in and see our horses whenever we like and be more or less undisturbed. It would be easy enough to give them a shot. Or something in an apple."

There was silence for a while. The only sound was the local drinker ordering another whisky.

"Do you suspect Jan?" I asked.

"No, not Janne."

Mia had been silent for a long time. Now she glanced up at me and the green eyelids glistened.

"Bengt thinks it was Anette who did it," she added playfully, and her husband looked daggers at her. "They were engaged at

53

one time, she and Bengt. A very handsome couple. She's pretty, and *so* willing. Bengt is merely willing."

"You're stoned," Ring said brutally.

I looked more closely at his wife and found he was right. She *was* drunk.

"In vino veritas," I remarked.

"What the hell did you say?"

"It's Latin and means you tell the truth when you're drunk," I explained.

"Oh."

In some odd way the conversation came to a dead end there. Ring stared blankly at his drink and his wife sat trying to get the clock on the wall into focus.

"Can you see what the time is?" she asked.

"Ten past ten," I replied politely.

"I'll go to bed then," she said.

We rose from the table. I felt quite sober. Mia swayed slightly and Ring steadied her. He seemed completely at ease.

I thanked them. Ring nodded in an offhand way. Just before we parted he suddenly turned to me.

"I'll give you a job if you like," he said. "Free lance. I pay well."

"How well?"

"Name your price."

"He's trying to bribe you," his wife said with her tipsy perspicacity.

"I'm afraid he is," I said.

"Go to hell," he snarled, and walked away.

So we were back where we started.

I went up to my room and then did something I had already decided upon earlier in the day.

I got my toilet case out of my suitcase and took out the blue syringe. Then I cut it into little bits with my nail scissors and flushed the lot down the toilet.

After that, I felt much calmer. I got into bed and fell asleep almost at once. Just before sleep overcame me, I had a hazy idea that I had stumbled onto something important but I forgot it as quickly.

Once during the night, I was roused by ambulance sirens but I soon fell asleep again.

The Fire

THE MINUTE I woke up in the morning I grabbed the phone and called the police. I wanted to know if anything special had happened during the night. I was put through to my friend Bodén.

"Has there been anything?" I asked intelligently.

"Well, yes there has," he replied calmly.

"Is it asking too much to be told what happened last night?" I said, trying to be polite.

"There has been a fire," the taciturn inspector replied.

"Where?"

"At the vet's."

"Then it was the fire brigade I heard last night," I said. "I thought it was an ambulance."

"Don't you want to know what burned?"

"Of course I do, but it seemes impossible to make you say anything of your own accord."

"His old barn burned down," Bodén informed me.

"Very exciting."

"Yes, isn't it? Especially since the carcass of that horse Sam Boy was inside it. Nothing was left of him but a few charred bones."

"Well, I'll be damned. Was the fire the work of an arsonist?"

"Everything points to it."

"No suspects?"

"No, not yet."

During the conversation I had managed to get out my notebook, in which I scribbled down his information.

"What does the vet say?" I asked.

"The carcass was to have been sent to Stockholm today. He couldn't arrange transport earlier."

"I suppose you know where he lives?"

"Yes."

"That barn is rather out of the way. He didn't want to be troubled by the smell if the horse began to rot in the heat."

I knew the vet's farm very well. It was only a ten-minute walk from the market place along the Arvika road. Nice and handy for anyone who wanted to set fire to the barn.

"Nobody saw or heard anything suspicious?"

"Nothing at all."

"Well, there's nothing much left for the autopsy," I said. "What are you going to do now?"

"We'll send what's left, of course, but the chances are small of finding out whether Sam Boy was doped or not."

"That must be a blow."

"Well, yes," the inspector replied without sounding too depressed.

We said goodbye and I ordered breakfast. After a while the girl came with the tray. She was wearing one of those white coats that all Swedish chambermaids wear for some reason. Otherwise she was pretty, and for a moment I considered making a pass at her.

I refrained. I usually do. I've had my littte flings, of course, but I never put myself out.

The coffee was drinkable and the egg edible. I like having breakfast in peace and quiet. The day and its possibilities are ahead of me. One seldom has the same feeling toward evening.

I swallowed the last piece of toast and put the tray outside the door, so I wouldn't be disturbed when the girl came to collect it.

I looked up the vet's number in the telephone directory. One of his many children answered.

"Is your father at home?" I asked.

"Who's calling, please?" the well-brought-up child asked.

I gave my name, and after half a minute or so I heard the vet's voice. We were casual acquaintances, but no more. I asked some routine questions about the fire and was given equally routine answers. Yes, he thought it was the work of an arsonist. Did he suspect anyone? Oh, no."

"Can anything be deduced from an examination of the bone remains?" I asked.

"Hard to say. I doubt it. But of course it's not impossible. I'm not a specialist in such matters."

It was on the tip of my tongue to ask him just what he was a specialist in, but checked myself in the nick of time.

"But as luck would have it, I had already taken some specimens," he went on.

"What specimens?"

"Blood, saliva, and urine. I sent the specimens to Stockholm yesterday."

"That was fortunate," I said. "It should mean that they can establish whether or not Sam Boy was doped."

"I presume so."

"When can they have the analyses ready?"

"They were going to try and do them this week. The police are anxious to get the results as soon as possible."

"I can well imagine," I said.

It would certainly be a disappointment for the murderer if he had hoped to remove important evidence by setting fire to the vet's barn.

"Do you think the horse was doped?" I asked.

"Impossible to say. It's not normal for horses to run straight into a wall, but it *has* happened before. A bite from a gadfly is enough."

"That possibility hadn't occurred to me," I admitted. "Someone told me it would be possible to achieve the same effect mechanically."

"You mean by putting something under the harness?"

"Yes."

"It's not very likely. Besides, it would be very hard to regulate. But of course . . ."

He checked himself.

"What were you going to say?"

"Nothing. Just a stray thought."

After a little persuasion I got it out of him. I seem to have a knack sometimes of making people disclose their innermost thoughts to me—against their better judgment, of course.

"Hypothetically, it's conceivable that the driver could fix something."

57

He said "the driver" when he really meant Håkan Lindgren, who was driving Sam Boy when the horse crashed into the stable wall.

"I see," I said. "Nothing else?"

"No, I don't think so."

My next call was to the paper. I asked them to send a photographer. I was told that one was already on his way.

"He's flying to Karlstad and will hire a car there."

"Good. How did my story go yesterday? The paper hasn't got here yet."

"It was nicely placed on the front page."

I told the assistant editor, at the other end of the line, that I'd have something else for him in the afternoon.

"Well, phone it in as early as possible," he said. "Since we got the computers and other technical junk, we have to go to press nearly a day ahead."

"Easy does it. You'll get the whole story before five o'clock."

Yesterday, I had been in the fortunate position of not having any competition from the other big papers, but I couldn't hope for that today. I thanked my lucky star for the vet's disclosure that the specimens had already been sent to Stockholm; that might give a nice little twist to my story.

In order to be a really good journalist, you need a large portion of disloyalty, a quality that flourishes in the press world. It's certainly no coincidence that the Journalists' Association, of all unions, signed a ten-year agreement with the employers. Pretty shrewd, because if there should be a general strike, the journalists can sit back and wait for other professional groups to get their demands through. Then the journalists have only to fall in line.

Sometimes, I wonder why I'm a journalist myself. But the answer is simple. I like it. Mostly, anyway. But it's no good being encumbered with self-esteem. On the other hand, you must think of yourself. What's good for the newspaper is good for you. If you take care always to keep this in mind, it's fun being a journalist.

So much for that.

I shaved and had a shower. Then I went down to the hall porter to tell him that I would be at the trotting track if anyone wanted me. As I came up to the reception desk, a journalist called Åke Bengtsson was signing the register.

Bengtsson is living proof of the corruption that is part of the Swedish press. He works as a freelancer and does very well. His method is this: There are several large auctioneering firms that arrange big horse sales all over the country. Bengtsson works as speaker at these events, presenting all the nags that are auctioned off as future stars. In this, he is successful. Naturally he takes a cut.

Beforehand, he writes an article about the auction. With the best will in the world, you can't call it anything else but editorial advertising. After the auction, Åke writes a report telling of all the incredible finds the lucky buyers have made at the expense of the poor sellers.

Occasionally, it happens that someone really does make a find. It's very rare, but it does happen. Åke never neglects to mention, in his account of the race, that the owner in question grabbed this champion at such and such an auction.

He's clever, Åke is. An excellent representative of Swedish journalism.

There he stood looking very smart in a light blue suit and pale gray hat bought in the U.S. His honest blue eyes turned on me and he greeted me like a long-lost friend whom he hadn't seen for at least twenty years. It wasn't more than two weeks since we last met.

"My old buddy," he gushed. "You're here. Well, isn't that just great."

"Hello," I said somewhat less effusively.

"Quite a lot seems to be happening in old Årjäng," he went on. "Murder and doping. Not bad, not bad."

I merely grunted.

"Wonderful, just wonderful that you've bought such a good horse," Bengtsson enthused with a broad smile and ice-cold eyes. "Are you thinking of selling? If so, I have a prospective buyer up my sleeve."

"Who?"

"He wants to be anonymous, old boy. Wants to be anonymous."

"Is it Bengt Ring?"

He looked blank. If he was lying, then he was a very good actor. In fact, I knew that already.

"I've no dealings with Benke any longer," he said. "He's a bit too smooth for my liking. A bit too smooth."

"It was just that he wanted to talk business the day before yesterday. I told him no. Anyway, Stylist isn't for sale. Not yet anyway."

"The price is good," Bengtsson said.

"How good?"

"You can probably get fifty thousand."

I made a rough calculation. Stylist had cost me forty. Add training fees and other expenses. Too littte profit.

"Not enough," I declared.

Bengtsson looked at me appraisingly. His internal calculator was evidently hard at work.

"I can't go any higher just now," he said. "But I'll have a word with my client. It's possible he can go up a fraction. Will Stylist be racing on Friday?"

"Yes."

"I'll take a look at him then. His blood's fine, but that's not always everything."

Say what you like about Åke, but he's probably the foremost Swedish expert on strains and lines of descent. There's not one Swedish horse whose pedigree four generations back he can't account for.

"I saw what you wrote about Sam Boy."

I made no reply. If he wanted to say anything, let him come out with it.

"Are you sure he was doped?" he asked.

"No, not at all."

"What you wrote gave that impression. Or was it merely to get a good story?"

I shrugged. His last words were uncomfortably near the truth; but, to be quite honest, I did have a suspicion of doping.

"I'm not sure," I replied truthfully. "What do you yourself think?"

60

"I don't think anything. But somehow doping and Janne Lindgren don't go together."

He sounded almost irritated at having to affirm this. And as a matter of fact, Åke Bengtsson and Jan Lindgren didn't get along very well.

I was about to go when the hall porter turned to me.

"You're wanted on the phone," he said. "I'll put the call through to the booth."

I nodded goodbye to Bengtsson and went into the phone booth.

"Berger," I said.

"Good morning, Mr. Berger," replied a voice with a slight Skåne accent. "My name's Norberg, head of police. I'd be glad of a word with you."

"Well, you're having it now."

"I meant here at the police station," he went on, ignoring my fatuous remark. "Have you time now? It's just across the market place."

"I know. I'll be there in five minutes."

The Head of Police

I WALKED the short distance to the police station. My old acquaintance Johansson with the side whiskers sat behind the counter.

"I've come to see Mr. Norberg," I said politely.

Johansson looked at me with large, vacant eyes. My words didn't seem to have registered.

"I want to see the head of police," I repeated. "He phoned me just now."

"Oh, him," he said, pointing inside. "The name on the door's Bodén."

The door was fitted with one of those gadgets that light up. I mistrust all such contraptions, just as I mistrust elevators, intercoms, and mysterious automatic machines of all kinds.

I knocked on the door and entered. Bodén was sitting in his small office together with a man whom I took to be the head of police. He was very large in every way. His jacket was stretched tight across his chest and his shirt collar seemed to be strangling him. He reminded me of Orson Welles.

"It was good of you to come," he said, when I had told him my name. "I know you were questioned yesterday by Inspector Bodén, but I'd like to check a few things."

"Why, of course."

He rubbed his chin, making a scraping noise on the stubble. He had short powerful fingers, one of which was being strangled by a wedding ring in the same way his neck was by the shirt.

"Would you mind telling me, in your own words, what happened when you found the murdered man?"

I obliged him by giving a short account of how the bulb in the stable was broken, how I had found Shag, how I had vomited, etc.

During my little speech, the head of police sat leaning back with his eyes closed and with that foolish expression that certain music lovers have when they're listening to their favorite record. It looked rather silly, and for that reason annoyed me.

He opened his eyes slowly and regarded me amiably.

"Good," he said. "Splendid."

I had no idea what was good and splendid. I sat there opposite him, waiting for him to go on. The tape recorder on the desk rotated dismally.

"It was an unusually brutal murder," the head of police said at last.

"I know," I replied. "I discovered it."

"The murderer must be exceptionally ruthless," he went on. All this time Bodén remained silent, studying some papers.

"And very desperate," I said.

"What do you mean, Mr. Berger?"

"He must have taken an enormous risk when he murdered Shag. He can't have had more than a few minutes."

"So you're sure it was a man who did it?"

"I haven't even reflected, but when you think of a murderer it's usually as a he, isn't it?"

"Yes, true enough. We've already questioned a lot of people but no one has noticed anything unusual. They were all minding their own business and were not interested in anything else."

"That's mostly the way," I said. "People don't want to get involved."

"Do you think someone knows more than he or she makes out?"

"It's not impossible," I said, thinking of myself.

Norberg closed his eyes again and sat there with a dreamy expression on his face. He clasped his hands behind his neck. This made the noose of the shirt collar still more effective and the jovial face got redder and redder. I was afraid he'd faint, but fortunately he didn't.

"You're more at home in these circles than I am," he said without opening his eyes. "What could Karlsson-Gren have known that was so dangerous for the murderer?"

"I haven't the vaguest idea."

"But surely you must have some theory," he insisted.

I began to lose my temper, but resolved not to.

"I've already given Inspector Bodén a couple of suggestions."

"So you have. About doping, and so on. And it looks as if you were right. The fire at the vet's last night was evidently an attempt to get rid of evidence."

"So it seems," I agreed. "But the arsonist went to all this trouble for nothing."

Norberg surprised me by suddenly opening his eyes and fixing them on me.

"What do you mean?"

Did he really not know that the specimens had already been sent to Stockholm? Surely the vet must have told him.

"You know quite well."

"I do *not* know," he snapped.

"The vet had already sent all the specimens to the laboratory in Stockholm," I informed him. "Presumably, they're analyzing them now."

"Well, I'll be damned!" he exclaimed.

"You mean to say the vet didn't tell you?"

"No," said Bodén, putting a word in for the first time. "I suppose it didn't occur to him. I know him slightly and he has always been rather absent-minded."

Norberg again raised his florid Santa Claus face to the ceiling.

"Tell me about a publisher called Bengt Ring," he said. "You know him, don't you?"

"Only slightly," I replied. "He has several horses in training with Jan Lindgren. He was engaged at one time to Håkan Lindgren's wife. He's said to have plenty of money, though there are rumors to the contrary. His wife's name is Mia and I had dinner with him last evening."

"So we heard," Bodén said. "Is it presumptuous to ask what lay behind that invitation? From what I hear, you're not the best friends in the world."

"You hear too damn much," I snapped. "He wanted to bury the hatchet after a little run-in we had the day before yesterday."

"What about?"

"I told him his credit was bad. He wanted to buy a horse from me. I didn't want to sell. It was as simple as that."

"Had you any grounds for saying that his credit was bad?"

"Well, yes, in a way."

That's all I said. It was some seconds before the head of police again spoke.

"In a way, you said. What do you mean by that?"

"Jan Lindgren told me that Ring was getting behind with the training fees. Lindgren concluded that it was because Ring's affairs were going badly. Which doesn't necessarily mean they are."

"No, of course not," he agreed.

I decided to put forward an idea.

"Ring always insures his horses heavily," I said.

Norberg took out a large handkerchief and carefully mopped his brow.

"Oh, does he," he said. "In other words, that means he might have a direct interest in his horse's death."

He had risen to the bait. I had no time for Ring and his bullying ways. But that didn't make him an insurance swindler and a murderer. I was well aware of that. All the same, I had no pangs of conscience. Besides, I had merely done my civic duty and given the police some valuable information.

"I didn't say that," I objected.

"And then we have Jan Lindgren," Norberg went on.

I was silent.

"I'd like you to tell me something about him," Norberg said after a few moments of intense silence.

"There's not much to tell, other than that he's an unusually successful trotting trainer, that he has never been mixed up in any scandals, and that his affairs are known to be in order."

"His business affairs, you mean?"

"Of course."

"I haven't had time yet to study the ins and outs of the case, but I seem to remember a witness saying that Lindgren showed a marked interest in Bengt Ring's wife."

"That's nothing to do with me."

"Then you can't confirm the report?"

"No," I lied. "Anyway I don't see what it has to do with the murder."

He almost drawled his reply.

"You're the one who supplied the information," he said. "I quote from a conversation you had with Inspector Bodén yesterday: 'A love affair, for instance, which the person in question didn't want to leak out.' That's what you said concerning possible motives for murdering Karlsson-Gren."

"But I never said I was thinking of Jan and Mia," I protested quickly.

"Who were you thinking of then?"

"Nobody in particular. It was just a general remark without any real background. Inspector Bodén asked me why anyone should murder Shag, and I answered him. There was nothing else behind it. I know nothing whatever about Lindgren's love affairs."

"I see."

He'll ask about Håkan next, I thought. I was quite right.

"As far as I know, Jan's brother Håkan is not a partner in the business," he said.

I confirmed this.

"So, he's no better paid than any other stableman," the indefatigable head of police went on.

"There's no system of wage adjustment and automatic promotion in a trotting stable," I said sarcastically. "I'm quite sure Håkan is well paid. In practice, he acts as an assistant trainer."

"What about his wife?"

"She's also employed by Jan."

"Isn't it unusual for a girl who has passed her university entrance exam to take that sort of job?"

"Don't you know that our country has been hit by an academic crisis? Joking aside, it may be simply that she likes the job. The best trotting trainer in Sweden is a constructional engineer."

"May I ask what the Lindgren brothers and Mrs. Lindgren were doing yesterday when you discovered the murder?"

"What they were doing at that precise moment I don't know, but soon afterwards I saw Håkan and Anette out on the track and Jan was on his way out for a practice run in the woods with a horse that was tenderfooted."

He consulted his notes.

"That tallies with their own account," he nodded. "Nothing else you'd like to say while you're here?"

I pretended to think hard.

"No," I said after a pause. "You've pumped me of all I know."

"I wonder," the head of police sighed. "I can't make head or tail of this. If anything fresh occurs to you, call me up."

"I promise," I said.

Norberg leant forward and switched off the tape recorder. I took my leave.

Conversation with a Gambler

AFTER MY VISIT to the police station, I went straight to the taxi stand in the middle of the market place, intending to take a cab out to the track. The time I spent with the police wasn't wasted; I had gotten good insight to their method of pursuing the investigation. It might be useful to me.

Evidently the police were very interested in Ring's shaky financial position. I had almost reached the taxi stand, when a thought struck me and I returned to the police station. I knocked at Bodén's door and went in. He was now alone.

"One thing that has just occurred to me as a journalist," I said. "Shouldn't the murderer have been covered with blood when he did Shag in?"

"The doctor says it's possible, but not certain," came the answer.

"That's all I wanted to know."

I pondered Bodén's words as I returned to the market place. Two taxis were standing at the curb, but I couldn't see any drivers. I went inside. No drivers there either, but to my surprise I found my corpulent friend, the professional gambler Bjarne Svensson.

"They're at Clara's having coffee," he said. "I'm minding the phone for them. They'll be back soon."

I remembered that Svensson often used to hang out at the taxi stand. It was almost a kind of office for him. Sometimes, too, there would be a cautious little game of poker. Svensson didn't despise small sources of income. I knew that.

"Are you going up to the track?"

"I was thinking of it," I replied.

Svensson stuffed half a bar of chocolate into his mouth all at once and held out the rest to me.

"Like some?"

"God no!"

"It's good," he stated.

I didn't believe him. The chocolate had some revolting sticky mess inside it. There's a limit to everything.

"I'll come with you to the track," the Railroader said.

The two taxi drivers came shambling across the market place. One was short and one was tall, and both were very lean. It was evidently the tall one's turn to drive. He looked as if he carried all the cares of the world on his narrow shoulders. He was never called anything but "A quarter past twelve." He'd been given this

67

strange nickname because of the angle at which he placed his feet when he stood talking to anyone.

The time was about a quarter past ten when he drove Svensson and me up to the track. A lot of people were there already, although the evening's races wouldn't begin until six o'clock. No doubt, many of them had also been drawn there by the events of yesterday.

I saw that the police still had the area around Shag's room roped off. I had not thought of going there, but I spotted the photographer from my paper in the crowd.

We had done a lot of jobs together and didn't need to waste any words. He knew what pictures to take and I did the writing. That's all there was to it.

When I'd straightened things out with the photographer, I went back to Svensson, and we sat down on a bench in the shade where the Railroader could check the horses' training laps. He wrote the times down in a little book.

As yet, he hadn't said a word about the murder.

I thought it was a pity, as he should have quite a lot to tell. Much valuable information must trickle in via his underground network.

I started the ball rolling.

"Well, what's your theory about the murder?" I asked.

"I expect he knew too much."

"Knew what?"

"Oh, you knew Shag. He wasn't half as stupid as people made out. It was just that he couldn't express himself properly. If you ask me, he was just as sane as you or I."

"No doubt, but you didn't answer my question. What did he know?"

"I don't know. But things are always happening that people are afraid will leak out. You've only to take Berggren . . ."

"Berggren!" I exclaimed in surprise.

"Yes, Berggren. Our fine secretary who's always so short of money."

"What's that got to do with Shag?"

"Quite a lot, if the track secretary is so badly off that he has to borrow from a trainer."

"Lindgren," I said.

"How did you know?" he asked.

"I didn't, but I heard a conversation the other day which I understand better now."

I recalled sitting in the restaurant at the Nordmarken and overhearing the quiet discussion between Berggren and Lindgren. It wasn't the track's affairs they had been talking about, but Berggren's. I realized that now.

"How much money do you think he's borrowed?" I asked.

"I can't say off hand, but I know it was enough for him to be able to pay a large installment on his nice new house. He wouldn't have done so otherwise, with his creditors practically standing outside waiting to repossess it."

"How did you find this out?"

He looked at me in astonishment.

"Shag told me. With a little patience you could get anything out of him."

"I think it's odd that Lindgren took such a risk," I said.

"For him, the risk isn't so big. It's worse for Berggren."

He was right, of course. Though Lindgren would be shown up in a bad light if the loan became public, Berggren would be in a hopeless position. He would have no alternative but to resign. But somehow I couldn't picture him as a murderer.

In a given situation, however, almost anybody can be driven to murder.

"Did Shag tell you anything else?" I asked.

Svensson clicked off his stop watch, looked at it, and wrote the time in his notebook. Then he scratched the back of his neck, or rather necks.

"Nothing that has anything to do with the murder at any rate," he replied.

I had drawn a blank. I would have to try different tactics.

"I saw you with Bengt Ring the other evening. Have you dealings together?"

I had hoped to throw him off balance, but failed miserably. The Railroader was quite unmoved. He turned his round poker face toward me.

"That depends on what you mean by dealings," he said. "We sometimes play poker together. That's all."

"What's he like as a poker player?"

"Pretty bad, actually. He bluffs far too much. It comes off sometimes, but never in the long run."

"Has he lost a lot of money?"

"I only keep count of my own ups and downs, but he has lost money all right."

"How much?"

"I don't know."

"You must have some idea."

"Why are you asking me all this?" Svensson asked in a gentle voice.

"Because I'm interested. I found Shag after all."

"Yes, you did. No, I don't know how much money he has lost on poker this summer, but it's more than a little."

I pricked up my ears at his last words. When the Railroader said "more than a little" he undoubtedly meant a lot of money. Perhaps tens of thousands of kronor. But even gambling losses of that size were hardly likely to make Ring insolvent. It would take more than that. But if his financial position was already undermined, then thirty or forty thousand could make a big difference.

I stored the Railroader's information away for possible future use. Perhaps he knew still more about Ring and his affairs. No harm in trying anyway.

"I heard someone say that Mia Ring is carrying on with Jan Lindgren," I remarked in that vague tone one uses when bringing up such matters.

"Who doesn't she carry on with," Svensson retorted. "She's like a bitch in heat."

Never once had I seen the Railroader with a woman. He seemed utterly disinterested in that aspect of human behavior. I know it'd be logical, in that case, to assume that he'd be interested instead in his own sex, but I hadn't even heard that he had those tendencies.

He had a single all-consuming interest in life, and that was gambling. The betting ticket and the playing card were substitutes for wine, women, and song.

He made the effort and got to his feet. Then he returned his notebook carefully to his breast pocket and heaved a sigh.

"I'm afraid Shag won't be the only one," he said.

"Do you mean someone else is in danger? In that case you should tell the police."

He shook his head.

"No, never mind. I don't want to meddle in things that are not my business. I—"

He broke off. For the moment I was at a loss to know why, but then I looked up and saw that Anette Lindgren was standing next to us. As usual she was dressed in jeans and overblouse. Moreover, she was barefooted. I suppose that's why I hadn't heard her approach.

"Hello," she said. "There were so many policemen around the stables that I went for a walk."

"Have they questioned you?" I asked.

"Yes, one guy asked me a few things."

"About what?"

"Oh, this and that. If I knew why anyone should want to kill Shag, what I was doing at the time, and so on."

The Railroader stood listening to us.

"I'll go and have something to eat," he said.

He plodded off in the direction of the stables.

"Let's sit down for a moment," Anette suggested.

A Wife's Confessions

THE RAILROADER disappeared. There I sat with Anette, feeling embarrassed. I'm no good at making polite conversation; and I don't like being left alone with people I don't know well enough to talk freely with. I get tongue-tied on such occasions, and this was one of them. For what seemed an eternity there was a painful silence. I felt as if I had been turned into a stone idol. Anette broke the silence and the spell.

"I'm so worried about Håkan," she said, and she certainly looked it.

My nervousness evaporated. The pit of my stomach no longer ached and I felt calm.

"Why?"

"He hasn't been himself lately."

"Why are you telling me?" I asked.

"I must talk to someone."

I couldn't quite see why I should be this someone, but I could hardly refuse.

"In what way hasn't he been himself?" I asked.

"He's so terribly nervous and restless," she replied. "He never is, as a rule. He has always been so quiet and easygoing."

"And you've no idea why he's become so nervous?"

She hesitated.

"No," she said, after a long pause.

"Are you quite sure?"

"I've nothing to go on, but I've got a feeling that he's gotten himself into a mess."

This was not very informative and might mean anything at all. Sometimes you get better results if you keep your mouth shut when you're interviewing. I chose these tactics now.

"I think Håkan has gotten mixed up with a gambling syndicate," she said.

I didn't think that sounded very convincing, but of course it has happened before that trotting people have gotten involved like that. There was a logical question to ask.

"Do you know if they're putting pressure on him?"

"I've wondered about that, but I can't put my finger on anything."

"You don't suspect anyone?"

"Yes," she said curtly.

"Ring?"

"Yes. It would be just like him to get at me through Håkan. Bengt is completely ruthless. I know that from experience."

"How long were you engaged to him?"

"Almost a year, but it has nothing to do with this."

72

"So you've nothing to go on?"

"Nothing at all. And don't think that I just want to get back at Bengt. I couldn't care less about him."

"Are you quite sure?" I said unthinkingly.

Her reaction took me by surprise. Without the slightest warning, Anette suddenly began to cry. It was a quiet sobbing, as if from a child.

I let her weep. After a while she pulled a checked handkerchief out of her pants pocket and blew her nose.

"Well, that's that," she murmured with a pathetic attempt at a smile.

"Feeling better now?"

I didn't know quite what to say. I wanted her to go on talking if she really felt like it. She sat there staring out at the dazzling sunshine and thinking her own gloomy thoughts.

"Yes, a bit," she said at last. "I hate Bengt, but at the same time I'm obsessed by him. He never leaves me alone and I can't keep away from him. Yet its Håkan I care for."

"Does Håkan know all about this?"

"Sometimes I feel he does, but mostly I'm pretty sure he hasn't a clue."

"If he really does know, then that explains his nervous irritation. I suppose you weren't describing yourself when you spoke of Håkan?"

"No, actually I wasn't. There's something on Håkan's mind."

"Presumably he knows quite well that you're still carrying on with Ring. That must be the most natural explanation."

"But Håkan has such a lot of money, too," she protested. "We've never been so well off as we are now."

"Maybe he gambles. With Janne winning so often, anyone could make quite a packet, if he was as well informed of the horses' form each day as Håkan must be."

"I never see him gambling," she said.

"That's easily fixed through stooges," I objected. "After all, it's very common, isn't it?"

"Yes, but I still think I'd have noticed something. But you never know."

A thought struck me.

"What about Mia Ring?" I asked. "Does she, by any chance, know of your affair with Bengt?"

"Oh, I expect he's told her. They usually entertain each other like that. But I don't think it worries her that Bengt sleeps around. And living as she does herself, she can hardly make any demands."

It was the second time that day I had heard of Mia Ring's easy virtue. I began to wonder what she was really like. I always get rather suspicious when too many people try to force their opinion of someone on me. A somewhat irrational reaction, no doubt, but that's the way I am.

"No, hardly. I've heard that she's having an affair with Janne," I said casually.

"That's a lie!" she exclaimed vehemently.

"How do you know?"

"Janne wouldn't look at her. She's not his type."

"What *is* his type then? Something more like you, perhaps?"

"Yes, perhaps," she snapped back.

"You seem to get a lot one way or another," I remarked. "And then you wonder why Håkan is worried. What husband wouldn't be?"

She took refuge in tears again. As before, they didn't last long, and the forlorn snuffling soon ceased. She sat there, small and lonely. I felt sorry for her.

"There, there, now," I said soothingly. "Don't worry."

"But it feels so *hopeless*," she sighed. "I don't know what to do. Whichever way I turn, I'm wrong. If I tell Håkan everything, he'll break down, and if I don't tell him, I'll break down. Can't you help me?"

"How could I help you?"

She looked at me with her large tear-stained eyes.

"You can try and find out what's making Håkan so nervous and edgy," she said.

"His actions are not so strange if he knows about your affairs."

"I don't think he has the vaguest idea. No, it's something else."

"OK, I'll try. That's all I can promise. I happen to have other things to do."

"Yes, I suppose so," she said.

We sat there for a while without speaking. I thought about what she had told me, while she seemed absorbed in herself and her thoughts. She was not building castles in the air, I was sure of that.

"It's not easy," she sighed.

"No, it isn't," I agreed. "But you don't exactly make it any easier. If I were you, I wouldn't say anything to Håkan. What he doesn't know won't hurt him."

"I do so want to be honest," she confessed. "I hate this pretense. I know the simplest thing would be to break it off with Bengt. I tell myself that over and over; and just as often, I find myself with him again."

My head was aching and I put my hand to my eyes. The hot air quivered as I took my fingers away. I felt sorry for Anette, but I don't like getting mixed up in other people's problems. Let them get on with it and I'll mind my own business. It's as much as I can do at times. And getting involved with Anette would only cause trouble. I knew that.

She stood up, but I didn't move. She looked down at me for a few seconds without speaking. Then she said:

"Thanks for listening to me. I feel better now that you've promised to help me with Håkan."

I mumbled an answer, and felt ashamed. I didn't take my eyes off her as she walked back to the stables.

The Vultures

I REMAINED SITTING on the bench for a while, turning over what the Railroader and Anette had told me. By far the most interesting, of course, was Svensson's disclosure that Berggren had borrowed money from Jan.

It's true that there had been a similar affair at Solvalla many years ago without any unpleasant consequences for the official concerned, but nowadays the Swedish Trotting Association was not likely to wink at such a thing. No, Allan Berggren might find himself in a nasty spot if certain newspapers got wind of his doings. And it was by no means sure that they would. I knew about it, but I had already decided to keep my mouth shut. For the time being, at any rate.

Then, there was Anette Lindgren's tangled love affairs. She had openly admitted that she was still having an affair with Bengt Ring and had, in addition, hinted that there was something going on between her and Jan. She seemed to be kept quite busy, that girl.

It is often said that routine and clichés are the journalist's worst enemies. If anything, the reverse is true. Routine is always good to fall back on, and when you're working under constant deadline pressure as a news journalist is, it's sheer self-preservation to have certain hackneyed phrases in reserve. The highbrows on the literary pages never seem to realize this. Anyone can write an acceptable article, if he's allowed to sit and polish it for a week.

What I'm trying to say is that no journalist has the time and energy to write things that are as well-documented and carefully prepared as he would like. Instead, he often has to neglect his own work and throw an article together on a subject he knows very little about. It is worse for the reporters on the evening papers, who every hour of their active life have to fight tooth and nail for the favor of the buying public. No wonder things turn out as they do. For a journalist of this kind, it's impossible to write a straightforward story. He must always keep this motto in mind: How can I angle this so that it will appeal to the readers and the editors?

I realized that this murder case had spicy ingredients which would attract the journalists who liked to stir the dregs. It had everything from a good-looking, well-known trainer to pretty girls and, above all, a porno publisher. And there's no denying that the word "porno" stands out well in the headlines.

Reluctantly, I made my way to the stable buildings where Shag had been murdered. I knew in advance what my colleagues would say. The usual empty chatter: the false congratulations on a good story, the sarcasms and the probing, and the anxious questions attempting to flesh out a background and find the detail that could be blown up into a salable front-page scoop.

There they were, the crime reporters, talking knowledgeably to the detectives. They were so honey-voiced, so friendly, and so polite that an outsider would have thought they were displaying their true selves. But all the time, the knives were hidden up their sleeves. They would not be taken out until the reporters sat safely behind their typewriters.

What is more, they knew that all the odds were on their side. Nobody can ever win against a newspaper. The editor always has the last word. And if anyone is so stupid as to go to the Press Fair Practices Commission, it's always the newspaper that comes out ahead. The retraction is placed away in a corner on a back page; the type is small and there is no trace of the skillful editing used when the original libelous story was splashed across the front page.

The journalists know all this. Their only restraint is their own self-respect, but that is soon forgotten for more important things: a fat salary, travel, an expense account, and a titillating sense of power. The fact is, no Swede is safe if a big newspaper gets the idea that he is to be put in his place. And having succeeded in its intent, the press expects to be praised. Surely it is the aim—and duty—of the press to criticize?

I myself once managed to get a league trainer dismissed, although I knew that he was right and the louts on the team were wrong. But you don't criticize popular heroes in this country and get away with it. Before you know what has happened you've been deported to some hole in the provinces and have to prowl around for news. What happened to the trainer I sacked? It was the ruin of him, but how was I to know he was so thin-skinned?

Only one of the journalists recognized me. He had made a dazzling career for himself on a big newspaper in Stockholm and was a specialist in the so-called human touch (even if, in his case, the prefix "in" should be put in front of "human.")

"Hi," he greeted me. "So here you are in clover, eh?"

I agreed.

"You sure had a great story on the front page today," he went on. "You seem to know the area all right."

"I was born and raised here."

I saw how his interest in me quickened. He had a good source to draw on here. He had only to choose the method. To hit on the right approach, the PR people would say. He decided on appealing to my loyalty as a colleague.

"You and I don't have to compete for the news, thank God," he said. "We can swap information. We each write for our own readers."

"Sure, sure," I said, without meaning it.

"Let's go and have some coffee," he suggested in order to avoid possible competitors for the source of information he had just seen spring up in the news desert.

We went to the stable café. He talked without stopping and kept firing questions at me.

"Do you know this porno guy?" he asked.

"Slightly."

I had a chance here to get at Ring.

"He's a bastard who has made a lot of money. Crazy about women."

His face lit up.

"Fine," he said. "What about this: 'Bengt Ring, as hard in business as he is tender in love.' Not a bad caption, eh?"

"Terrific," I agreed.

"What about this Lindgren?"

"Which one?"

"Is there more than one?"

I filled him in on the details. He had, of course, meant Jan Lindgren, who I concentrated upon at once. I told him that Jan was a conscientious young man and that everyone spoke well of him.

"But if this horse was doped, Lindgren did have the responsibility in the stable?"

"Yes. Technically at any rate."

"That could all be written up," he said eagerly. "His successful career in danger and so on. Perhaps I can put something together today after all. It was decent of you to help me."

He rushed off, self-centered and programmed. The day was saved. I knew exactly what he would do. His study of sources was

78

completed. I had supplied him with what he needed. Now he would drive straight to the hotel and write his story.

He always wrote in short sentences, each of which dripped with the sort of unctuous nonsense used by a religious crank. Something like this:

> Bengt Ring is used to handling big money and lovely women.
> But now there's a new factor:
> A brutal murder!
> But the drama has several leading actors.
> Jan Lindgren, successful trainer with a fantastic career behind him.
> A career which, perhaps, is now finished.

And so on, and so on. The reader who hopes to find any information in this rubbish will look in vain. But does the crime reporter care? He has his salary of six thousand kronor a month, an incipient stomach ulcer, and thinks life is just fine.

But was I really any better myself? The only difference between us was a chief editor who perhaps aimed at more serious readers. There are those in the editorial office who say that murder doesn't sell very well. At least that's what they say when they take part in a public discussion. Internally, the message is quite different. Our crime reporters are in an extremely strong position, which they know how to exploit. And who wouldn't?

I myself knew one thing that no one else did: the vet's precaution in taking various specimens immediately. I decided to make sure I did have the sole rights. I hunted about for a telephone and called the police station.

I was in luck and got hold of Norberg. His telephone voice didn't match his large build.

"Why, hello, Mr. Berger," he said. "Is there anything we can do for you?"

"Can't we drop the mister?"

"By all means. My first name is Sven."

"Mine's Kalle."

"I know," he said.

"I was only wondering whether my colleagues had found out that the vet took specimens from Sam Boy yesterday?"

The head of police burst out laughing, his voice rising to falsetto.

"No," he said. "You can put your mind at rest. Only you, we, and the vet know it."

"He might tell the others."

Another burst of laughter. I was beginning to tire of this uncalled-for hilarity.

"Don't worry," he said. "We've made the vet promise to keep quiet. That will give us breathing space on that point until tomorrow. I presume it will then be your—what do you call it again?—oh yes, your scoop."

"That was damn nice of you," I said, sounding like a fool.

"The police do all in their power to improve relations with the fourth estate," Norberg declared, as if reading aloud from a book of instructions.

"Are you as square and pompous as you sound?" I asked.

He nearly choked with laughter now.

"No, actually, I'm not."

I believed him.

Ring's Buddy

I REMAINED at the track for a couple of hours. I like poking around up there. However often I visit a racecourse, I'm always fascinated by the atmosphere. In one way, it's a world of its own, but at the same time, it reflects so much of what happens round about us.

I ran across several people I knew, and one of them was Rickard. A big, heavily built guy who was always dreaming of owning a champion. He had owned many horses, but none of them had ever been above average. He was always being cheated by unscrupulous horse dealers and trainers with no sense of morals.

The trainers often help with the sales. Inexperienced buyers ask their advice, not knowing that the trainer is, at the same time, the seller's agent.

Of course, not all trainers are a party to this system, but a good many are.

Rickard and I had known each other rather well at one time. I was even part owner of a horse we had together with a couple of other guys. It was a miserable scarecrow which won a total of six hundred kronor in a year and cost us at least ten times as much.

"That's a damn good horse you have," Rickard said.

I agreed that Stylist *was* a good horse.

"But I wonder if he has the speed of mine," Rickard went on, his eyes shining with enthusiasm.

"Well, well, what have you got hold of now?"

"A mare out of Frenzy," he replied.

Frenzy, I thought. Hardly a star stallion. But you never know. There are horses with no pedigree that turn out very well indeed—but they're the exceptions.

"What about the mother's side?" I asked.

"Kismet and Deaner," he said. "Plenty of speed there."

Oh, sure, I thought, but plenty of dishonesty, too. I usually compare dishonest horses with Göran Claeson in skating. They have every qualification—strength, speed, and the right build—but they lack the proper kick. When everything agrees, they couldn't be better, but if there's one discrepancy they're out of the running.

"How big is she?" I asked.

He hesitated, looking rather anxious.

"No higher than a hundred and fifty-three, but that doesn't matter. She moves nice and low, and has been carefully handled."

I jumped to the conclusion that Rickard had been duped yet again. Small horses can turn out all right, I know of many examples, but the bigger the horse, the bigger the chances.

"She has already speeded 1.20," Rickard went on. "We've entered her for Färjestad's next meeting. If you've money to spare, then back her. Sven says she'll romp home."

So Sven Nilsson was training Rickard's meteor. Then I'd be wise not to put any money on the horse.

Rickard was an unsuspicious man. At the same time, he was

not as stupid as people thought. Except for horse dealing when he was himself involved, he had a good knowledge of human nature. He worked as an ordinary factory hand, but since he had had the luck to marry a high school teacher, he didn't have to worry too much about making ends meet.

He spent most of his spare time at trotting tracks. Maybe it would be a good idea to lead the conversation around to the events of the last day or two.

"I'll risk ten kronor," I said.

"Ten kronor! You can put down everything you have. She'll win by a mile. You'll see!"

"I haven't much left," I lied. "But, I'll remember what you said."

There was a short pause. Then I changed the subject.

"What do you think about Shag's murder?"

Rickard frowned.

"I think it's all very odd. I can't understand why anyone would want to kill him."

"Nor can I," I said, though several motives for putting Shag out of the way had crossed my mind.

It was obviously useless to pump Rickard about the actual murder. But there were a number of obscure points.

"It was a funny business about Sam Boy," I said, putting out a feeler.

"Yes, wasn't it. I could have understood it in another stable. But Janne's as honest as my old mom."

"What about Håkan and Anette?"

"I think Håkan might be tempted sometimes to make a bit on the side, but he can't bring himself to do it. As for Anette . . ."

He shrugged. I kept quiet, hoping he would go on.

"I can never make that girl out," he said. "She's damned efficient in the stable, as well as being pleasant and agreeable . . ."

He fell silent, evidently waiting for me to put in a word. I decided to humor him.

"I've heard she's pretty active with the men," I said, and felt ashamed.

It was only a couple of hours since I had promised to help the same girl I was now doing my best to slander.

Rickard licked his lips.

"Yes, by Christ," he said. "She's really something all right."

"Wasn't she once engaged to Bengt Ring?"

"Yes, that was before he moved to Stockholm and started printing all those dirty magazines."

"Do you think they still meet?" I asked.

"Why else should he come all the way to Värmland every weekend?"

"Perhaps he wants to look at his horses," I objected.

"Ring doesn't give a damn for his horses. He's a gambler and nothing else."

"But he has a lot of horses, hasn't he?"

Rickard looked at me as if I were soft in the head.

"Tax losses," he said. "Ring buys dozens of horses just for depreciation. Lots of people do, you know that."

Yes, I knew that. I recalled a florist in Stockholm who was a genius at that game. With a few important exceptions, all his horses were put out to graze at his farm in the country, where they were looked after by his irresponsible son. I don't think they were ever trained. Now and again he would start one of them and it was always among the also-rans. But at the same time, he was aware of the power of publicity and would send a couple of horses to Sören Nordin. This trainer, who can put the fear of God into any scarecrow, would make trotters out of them, and all this was very good for the florist's business. But of course, the most important thing was that all the horses at home on the farm were a dead loss.

The tax regulations for trotting horses are in fact rather peculiar. You can have two horses without paying a cent in taxes if they win and make money. On the other hand, you can't deduct anything if they run at a loss. The shrewd minister of finance has worked it out that the state earns money in that way. True, it does happen that someone gets hold of a champion which gives him a tax-free income of a hundred thousand a year or so, but not often.

It is much more usual for the horse owners to lose. And if they have no more than two horses, that's their own affair—their activities count as a hobby. If, however, they have three horses or more, then it's business and is taxed in the ordinary way.

"It must have been a shock for Ring when Sam Boy turned out to be such a good investment," I said.

"I expect so," Rickard agreed. "On the other hand, when he found out how good he was, he could rake in a lot on bets."

"Rumor has it that Ring's finances are a bit shaky," I said.

Rickard smiled so broadly that his upper dentures clicked.

"Yes, so I heard," he said. "But you probably know more about that than I do."

"What do you know?" I persisted.

"Not much."

"You must know something."

Rickard hesitated again.

"You may have heard that Ring is mixed up a bit with gambling in other forms?"

"Yes, I did hear something to that effect."

"I don't know much, living in this hole, but word is going around that Ring has borrowed money from big guys in the syndicate."

"And who would they be?"

"I haven't a clue. It might be someone from Stockholm or Gothenburg. Or even Copenhagen. Ring often buys horses from Denmark and they say he makes other big deals down there."

"So I imagine," I said. "The Danes still have a head start in the pornography game."

Rickard looked at me with his big, brown, ingenuous eyes.

"You hear such a lot of talk," he said. "But a syndicate man turned up in Årjäng yesterday and checked in at the Grand."

"Oh?"

"I saw him together with Ring not long ago."

"Do you know who it is?"

"No idea, but he doesn't look Swedish."

"No?"

"No. He looked like the villain in an Italian western."

"And he's staying at the Grand?"

"Yes, I had a word with the headwaiter—you know, Nils-Erik
—and he said that this foreign guy has two rooms."
"Well, well. Do you think Sam Boy was doped?"
"How the hell do I know?"
"But it seems like it, doesn't it?"
"Ye-es."
He drew the word out.
Obviously, Rickard didn't believe much in the doping theory.
We chatted for a while longer about nothing and then parted.
I now had food for thought.

The Buddy

I RECALLED what Berggren had said about Ring and his
passion for gambling. No doubt that Rickard's remark fitted into
that pattern.

I should have nosed around a little more, but by this time I was
rather tired of the whole thing. I went to a phone booth and tried
to call a taxi, but no one answered. In a bad mood, I started to
walk down to town.

I had gotten as far as the old brewery, long since closed down,
when a car pulled up sharply beside me.

Mia Ring was at the wheel. In the back seat, in addition to her
husband, was a man whom I instantly recognized as the
mysterious guest at the Grand Hotel.

"Like a lift?" she asked.

"Thanks," I said, getting into the front seat of the big American
car.

I glanced over my shoulder and eyed Ring's companion.
Rickard was right. The man didn't look Swedish.

He was immaculately dressed in a light blue summer suit and a
fancy shirt. His tie had a gigantic knot. He was rather slim, but his
fingers were short and thick. A tiepin and a large signet ring
completed his outfit.

85

I had a vague notion at the back of my mind that I had seen the man before, but I couldn't recall where and when. Nobody spoke until we reached the market place.

"Shall I drop you here?" Mia asked.

"No, I was going down to the Grand for a cup of coffee," I lied.

"Oh, good," Mia twittered. "That's where we're taking Milan."

Milan, Milan . . . Now I knew where I had seen the man before.

"Milan here is a business acquaintance of mine," Ring filled in, his voice sounding rather uncertain.

"Oh, so you're both in the porno trade?"

"That's right," Ring agreed hastily. "In this business you have to have good foreign contacts. Milan knows the right people on the Continent."

Milan had still not said a word. He sucked greedily at a fat cigar, now and then sticking his hand through the window and knocking off the ash. He appeared totally indifferent to our conversation.

Mia stopped the car outside the hotel, which was anything but grand, and I got out. A few seconds later, Milan climbed out. He had a patch of sweat under one arm.

"See you this evening then," Ring called.

Milan waved his cigar vaguely by way of answer. Then we walked side by side into the vestibule. There wasn't a soul inside. Milan drummed his short fingers on the reception desk. Nothing happened.

"There doesn't seem to be anyone here," I said. "May I buy you a cup of coffee?"

For the first time he looked me straight in the face. He had large brown eyes. Their expression was quite neutral.

"Do you think there's anyone to serve it?"

He spoke Swedish almost without an accent. But the soft Slav intonation, though very slight, was unmistakable.

We went in and sat down at one of the tables. After a couple of minutes a waiter did, in fact, appear.

"Two coffees, please," I ordered. "Would you like something to drink?"

"Yes, perhaps some mineral water," Milan replied. "I'm very thirsty. It's so hot."

As we sipped our coffee, I gathered my courage and said:

"As a matter of fact, we met briefly once a couple of years ago."

"Oh, did we?"

The voice couldn't have sounded less interested.

"Perhaps I can refresh your memory," I went on. "It was in connection with a trial in Stockholm. A slight row between rival Yugoslavian emigrant groups."

Now there was a flicker of interest in the brown eyes. He took out another cigar, which he carefully clipped and put into his mouth. Some gold crowns glistened.

"You don't say," he said slowly.

"At that time, you were not in the porno trade. Anyway, the cops I spoke to didn't seem to think so."

"Well, things change, you know."

"Of course. But it would surprise me very much if porno magazines are more profitable than gambling clubs."

He smiled and scratched his head with his little finger.

"You seem to know quite a lot, Mr. Berger," he said. "I'm sure it's very useful to you in your profession."

Oh, so he knew my name. Ring must have told him before the car stopped to pick me up.

"How long have you been in Årjäng?" I asked. "And I don't think I caught your surname."

"No, it was very rude of Mr. Ring not to introduce me. My name is Milan Stayovic."

"And when did you arrive in Årjäng?"

Again he smiled.

"I arrived the evening before last. I've heard such a lot about this place from Mr. Ring."

"And what do you think of it?"

"Very charming and peaceful."

"The charm is perhaps questionable," I said. "And it's not very peaceful, is it, with murder and doping."

"Yes, I heard that some poor wretch had been murdered at the race track. But that can happen in any paradise."

"What about the doping?"

"If you mean Mr. Ring's horse that died so suddenly; there's no proof that it was doped. Anyway, I know nothing about horses."

"But you do about gambling," I filled in.

"It's you who say that I own a gambling club," he said.

"And don't you?"

"You heard Mr. Ring say that I dealt in porno."

"One needn't exclude the other. On the contrary, certain connecting links are rather common."

"Well, if that's what the papers say, then it must be true."

His voice sounded serious, as if he meant what he said. But I knew that he was being sarcastic. Anyone in search of the truth seldom finds it in the newspapers.

"If you're not interested in horses, why have you come here?"

"Just for a vacation." He smiled.

I was afraid, all along, that he would leave, but it appeared as if he had all the time in the world to talk to me. This irritated me in some way. People are mostly on their guard when talking to a journalist. But not Milan Stayovic, who, according to my information, ran a couple of the most frequented gambling clubs in Stockholm.

At the Stockholm trial I had taken over at short notice as crime reporter; at one time, that had been my job when I was with my old firm. One of my police contacts informed me that Stayovic owned gambling establishments. He was in no way mixed up in the trial itself. But every day he sat in the public gallery, according to the police, acting as leader of one of the national groups that were at odds with each other.

Although it was nearly three years ago, I found it hard to believe that Stayovic would have changed to another line of business. It was therefore interesting, to say the least, that he had come to this hole in the provinces with Bengt Ring.

Stayovic broke my train of thought.

"I thought you were a sports journalist nowadays," he said.

"So I am, but as I was here anyway, the paper thought I could cover this murder."

"I see. If I were a journalist"—he smiled again—"I would hesitate about switching from one specialty to another like that."

Was there a veiled threat behind his remark or was it only my imagination?

"You said yourself that you'd switched *your* line of business," I said, feeling anger beginning to stir in the pit of my stomach.

"I think you quite misunderstand me. As far as I know I have never said I have anything to do with gambling clubs."

"You must forgive me, but in this case I prefer to believe the police."

"It's entirely up to you to believe what you will, Mr. Berger, but it's not always wise to jump to conclusions. In fact, it may even be dangerous."

"You wouldn't be trying to threaten me, would you?" I said, making an effort to sound as calm as possible.

"Why in heaven's name should I threaten you?" he guffawed.

"I could write that one of Stockholm's gambling kings was honoring Årjäng with a visit."

"Who's threatening now?" he said softly, staring me straight in the face.

Blast the man, maneuvering me into a corner like that. I shut my eyes, thinking I must do something about my temper.

It required an enormous effort of will for me to calm down.

"I'm sorry if I flared up," I said. "I didn't mean to threaten you."

"Oh yes you did," he retorted. "But I've been in this game so long that I've developed a thick skin. I can tell you, Mr. Berger, that I'm not easily frightened."

He drained his glass of mineral water.

"But I don't know how it is with you," he said and stood up.

He was gone before I could think of a suitable reply. Unfortunately he was right. A shiver of fear *had* run down my spine as Stayovic got up and walked away. It was odd, because I am seldom afraid.

The Evening

I FELT DEFEATED when I beckoned the waiter and ordered a whisky to calm my nerves. It is not very pleasant to have the syndicate after you. There are many stories told in Stockholm of how the syndicates handle people who are troublesome. Blackmail, assault, and even murder—the same working methods as those used by the prototypes abroad.

All the same, I wondered whether they would dare to go after journalists who have resources with which to hit back. These coldly calculating gangsters usually avoid such risks.

That's how I reasoned, but it didn't help much. I still felt worried and uneasy.

I left the Grand and walked up Main Street to the market place. I stopped at the newsstand and bought the evening papers, which had just come. Oh yes, my colleague had made the most of Ring's contacts with the porno market and of Janne Lindgren's threatened career.

There was no news, and, above all, the reporters were ignorant of the doping specimens waiting at the lab. I could see, too, that they knew very little about trotting.

I left the newsstand, having half a mind to go up to the race track, but decided not to. What was the use?

Instead, I went to the police station. Inspector Bodén assured me that nothing sensational had happened.

"We're just a little afraid that the homicide squad will turn up, because then we might just as well write the murder off and wait for the statute of limitations to expire," he laughed.

No, the homicide squad is certainly not one of the institutions that wins laurels in the provinces. On the contrary, the county police commissioners usually ward off "help" from the capital for as long as possible.

"May I quote you on that?" I asked Bodén.

"Good God, no!" he exclaimed, looking quite scared.

"Don't worry," I said reassuringly. "Not a word will cross my lips."

"Nor slip out through your fingers either, I hope," Bodén said. He was evidently the suspicious type.

I couldn't help laughing.

"No, I won't write anything either," I said.

"I hope I can rely on that," he persisted.

"Do you really think I would spoil a good contact by quoting you when you don't want me to?"

I felt a pang of conscience as I said that, for it *has* happened that I have written about what has been told to me in strict confidence. But now it was in my own interest to keep on a good footing with Bodén and his colleagues.

"It wasn't meant personally," he said. "But you never know. I skimmed through the evening papers just before you came and what they have to say has very little to do with reality."

"It never has," I said.

I went back to the hotel and concocted my text for the day. I felt slightly ashamed not mentioning Stayovic and his presence in Årjäng. My excuse to myself was that he needn't have the slightest connection with the murder.

But I did make the most of Sam Boy's specimens. To be on the safe side, I called up the laboratory and asked if they knew the result of the tests.

"No, not yet," a woman assistant told me. "But of course, we're giving this priority."

"When do you think they'll be ready?"

"Hard to say in vacation time like this, but I can probably let you know at the beginning of next week."

I pretended to be satisfied with this answer, but in fact I wasn't. She had no doubt added on a couple of days so that the laboratory could work in peace and quiet. I had better call up on Friday, too.

Then I called the paper and gave in my story. The receptionist was new and this annoyed me, but I make it a golden rule always to have the best possible relations with switchboard operators and people in the reception office, so I kept my thoughts to myself.

I have the reputation of getting my calls through quickly from abroad, and I think it's because I'm always pleasant toward the operators, especially in the East European states, of course.

When I was finished, I drank a beer and lay down. I dozed off and lay there between dream and waking. Over the years, I've learned to put myself into this state to give my thoughts a free rein. Association of ideas and all that. I am never so clear in the head as under this self-hypnosis. Everything is so distinct and clear-cut. A pity that I never remember much when I wake up again. I lay there now, the images flickering past as though on an old newsreel.

Sam Boy's glazed eyes.

The pitchfork, the flies.

He buys one dud of a horse after the other, hoping to make them trot.

Anette Lindgren in an orgy together with Håkan, Jan, Ring, and who is the fourth?–oh yes, it's me.

The flies.

Stayovic smiling, but the eyes are cold.

Norberg sitting in his chair, strangled by his own tie.

Sometimes I find it very hard to shake myself out of my dream world. I lie there with eyes open, apparently awake. I roused myself and came back to reality.

As always after one of these seances, I felt a great relief.

The phone rang. I picked it up without any great enthusiasm. Bell's infernal machine is my constant working equipment, but I always regard it as my personal enemy.

"Berger," I said.

"Hi."

I recognized Janne Lindgren's voice.

"Doing anything this evening?" he asked.

"No. Why?"

"I wondered if you'd like to come to a barn dance. It's a lot of fun. Håkan and Anette are coming along."

My dream image of Anette flashed past my eyes. I delayed my answer.

"Well, what do you say?" Lindgren asked.

"I might as well come as sit around here. What time do we go?"

"We'll leave the hotel about eight thirty."

I wasn't particularly anxious to go to a barn dance, but on the other hand I'd have an opportunity of meeting the Lindgren clan, and that might be useful for several reasons.

I looked at my watch and saw that I had plenty of time to go to the dining room and have dinner. I ordered fish and avoided all liquor. There had been a little too much of that commodity the last few days.

I can't say that I'm addicted to drink. Compared with some of my fellow sports writers, I am very moderate in my drinking habits.

Owing to my manner, I am tolerated by other journalists. I keep aloof and that is not always popular. But I've no call to complain. I've never been the target of their conspiracies.

At eight thirty sharp, I went down to the vestibule. Anette was already there waiting. She looked very nice in a thin jacket and trousers. Very thin, in fact . . .

"Hello," she greeted me. "I'm so glad you wanted to come."

I muttered something by way of answer. Actually I hate dances. I can do only the most elementary steps and move like a tailor's dummy.

"Do you know where we're going?" I asked.

"I think Janne said the place is called Näs," she replied.

I knew where that was. My old home was close by. My parents had been dead for many years and the place had been sold. I never went that way when I was in Årjäng. For some reason, I always had a guilty conscience when I saw the old farm that generation after generation of my ancestors had cultivated and cared for.

Janne and Håkan arrived together. Håkan looked rather sleazy in his baggy, grubby jeans and T-shirt; Janne was like a male mannequin in flared, skintight pants, striped pullover, and scarf tied in a Western fashion.

I noticed at once that Håkan was slightly drunk. He walked unsteadily and his eyes were bleary. He still had large bandages on his arm from the accident with Sam Boy.

93

We squeezed into Janne's car and I found myself in the back with Anette. We sat pressed against each other in the cramped space and it was not altogether unpleasant.

We had hardly gotten settled before Håkan pulled a bottle of whisky out of his pants. He passed it back to me.

"Have a swig," he said.

To oblige him, I put the bottle to my lips and moistened them.

"Go on, Anette, you next."

She took a sip and handed the bottle back to Håkan, who held it up and inspected it.

"You drink no more than an ant pisses, either of you," he declared. "This is the way to do it."

He gulped down the whisky, so that his Adam's apple bobbed up and down.

"That can't be good for you," I said to him.

"There's not much I can do," he replied. "But I'll tell you this: I can hold my liquor better than anyone I know."

"Don't be such a fool," Anette said. "I know you can hold your liquor, but we're not going to spend the evening drinking."

"Well, I'm going to, even if you're not," Håkan insisted truculently.

Anette didn't answer him. Jan kept quiet and concentrated on his driving. He never left anything to chance.

We drove past Kyrkerud School and along the Skrä ridge with its beautiful view over Västra Silen. Then we swept down the hill to Lysed and turned left toward Näs.

It was not hard to find the scene of festivity. A stream of cars showed the way.

An enterprising farmer had turned his unused barn into a dance hall. He himself sat collecting the admission and looked surprised when he saw me.

"You haven't been out this way for ages," he said.

"No, it's been quite a long time now."

"You're a journalist, I've heard."

"That's right."

He looked as if he wanted to go on talking to me, but people were pushing from behind, so I paid my five kronor and entered the barn. It was noisy and packed with people, most of whom were drunk.

I recognized some of them but many were strangers to me, tourists, most likely. The band consisted of an accordion, guitar, double bass, and drums. It sounded ghastly.

The farmer's wife was in charge of the open-air café. By standing ready to pounce, Jan soon got hold of a table. We ordered coffee. Håkan filled half his cup with whisky. He had evidently spoken the truth when he boasted he could hold a lot of liquor. By rights, he should have been stoned by now, but he looked just as he had done when we met at the hotel.

Jan asked Anette for a dance and they launched out into a waltz.

"A handsome couple, aren't they?" Håkan remarked.

"Yes," I said lamely.

"They have sex together, too, sometimes," he confided. "They think I don't know, but I do."

I didn't know what to say.

"So long as she comes back to me, she can fuck the devil himself," he went on. "I saw how you two sat cuddling in the back of the car. Have a go at her. She never says no."

The conversation had taken an unpleasant turn, and I reacted by remaining silent. I couldn't for the life of me think of anything sensible to say to this cuckold who was so very much aware of what his wife was up to.

Anette and Jan came back to the table. I wanted to talk to Anette and there was only one way of doing so. I asked her for the next dance, which I took to be a fox trot.

The dance floor was crowded and everyone was very boisterous.

"I was talking to Håkan just now," I said.

"I can't make him out. He never drinks like this."

"Remember our talk this morning? It seems ages ago. You needn't worry about any confession. He knows about your affair with Jan."

She stopped dead in the middle of the dance and stared at me.

"You're lying."

95

"Indeed, I'm not. He said that you two have sex together sometimes."

We shuffled around, around, in a pattern that had very little to do with dancing.

"Did he say anything else?"

"Yes. That he doesn't care whom you sleep with so long as you come back to him."

"Anything else?"

"That I should have a go at you. You never say no, he said. Shall I try?"

Her thick underlip quivered and I saw that tears were not far away.

"Don't make a scene on the dance floor, please. Pull yourself together."

"I think you've made it all up," she insisted.

"Ask him then."

"I don't dare."

"Don't you realize you're playing with dynamite, Anette? You'll soon have to pick sides. You can't go on like this, either for your own sake or Håkan's."

The music stopped and we threaded our way toward our table. We had gotten about half way there when someone grabbed me by the shoulder and I heard a voice with an unmistakable Gothenburg accent.

"Watch where you're going, you peasant bastard. You knocked my glass over."

My whole body stiffened. I was certain that I hadn't even knocked against a table, let alone a glass. I dropped Anette's arm and gave her a little push toward the Lindgren brothers' table. At the same moment, I wrenched free of the man's grip and turned toward him.

I saw a heavily built man of about thirty with thick hairy arms. The eyes he fixed on me were quite blank. A couple of other men were sitting at the table, looking on with interest.

"I think you're mistaken," I said quietly, but I felt anger boiling up inside me.

"Like hell I am, you knocked my glass over," he snarled.

The expressionless eyes remained fixed on me. Out of the corner of my eye, I saw that he was fumbling with something between his hands. There was a glint of metal. A knife? No—brass knuckles.

Without another thought I kicked him as hard as I could just below the knee. It's an old combat trick that I learned in the army, so I guess National Service has some use after all. He screamed with pain and collapsed. On his way down, I jabbed my knee in his face to make sure. There was a clatter as he dropped the brass knuckles, which was an ugly-looking thing made from a piece of piping.

His buddies jumped to their feet but quickly changed their minds when a couple of bouncers appeared out of thin air.

"Making trouble, are you, Kalle?" one of them asked. I knew him from the old days in the people's amusement park.

An onlooker came to my help.

"This guy was just going to hit him with brass knuckles," he said.

Several other voices chimed in.

My antagonist was still lying where he had fallen. He was bleeding profusely from the mouth. One of the bouncers bent down and felt his leg.

"We'll have to get him to hospital," he said. "I think his leg's broken. You'd better come along with us to the police, Kalle."

"With pleasure," I said. "But take the names of the witnesses here, and take charge of those brass knuckles too."

"Sure, sure," the bouncer said, doing as I told him.

I accompanied him, and actually, I was only too pleased to get away from the place. I was just about to get into the car, when Anette and Jan caught up with me.

"What did that horrible man mean?" she said hotly. "We weren't anywhere near his table."

"I expect he made a mistake," I suggested.

"No, no, no. He was after you, that's for sure."

I was pleasantly touched by her interest in me.

"I hardly think that."

Jan Lindgren looked at me thoughtfully.

97

"I didn't know you could fight so well," he said.

"I didn't either," I replied. "It was just luck. I've used the same trick once or twice abroad. It's not pretty, but it's effective."

"Damned effective," the bouncer agreed. "It'll be a long time before that knee heals up."

"Damn well serve him right," I muttered. "Did you recognize him, by the way?"

"No, I've never seen him before. Have you?"

I shook my head.

But only for the sake of appearances. I was pretty sure that my friend Milan Stayovic had hired the thug from Gothenburg.

The bouncer drove me to the police station.

"Well, let's go in," he said.

And we did.

At the Police Station

I HAD TO WAIT for almost an hour before being admitted to my old friend Bodén. I heard telephones ringing and policemen coming and going. The county police commissioner, with the murder in mind, was evidently ordering reinforcements to Årjäng.

In due course Bodén came gliding out.

"So here's the brawler," he said. "Come in, will you."

We went into his office. I was surprised to find Norberg in there. To my relief, I saw that the noose was no longer around his neck. Instead, he was wearing a pullover that was far too short in front.

"Sit down," Bodén said.

Nordberg nodded to me and Bodén switched on a tape recorder.

"Interrogation with Mr. Karl Berger, Thursday July 19, 11:30 p.m."

"Being rather formal, aren't you?" I asked.

"We have to be in a case of suspected assault and battery."

"Am I really suspected of that?"

Bodén hesitated.

"Not exactly, but the fact is that you broke the other man's leg. Will you please give an account of what happened."

I did as he asked and kept to the truth as far as possible, avoiding, of course, any mention of my conversation with Anette or of my suspicions of Stayovic.

"And you're quite sure you've never seen the man before?" Bodén asked.

"Quite sure," I replied truthfully.

"His name's Conny Eng and he's an ugly customer," Norberg announced unexpectedly.

I received this information without comment. Bodén, however, glanced rather reproachfully at his chief, evidently not very pleased by Norberg's intervention.

But Bodén's annoyance didn't seem to worry the fat chief of police in the slightest.

"In point of fact, you did us a service when you broke his leg," he went on. "Eng has been sentenced for assault a couple of times and should be sitting behind bars right now. He escaped from Härlanda a couple of weeks ago. Not that there's anything remarkable in that; it's unusual nowadays for prisons to be able to keep their inmates. I've a suspicion there's a diabolical conspiracy behind it all. The Prisons Board wants to earn money at the expense of the police force. The fewer the prisoners, the cheaper it is."

After this long, somewhat reactionary address, the chief of police leaned back in his chair and said no more.

"Do you mind if I go on now?" Bodén asked, a note of sarcasm in his voice.

"Of course not, that's why we're here. Crack down on this assailant now, so that he'll know in the future that it's forbidden to defend oneself when attacked by someone armed with a murder weapon."

The chief of police bent down and brought out Eng's brass knuckles. I shuddered when I saw the great clump of iron. The projecting part would easily have smashed every bone in my face.

"I've never said he was an assailant," Bodén protested.

"I thought you said I was suspected of assault and battery," I objected. "If I'm not mistaken, the minimum sentence for a crime of that kind is a couple of years."

"The fact that the victim happens to be an escaped prisoner doesn't automatically turn him into an outlaw."

Evidently Bodén's attitude to crime and criminals was a little more modern than the chief's.

"Anyway, it's a fact that he attacked me with a dangerous weapon," I said.

"Ah, but did he?" Bodén retorted. "I gather that he never had time to strike you before you kicked him."

"So you mean I should have waited until he had smashed my face in? If someone takes out a gun with the obvious intention of shooting you, do you wait for the shot before making a defensive move?"

Bodén looked as if he was about to protest, but he changed his mind.

"It's only fair to say that your account tallies with that given by the bouncer. Have you any idea why he was after you?"

"No, not the faintest," I replied. "As I said, I've never seen him before. Maybe he only wanted to pick a quarrel with someone he thought looked harmless."

"Well, *I* wouldn't say you looked harmless," Norberg remarked.

"I suppose he thought it was safe to pick on me. And it was pure chance that the kick landed where it did."

"I'm not so sure," Bodén said. "The bouncer in fact thought that you were unusually cold-blooded."

"No, not cold-blooded—just plain scared. And when you're scared, you often act automatically. Instinct of self-preservation and all that."

"But I don't think many people would automatically think of such a dirty trick as that kick." Bodén was not giving in.

"I learned it in the army," I said. "We were given special commando training."

"Aha, I see. Now I understand better. I myself would never have hit on the idea."

I made no comment. Bodén fixed his eyes on me and I stared

back. Then he glanced swiftly at Norberg and went on with the interrogation.

"We haven't been able to question Eng yet, since he's in the hospital being operated on."

"Operated on? I thought it was only long-term care there nowadays."

"They can manage fractures. It's very common for old people and cripples to break a leg," he said like a schoolmaster. "As I said, we haven't been able to question Eng yet, but we know that he has been a sort of strong-arm for gambling clubs in Gothenburg."

"Oh, has he," I said, merely for something to say.

"So now we're wondering whether Eng's relations with the illegal gambling clubs can have any connection with his aggressive attitude toward you."

"Aggressive attitude!" I exclaimed sarcastically. "He was going to smash my face in."

"You didn't answer my question."

"Was it a question? No, I can't see any connection between Eng and me, even if he had been hired by ten gambling kings."

"So you've nothing to do with clubs of that kind?"

"To be honest, I'll admit I have visited a couple in Stockholm, but never in Gothenburg."

"The owners are often the same," Norberg put in.

"So I've heard. But if you think I have any close dealings with those circles, you're barking up the wrong tree."

"Close," Bodén repeated. "Am I to take it that you do have some dealings with these clubs?"

"Don't split hairs," I snapped. "My only contact with the clubs is that I have visited them as a customer on several occasions. It may be a criminal offense, but in that case there are thousands like me."

"Did you lose a lot of money?" Bodén asked.

"No, not at all. I'm not a big gambler nowadays. If I remember rightly, I've been to gambling clubs three times. On two occasions, I won a couple of hundred and the third time I suppose I lost just as much."

"What did you play?"

"Poker. I don't care for games of pure chance."

"You say you're not a big gambler nowadays. Does that mean that you used to gamble heavily?"

"I wouldn't say heavily. A couple of years ago I did bet quite a lot on horses."

"By the way," Bodén went on. "When you bought your horse, where did you get the money from? I've heard that he cost you something in the region of fifty thousand."

"I had the same five figures on a betting ticket every week at Solvalla," I told him. "My old phone number when I lived out of town. I made myself hand it in every week, and last winter I got lucky and won over eighty thousand."

"Lucky indeed."

"Yes, wasn't it."

"And then you bought your horse for fifty thousand?"

"He didn't cost all that," I said. "You can go down ten thousand."

"It costs a lot to keep a horse in training, doesn't it?" Bodén asked.

"By God, I'll say it does."

"So you've been eating into your capital?"

"That's right."

"May I ask another question. You live in Stockholm now. How did you happen to put your horse in training with a Värmland trainer?"

"I didn't want to expose him to the conditions at Solvalla. It's not at all unusual for horse owners from Stockholm to engage provincial trainers. It's much cheaper to have a horse in training in the provinces."

"I see. And why did you go to Lindgren?"

"He's an outstanding trainer. Also, I knew him slightly from the old days."

"I see. And you're satisfied with his care of the horse?"

"I certainly am."

"What about your acquaintance with Bengt Ring?"

"Oh, I've known him casually for several years. He's anything but a friend of mine, but we always say hello when we meet."

"No business dealings with him?"

"Never."

"It's said that Ring is mixed up in a shady way with gambling clubs. Have you heard anything to that effect?"

"I think it was Berggren who told me that the Central Association was looking into Ring's affairs."

"What central association?"

"The Central Association of Swedish Trotting which administers trotting in Sweden."

Bodén made notes busily and the tape recorder went on revolving. Norberg, as usual, was deep in his nirvana.

"Why should the Central Association be interested in Ring's affairs?" Bodén asked.

"There's a ruling which says that horse owners and trainers must not have anything to do with illegal gambling. If it can be proved that there *is* such a connection, the person concerned can be expelled, usually for life."

"How very interesting," Bodén said. "So, by rights, you shouldn't be allowed to have a trotting horse then?"

The cunning bastard.

"It's over a year since I was at a gambling club," I retorted.

Norberg slowly opened his eyes. It seemed to cost him an enormous effort.

"What do you think about Ring?" he asked.

"How do you mean, think?"

"Does he have gambling clubs?"

"I don't know, but it wouldn't surprise me."

"After your disclosures, we amused ourselves by looking into his financial position. It's anything but healthy. He seems to be teetering on the verge of bankruptcy. But of course, we can't get at any crooked dealings he may have. Sometimes it can be very lucrative to go bankrupt."

"If you've looked into his affairs, then you must surely have investigated his gambling interests?"

"We've tried, but our valued colleagues in Stockholm contend that the business is so interwoven that it's impossible to make any definite statement."

I decided to make another disclosure.

"One of the big sharks is here in Årjäng," I said.

103

I had the satisfaction of seeing both of them gape with astonishment.

"How do you know?" Bodén asked quickly.

"I've seen him," I replied.

"Tell us about it," Norberg requested.

I obliged him by sketching in Milan Stayovic's background. I even mentioned that we had had coffee together, but this had been mere chance.

"Ring gave us a lift down to the Grand, you see."

"And why did you want to go to the Grand when you're staying at the Nordmarken?" asked the ever suspicious Bodén.

"I think their coffee's better," I replied, aware that the reason was not very convincing.

They asked a lot more about Stayovic, but I stuck to what I had said. It didn't seem to occur to either of them that the Yugoslav might have been behind the nasty incident of the evening.

"Anything more?" I asked at length. "It's late and I'm tired."

"No, we're satisfied for the time being," Norberg said.

"May I go home, or am I to be locked up?"

"We'll risk it and let you remain at large a couple of days longer," Norberg replied, smiling like Santa Claus.

"No news about the murder?"

Norberg sighed as if he had all the sorrows of the world on his broad shoulders.

"No, only that the homicide squad have advised us of their arrival tomorrow."

"Congratulations," I said. "Then you've nothing more to worry about."

"I wish I could say the same," the police chief sighed. "Now is when the trouble starts. If there's one thing I hate, it's when several different divisions work on the same case. The chief constable is coming too, and he's always at odds with the homicide squad."

"Good luck," I said.

I left the police station and walked back to the hotel, looking around me carefully. I had not forgotten Eng's pals who suddenly disappeared the minute it was all over.

But there was no sign of them. I got back safely and went to bed. Although I was dead tired in body and soul, I tossed and turned for a couple of hours before getting to sleep.

Friday

NORDMARKEN'S RACE TRACK usually has legendary luck with the weather; but on this Friday, God the Father failed in his duty—or possibly it's some other potentate who is responsible for it all.

A fine rain had set in and the clouds grazed the high ridges. I ran out and bought the early newspapers. To my relief, I found that the *Gothenburg Post* and the Värmland papers contained nothing of any importance that I had missed. I also searched for any report of the incident at Näs on Thursday evening, but there was nothing. As a rule, the local correspondents make all they can of such things.

The racecourse looks very inviting when the sun shines, but is inhospitable in bad weather. There is very little shelter from the rain and the spectators huddle under the restaurant. But despite the wet, there were a lot of people on this Friday, too. Wise from experience of such weather, I had put on rubber boots as well as a raincoat and was very glad I had, for it was indescribably muddy around the stables. Big puddles everywhere, stained yellow-green by all the horse droppings. The horses for the first race were being warmed up, and the farmers went around and around with their small steeds.

I went straight to the Lindgren stable. Everything was in meticulous order, as usual. Stylist, who was to start in the second race, stood already harnessed in the paddock, looking very melancholy. Perhaps he was only putting it on, because he scraped cautiously with one hoof, and that is usually a sign of slight nervousness. Otherwise, he hung his head and seemed the picture of misery.

Anette was standing beside him, winding bandages around his hind legs.

"Hi," I said. "He doesn't usually have bandages."

"It's the first time he's racing on such a bad surface and we're not taking any risks."

"How are things today?" I asked.

"Oh, not so bad. How are you?"

"Just fine. What about Håkan?"

She didn't look up as she answered, "He's not well today, so he took the day off."

"Have you spoken to him?"

"Of course I have."

"You know quite well what I mean," I said.

"He hasn't been in a fit state for a sensible conversation."

Jan Lindgren appeared, picking his way. He was wearing my jacket and colors, with gray nylon pants. A pair of goggles hung around his neck.

"He looks sluggish, if you ask me," I said, pointing to Stylist.

"He's always like that," Jan replied. "If you didn't know him, you'd think he was ready for the glue factory any minute."

As though to emphasize the truth of Lindgren's remark, the rascal suddenly shoved at my back, nearly knocking me over.

"You've forgotten to give him sugar," Lindgren said. "He never forgets anything. I don't think I've ever come across a more trainable horse."

I hunted desperately in my pockets and finally found a small restaurant package of sugar. I gave Stylist both lumps. He munched them and resumed his slack position.

"Isn't there a danger in his having such a good memory?" I asked. "In that case, he probably remembers everything that goes against him too. Rubber bands that sting his legs, bits of paper fluttering about on the track, people shouting in his ears, other drivers lashing at him with the whip—all that, you know."

"Oh yes, he remembers all right, but it doesn't scare him. He just watches out. By the way, I've a confession to make," Lindgren said.

Anette jumped up and I stared at him.

"Don't get alarmed!" he laughed. "I only wanted to tell you

that he'll be starting at Solvalla next week—if you're agreeable, that is. I entered him for the July meeting without asking you."

"Has he any chance?"

"That's what I want to find out. Myself, I think he'll win, but there's quite a difference in the competition at Solvalla."

"If you think he's ready, then I've nothing against it. When is it to be?"

"Next Thursday."

"That's settled then."

"Good."

Jan gathered up Stylist's reins carefully and drove out with him. The minute Lindgren took charge of him, the horse's attitude changed as if by magic. He began to twitch his ears and stretch his neck.

No, I had no cause to worry. There was nothing wrong with him.

I sauntered off toward the track. It was still raining with the same persistence, and I went up to the restaurant to see if there was a vacant table.

"No, I'm sorry," the headwaiter said. "We're full."

I looked around the room in search of someone I knew. Sure enough, at a window table sat the Rings and the big gambler Stayovic.

I saw Mia Ring spot me and tell her husband. He glanced over and his face beamed with good will.

He got up and almost ran toward me.

"Hiya," he said, behaving as if I were a long-lost friend he hadn't seen for the last ten years. "Won't you join us? We've room for one more at our table."

"Thanks, I'd like to," I answered. "But may I come after this race? My horse is running and I'd like to see the start at close quarters. You don't mind, do you?"

"Not in the least, old pal."

Old pal, hmm. I tried to catch Stayovic's eye, but failed. He was busy with whatever he had on his plate.

There was plenty of time until the start of the second race. When I got down to the track, the victory parade from the first race was just going past.

107

Suddenly I remembered something and ran as fast as I could up the stairs to the press tower. One of the telephones was free, and to avert suspicion from any of the other journalists, I walked with slow dignity into the cubicle.

I closed the door carefully behind me and phoned the laboratory in Stockholm. It was after four o'clock and I had no great hope that anyone would still be there.

But wonder of wonders, I was put through to the same girl I had spoken to the day before. Her laughter rippled over the line.

"I told you we wouldn't be ready until the beginning of next week."

"So you haven't any results yet?"

"Well, as a matter of fact we have," the angel replied.

"What are they?"

"I'm sorry to say they're negative in every respect. No drug substances in either blood, saliva, or urine."

"Are you sure?"

"Dead sure."

"Well I'll be damned," escaped me.

"The police said exactly the same," she said.

"Can you remember who it was you spoke to?"

"I think his name was Bodin or something like that."

"Has any other newspaper called up yet?"

She laughed again.

"No," she said. "You're the first."

"If anyone else rings, please say you're not ready yet. Promise!"

"You're joking. I can't promise anything like that. But it won't be easy to get hold of us later today because I have my coat on and am just about to leave."

"Fine," I said. "Thanks a lot and have a nice weekend."

"The same to you."

Then I called the paper and told them I'd have a story for them within two hours.

"That's rather late," a sulky assistant editor muttered.

No scoop in the world could stop me from watching Stylist's race, so I said:

"Take it easy now, Fredrik. I've a good story coming up. I promise you it's worth waiting for."

"Well, you haven't been too bad up to now, so I suppose we'd better keep some space for you in the national edition."

My old acquaintance Olsson stopped me as I left the cubicle. As usual he looked scared stiff.

"The police told me you were mixed up in a brawl at Näs last night," he said.

"That's right," I confirmed.

"And you've nothing to add over and above what the police say?"

"No."

"He'll be on the sick list for at least two months."

"I suppose you know he had escaped from Härlanda?" I said.

"Yes, so Bodén said."

He scribbled something in a minute notebook.

"It was he who attacked *me,*" I said. "Self-defense on my part."

"So I gather."

"Are you going to write it up?" I asked.

"I'll put something together."

"You won't mention any names?"

"Oh no," he assured me.

"And you needn't say I'm a journalist either. Just call me a Stockholmer."

"Sure, I'll do that," he promised.

I left him and went down and stood by the railing. There was plenty of room in the pouring rain. Jan Lindgren was just trying Stylist out for his start and it looked good.

I went to the betting window and bet three hundred on him to win. He was the favorite, so there wouldn't be much of a dividend.

At Årjäng, unlike other big race tracks, there is no tote board that tells the bettors how the money is being wagered on the different horses. In order to get an idea of this, the big gamblers must hang around the fifty-kronor windows and in this way find out who is the favorite.

I remember once, before I was a journalist, I was working in an office and we went to Örebro to back an Årjäng horse that was a dead cert.

Soltuna, I think her name was. Our tactics were good. As late as possible, I was to sneak in and put everything we possessed on her while my pals blocked the window so that no one else could back the same horse. Everything went according to plan. I got the money in just as the window closed and those behind me didn't have a chance. There was just one slight hitch. Soltuna galloped at the start, and despite a magnificent recovery she came in only second. But even in those days I was very cautious, so without the others knowing I had put a couple of hundred on a place too. This meant that we got enough money back to live it up that night, but that was all.

And here I stood now, waiting to see how my own horse performed.

Competition was keener this time. I had the utmost respect for the Gothenburg trainer Enar Brogren, who was visiting the track with a promising three-year-old that had already won at Åby and had thus attracted a lot of money.

But it didn't matter so much, since the prize money was calculated from the beginning of the meeting, which meant that he now stood at the start together with Stylist and five other horses.

Stylist had track three and Brogren's horse, Rodney's Pride, had track four. Matters were not improved by the fact that Janne and Brogren disliked each other. At one time they had both worked as apprentices with the same trainer and their hostility dated from then. Both were successful, but perhaps Lindgren had drawn ahead of Brogren of late, despite Brogren's advantage in having a license at a big track like Åby.

The horses were very restless and there was a false start. I had concentrated on Stylist and thought he was being hemmed in by Rodney's Pride.

Volting for a restart.

One of the horses was unruly and it took a couple of minutes before the chief starter raised his flag, thereby signaling to the judges' tower that everything was ready.

Stylist trotted around without paying any attention to all the fuss. Rodney's Pride, too, seemed quite unruffled.

As the horses turned into the straight, I realized what was

happening. Brogren was heading down at an angle to the left, squeezing Janne in.

"Keep to your track, you goddam idiot," Janne shouted.

But Brogren ignored him. There was no room left for Stylist, who took a couple of galloping leaps and then stood practically still while the whole field rushed past him. He must have been at least sixty yards behind Rodney's Pride when he got going again.

There goes my three hundred, I thought bitterly.

At first, it seemed as if Lindgren would give up and drive back to the stable, but he chose to complete the course. After the first lap, he was in touch with the others. Then, right in front of the spectators, he made a little rush, and as they turned into the curve by the stables he had only one horse in front of him—Rodney's Pride.

Brogren was driving for all he was worth and was at least twenty yards ahead of my horse. But perhaps the Gothenburg trainer was a little too sure of himself. With only five hundred yards to go, he was being shadowed by Stylist, who stole up close behind him.

I could plainly see Brogren turn his head and brandish his riding whip at Stylist's nose. Lindgren saw the danger and backed away. For that matter, it was quite possible that Stylist was tired from the effort of catching up and had nothing more to give.

Lindgren hung on all the way around the curve into the straight, and when the bell rang he was still close on the heels of Rodney's Pride. Not until there was only a hundred yards to go did he suddenly steer clear and attack.

Brogren was using the whip hard. At seventy-five yards the two horses were side by side, but then the fight was over. While Stylist maintained his speed, Rodney's Pride slowed down and when they passed the finish line, Lindgren was a good sulky's length ahead.

I could feel myself sweating from the nervous strain. I looked over toward the stable bend where Janne was preparing Stylist for the post parade. Brogren was doing the same at a safe distance from Lindgren.

I waited until Lindgren drove past me as the first of the three

111

place horses. He was coal black in the face from the mud splashed up by the horses in front of him. He had taken off his goggles. He was white where they had protected him and this made the contrast all the greater.

Janne looked pretty grim, but his face relaxed when he saw me.

"There's no beating this one, even with foul driving," he shouted.

Brogren was only a few yards behind him and must have heard. He kept his eyes fixed on the ground and seemed to take his defeat very hard.

Ring and Stayovic

AFTER THE RACE, I went up to the press tower and improvised a report on the murder investigation, basing it, of course, on the negative result of the drug analyses.

When I had finished dictating, I asked to speak to an assistant editor.

"Well, that's the lot for now," I said.

"You can ease up a bit now on this story," he said. "Keep an eye on things, but otherwise you can resume your vacation."

"Thanks."

"We've got a lot anyway. A sex murder here in Stockholm today and that sells better."

"So I imagine."

"This time of year, we always have a sex murder," he harped. "It never fails."

So poor old Shag was removed from the front pages of the Stockholm papers. I could picture the crime reporters who had been sent to Årjäng now making a beeline back to the capital.

Just as well, too.

Only now did I remember that I had promised to call on the Ring-Stayovic team. I went down to the restaurant and over to the table where they sat.

112

"May I join you?" I asked.

Ring exuded benevolence.

"You sure may," he said. "That's one hell of a good horse you have."

"Yes, he's not so bad."

I had difficulty in concealing my pride.

"And he gave good odds, too," Ring went on.

"Oh, did he? I haven't heard yet."

"Two seventy-five," he informed me.

"Then Rodney's Pride must have been the favorite," I said.

"Well, you know what Gothenburgers are like. They always back their own horses."

Stayovic sat picking his teeth with what amounted to frenzy. He drove the toothpick in as if it were a murder weapon which he then twisted in order to cause the greatest possible injury. The process looked extremely dangerous.

"All I can say is that Brogren did his best to win," I said. "He's got a big fine coming to him, if I'm not mistaken."

"Yes, the start was a bit cramped," Ring agreed, glancing rather furtively at Stayovic.

But the Yugoslav was still busy cleaning his teeth. Mia Ring had not yet said a word.

"You saw as well as I did that Enar did all he could to trip Kalle's horse," she snapped.

"It might have been sheer bad luck," Ring said.

"Like hell it was," I protested. "I was standing less than five yards away and saw the whole thing. Brogren was out to spoil Stylist's start and he succeeded. I hope he'll be suspended for six months."

Ring again tried to catch Stayovic's eye. The latter's dental operation was now complete, and he emphasized the fact by breaking the little wooden pick into three pieces and tossing them onto the floor. Suddenly he turned to me.

"I lost three thousand on your blasted horse," he snarled.

"But he won."

"I backed Rodney's Pride."

I shrugged.

"Those are the risks a gambler must take."

113

Stayovic stared at me. Ring was unnecessarily busy soaking up the last small pools of gravy on his plate with a piece of bread. Mia sipped the glass in front of her. It looked like a coke, but the color was suspiciously diluted. The disgusting American drink was no doubt laced with something very much stronger.

In fact, studying her closer I saw that her eyes were rather misty. She was in much the same state as during the big party a couple of days earlier.

"Kalle," she purred seductively, "surely you know that it's Milan who owns Rodney's Pride?"

Her surprising disclosure earned her a furious glare from her husband. Stayovic on the other hand didn't bat an eyelid.

"I bought him yesterday," he said. "Brogren guaranteed that he would win."

"Well, it certainly wasn't Brogren's fault that he lost," I said. "Did he have instructions to drive as he did?"

It was an insolent question, but Stayovic's poker face never altered.

"He had instructions to drive to win," he said.

"Very ambiguous," I said. "Have you any more horses?"

"No, this is the first time I've bought one," he replied.

"He didn't need to buy it," Mia blurted out. "The former owner owed Milan so much money that he got the horse for nothing."

"And who did you buy it from?"

I looked through the program and saw that "Stall Rail" was given as the owner. That didn't tell me much. Stayovic didn't seem inclined to say who the seller was.

"I don't recognize that pseudonym," I said. "But it's easy enough to find out the owner's name."

"Can't you see who it was?" Mia asked. "It's a riddle, see."

I began to think. The rail on a stall . . . That didn't make much sense . . . Rail . . . What other kind of rail was there? . . . Why, of course! Railroad!

"You don't mean it was the Railroader's horse?" I exclaimed.

"Sure."

"He must have been pretty expensive," I said to Stayovic.

"Oh, not so very," he said in a bored tone.

114

"How much did the Railroader owe you?"

"I'm not going to sit here telling business secrets to a journalist," he said with a smile.

"You know quite well that people who are mixed up with illegal gambling are not allowed to own horses," I said.

"Who says I've anything to do with illegal gambling?" Stayovic retorted. "I'm in the publishing business now."

"They say it's not so lucrative any more, eh, Bengt?"

"It all depends," he said.

I decided to change the subject.

"I think you'll get your insurance money on Sam Boy all right," I said to Ring.

He looked first at me, then at his wife, and finally at Stayovic. None of them made any comment.

"The analyses have been made," I said. "The results are negative."

"How do you know?"

There was an eager undertone in Ring's voice.

"I just spoke to the laboratory."

"Is it true?"

Now he sounded still more eager. Cheerful, too.

"Did you have him *so* heavily insured?" I asked.

Ring quickly tried to make his face a blank again. He almost succeeded, but not quite. A little gleam of satisfaction lingered in the corner of his eye.

"I had him insured to his full value," he said.

"That doesn't say much. What was he worth?"

"How much would you have given for him?"

"Twenty thousand, at the most."

"Being rather modest, aren't you?" Ring protested. "There was still a lot of money to be made out of him."

"Maybe."

It was obvious that Ring had had Sam Boy insured for a lot more than his real sale value. It's very expensive to insure race horses, so I was surprised that Ring put out so much money on a thing like that. It needn't mean anything in itself, but there was something fishy about it all the same.

I caught the waiter as he went past and ordered a couple of

115

sandwiches and a bottle of beer. I was not very hungry. The taciturn Stayovic sat opposite me looking rather glum.

Just as I took the first bite of my cheese sandwich, he asked:
"You don't want to sell your horse, do you?"

I took my time, chewing like someone in a film for children about dental care.

"That depends."

"I'll give you a good price."

"Yes, you'd have to."

He took a cigar out of his breast pocket and set about clipping it carefully.

"Name it."

That put me in an awkward position, as I knew very little about such affairs.

"I'll talk it over with Janne first," I said at length.

"Yes, do," Stayovic said generously.

"For your information, I can tell you that I've already been offered fifty thousand."

That was the price that the trotting journalist Åke Bengtsson had mentioned when we met.

"Sounds reasonable enough," Stayovic declared.

Nothing more was said on that subject. I finished my sandwiches and Ring offered me a whisky. I refused.

I had not yet brought up my encounter of the previous evening with Eng, the ugly customer from Gothenburg. There wasn't a vestige of evidence that Stayovic was mixed up in it, but I wanted *him* to be the one who hired thugs to beat me up.

So I steeled myself and launched out.

"Do you know a guy called Conny Eng?" I asked, turning to Stayovic.

"Never heard the name," he replied.

Was it only my imagination, or was there a flicker of discomfort on Ring's face? Stayovic, on the other hand, looked just as usual. He didn't seem as if he had ever heard Eng's name before. But Ring . . .

"He's said to work as a bouncer for your colleagues in Gothenburg," I said to Stayovic.

"Which publishing house are you thinking of?"

I couldn't check a wry smile. He was as smooth as they come, this Serb.

"Eng is usually a strong arm for the gambling kings in Gothenburg," I informed him. "Last night he attacked me, for no reason, at a dance."

"You don't seem any the worse for it," Stayovic said.

"No, but Eng's in the hospital."

"Just goes to show."

He didn't seem in the least interested. I tried to study Ring, but he too seemed quite indifferent. But I can be stubborn, so I went on:

"You don't know Eng either, Bengt?"

"The name rings a bell," he replied. "Wasn't there a boxer called that who was Swedish champion a few years ago?"

I ransacked my memory. Ring was right. A guy called Conny Eng did win the Swedish championship in middle weight three or four years ago. Could it possibly be the same man?

Ring looked at me and managed to achieve a hurt expression.

"You surely don't think that any of us would send a guy like that after you?"

"I must admit the thought did occur to me," I replied.

"Then I can assure you that you're quite wrong. We don't go in for such methods."

"Sometimes I wonder."

Stayovic, who had been silent, now spoke up:

"You're evidently a very suspicious man. Perhaps it's part of your job. But you should never let suspicion go too far."

"I think my suspicions were well-founded after our conversation at the Grand yesterday."

"Yes, I remember you took something I said as a threat. You have far too lively an imagination, Mr. Berger. By the way, was it you who tried to make the police believe that I'm a professional gambler?"

"No," I lied. "I expect they found that out themselves. The cops aren't as stupid as many shady individuals think."

At last I had stung him into reacting. His brown eyes glinted with anger.

"Are you insinuating that I'm dishonest?"

117

"I never said so," I replied. "But if the shoe fits— You're evidently very touchy and that doesn't inspire confidence."

Stayovic's anger vanished as quickly as it came. He was now his old self again.

"I don't take offense at that sort of thing," he said. "I only wanted to assure you that your suspicions concerning me and Mr. Ring are quite unfounded."

"Well, that's fine," I said.

I got up to go.

"Don't forget I'm interested in your horse," Stayovic reminded me.

Judging by his voice and behavior, you wouldn't think anything out of the ordinary had passed between us.

I went back to the press room and looked at the judges' report from Stylist's race. I felt genuine *pleasure* as I read:

"Enar Brogren fined three hundred kronor and suspended for the period July 23–August 15 for taking someone else's track at the start, for gross disturbance of fellow competitor, and for disobeying an official."

Not at all bad.

I sauntered over to Lindgren's stable.

"Oh, there you are," said Janne, who was sitting having coffee between two races. "I thought you were never coming to congratulate us."

"Congratulations," I said. "I'm beginning to think you're right when you say that he's a champion."

"There's no limit to what he can do."

"You don't think he'll suffer any aftereffects of the collision at the start?"

"No, he's too wise for that."

"You didn't use everything he had today?"

"Almost, but not quite. He was a bit tired at the finish, but it won't hurt him to see how it feels."

"I suppose you saw that Brogren has been suspended," I said.

"He got off far too lightly. Any other horse would have galloped when Enar brandished his whip at Stylist's nose."

" 'Disobeying an official' it says in the judges' report. What was that?"

"He didn't bother to go to the judges' tower, although they sent for him several times."

"Did you know that it was the Railroader who owned Rodney's Pride?" I asked.

Janne gaped in genuine astonishment.

"No, I certainly didn't."

"But I'm told he sold him yesterday."

"To whom?"

"A business acquaintance of Ring's. A Yugoslav named Stayovic."

"I've heard of him."

"In what connection?"

"Gambling, of course."

"Roulette?"

"Roulette, poker, horses, betting. Take your choice."

"I heard that the Railroader owed him money," I said.

"That's quite possible. There are rumors that the Railroader has lost a lot of money lately."

"He doesn't usually."

"No one can get the better of the roulette wheel," Lindgren said. "So long as you stick to horses and poker you've got a chance, but that littte ball spinning around and around can be your downfall."

"It's not like the Railroader to trust to pure chance."

"No, but I think what happened was that he had a go at roulette once when he was in Gothenburg just for the hell of it, and had the bad luck to win thirty or forty thousand. Then he was done for."

I wandered in to see Stylist, who was his usual indolent self. I gave him some sugar, which he ate up without even favoring me with a glance.

I didn't see a sign of Håkan Lindgren. Anette was toiling like a slave washing down muddy horses.

"Hasn't Håkan come?" I asked her.

"I told you, he's resting today. Anything in particular you want him for?"

"I just wondered."

Number Two

I ARRANGED with Lindgren that I would travel with the horse transport to Solvalla next week.

"You don't think he's any the worse after today's race? It won't make it harder for him at Solvalla?"

"Not in the least," Lindgren assured me. "You can see for yourself that he's just as usual. You're so pessimistic, Kalle. He can easily stand up to this sort of strain."

I tried to believe him, but wasn't quite convinced. I still didn't dare to hope that Stylist would be a winner and yield a profit.

There were still a couple of races to be run, but I decided to go back to the hotel. I was pretty tired. I had been late getting to bed the night before.

I was just about to phone for a taxi when I heard the loudspeaker blare out:

"If Karl Berger is at the track, will he please contact his paper at once."

What was this all about? I felt in my pants pocket and found a few coins. They would do to feed the phone for a call to Stockholm. I dialed 08 and then the number of the paper, and eventually got through to the editorial desk via a panic-stricken relief operator. But after I'd spoken a few kind words to her she gave me the right connection.

It was the same guy I had spoken to earlier in the day.

"I think we were a bit hasty today," he said.

"In what way?"

"With the murder coverage."

I had no idea what he was getting at.

"I just heard the news on the radio. They've found a man murdered at Årjäng."

"What! Did they say who?"

"A man of about thirty-five."

"Look, I'll phone back."

"Do."

My next call was to the police. The constable on duty was a complete stranger to me. I introduced myself and asked if it was true that a man had been found murdered.

"I'll put you through to the inspector," the constable said.

It took a long time, but at last I heard a voice with a Småland accent at the other end of the line.

"Ivarsson," he said. "Ivarsson of the homicide squad."

"I hear you've been saddled with another murder."

"That is correct."

"May I ask who it is?"

"The next of kin have not yet been informed, so I'd rather not give the name."

"Surely you realize I can find out the name in two minutes in a small town like this."

"Yes, yes, but it's against regulations," Ivarsson said.

"This is ridiculous," I shouted.

"Easy now. In confidence, I can tell you that the victim is a man of thirty-six called Bjarne Svensson."

"The Railroader!" I exclaimed.

"What's that you say?" Ivarsson asked.

"He was never called anything but the Railroader," I told him.

"Did you know him?"

"Fairly well. He was a professional gambler."

There was silence for a moment.

"Yes, so I heard," the Småland voice said.

"Where was he found?"

"At home."

"Who found him?"

"The cleaning woman. I gather he lived alone, but a woman used to come in and clean the house once or twice a week."

"How did he die?"

"He was hit on the head," Ivarsson said. "From behind. He hadn't a chance to defend himself, apparently."

"It must have been someone he relied on."

"Not necessarily, Mr. Berger. Svensson was sitting in an armchair. The door was open. The murderer may have sneaked up on him."

"Does that sound feasible?"

"Yes, I would say so."

"While I've got you on the line, Inspector, something just occurred to me. I presume that by now you're able to establish whether there were any fingerprints on the pitchfork that was used in Karlsson-Gren's murder."

No answer.

"I suppose there weren't any."

"Why do you assume that?" Ivarsson asked.

"Well, if that weren't the case, you'd have caught the murderer by now."

"It's just possible we haven't had time to take the fingerprints of all the suspects."

"I didn't think of that," I admitted.

"At any rate you're right," Ivarsson squeaked in his horrible Småland dialect. "There weren't any fingerprints on the pitchfork. The murderer must have been wearing gloves."

"There are plenty of those around in a trotting stable," I reflected.

"What do you mean by that?"

"The stablemen often wear gloves when they clean out the manure, and the drivers often have motoring gloves."

"Oh, that may be."

"It not only may be. That's how it *is*."

"That may be."

God, what a blockhead. Typical of the homicide squad.

"Well, that's all for now," I said. "But just as a matter of record, you haven't caught any suspects?"

"Not yet."

"So the investigation is following a certain trail?"

"No," Ivarsson replied. "That's not how I would interpret my remark."

"How would you interpret it then?"

"I'd say that we're doing all in our power to catch the murderer. May I ask something in return?"

"Of course."

"You seem to take it for granted that this latest murder is connected with the first."

"Yes. Don't you?"

He made no reply. His silence made me feel I must say something.

"Svensson moved in the same circles. The murderer seems to have gone about it in the same way, too. Do you know anything about the murder weapon?"

"We have our suspicions. It was apparently an old ax that used to stand out on the porch."

"That seems to indicate that it was someone who knew the house," I said. "Provided, of course, that he went there in order to murder Svensson. Do you think he got any blood on himself?"

"I don't know. Svensson was struck by a single violent blow on the back of the head. He didn't bleed much. But of course, there might have been a spattering."

"Have you established when the murder took place?"

"We know that he was alive late last evening. Several people saw him then. The doctor's inclined to think he died sometime last night or early this morning."

"Anything else worthy of note?"

"No. Only that everything in Svensson's house was undisturbed. Nothing was stolen, at any rate."

I thanked him and began writing. It was soon done. I'm usually a fast worker. Then I phoned in my report. Among the others in the press room, I spotted the local woman editor of the provincial paper. On an impulse of rare fellow feeling I told her what had happened.

She was overjoyed.

The Rescuer in Need

THERE WAS LITTLE I could do except trudge back to Lindgren's stable. I was wondering what on earth I should say or not say when I got there.

Janne had finished driving for the day and was changing when I entered. Washing facilities were not of the best and he was scrubbing his face in a bucket of water.

"May I have a few words with you?" I asked.

"Sure, go ahead," he said, starting to comb his coppery hair.

"Someone has killed the Railroader," I said.

The comb stopped halfway through the thick mop.

"What the hell are you saying? When did it happen?"

"They found him a couple of hours ago but he was evidently murdered last night or early this morning."

"I saw him on my way home last night."

"What was the time then?"

"Twelve, or thereabouts. I dropped Anette and Håkan off; he was stoned. He never is, as a rule. Then I drove a girl home to Höglian, I think it's called."

"And you stayed there?"

"No, not more than an hour. She was pretty boring."

"Was the Railroader with anyone when you saw him?"

"No, he was sitting on the bench outside the taxi station. I suppose he was waiting for a cab. There were none in at the time."

"He wasn't still there when you came back?"

"No, I don't think so. I didn't look, come to think of it."

"Why do you think he was murdered?"

"How should I know. The most logical thing is that he knew something about Shag's murder."

I scratched my head.

"He knew quite a lot, the Railroader did."

124

"He was like the eyes and ears of the world. He heard and saw everything."

"He knew, for instance, that you had lent Berggren money."

I had hoped to throw Lindgren off balance with this bit of information but I failed.

"Did he now," was all he said. "Did he tell you?"

"Yes. How much money was it?"

"Only four thousand."

"Isn't it a bit risky lending money to an official like that?"

"Yes, naturally. Not so much for me as for Berggren."

"Has he paid anything back?"

"About half. I just wanted to do him a good turn. He's always been decent to me."

"Do you think anyone else knows about the loan?"

"No. I can't understand how the Railroader found out about it, still less why he told you. He wasn't a gossip."

"Did you put the loan down in black and white?"

"Good God, no! I have *some* instinct of self-preservation. It's quite impossible to prove that I have loaned anyone anything."

He looked at me and smiled.

"I'm glad," I said. "Because I'd like you to keep your trainer's license so that you can look after Stylist."

Stylist—that reminded me.

"I have a prospective buyer for the horse," I said. "Stayovic wants him. He asked me to name a price."

"If I were you I'd never sell him."

"Thanks. That's all I wanted to hear. I can tell you something else that may please you. Sam Boy was not doped."

"Who said so?"

"I've spoken to the laboratory. So he must simply have gone crazy or been stung by a gadfly."

"Yes, I suppose so," Lindgren said, looking thoughtful.

"Did you expect the tests to be positive?"

"I think it was the most reasonable explanation."

"What about the syringe?"

"What syringe?"

"That Shag saw in your cupboard."

125

"He only imagined it. There wasn't one."

"Oh yes, there was," I retorted. "I took charge of it just before Berggren came here to investigate."

Lindgren looked thunderstruck.

"Why didn't you say so earlier?"

"I wanted to protect you."

"I don't need protecting," he snapped.

"How do you explain the syringe then?"

"The vet must have left it behind when he was here last giving the horses vitamin injections."

It certainly sounded plausible. The explanation could, in fact, be so simple. But in that case, why was the syringe lying in a cupboard?

"But why should the syringe be lying hidden away in a cupboard?" I asked.

"One of the stablemen might have put it there absent-mindedly. What did you do with it, by the way?"

"Flushed it down the toilet at the hotel."

Lindgren's irritation was gone and he laughed out loud.

"So now you can hardly go to the police?"

"No, hardly."

"Then we might as well continue to keep our mouths shut," he said.

"Yes, I suppose so," I agreed halfheartedly.

I wasn't entirely satisfied, but on the other hand, it *was* possible that the vet had forgotten the syringe. I decided to accept the explanation. There was one big advantage to this solution: it eased my conscience.

Jan had now finished dressing, and we left his little cubby hole and went out into the stable, where everyone was working feverishly to finish up as soon as possible.

"Like a lift down?" Lindgren asked.

"I thought of going to the Railroader's house," I replied. "Must show that I do some work."

"I can drop you there," he said.

The Railroader's little house lay isolated in a district called Östtomta. He had lived there as long as I could remember with his parents, who were now both dead.

Lindgren drove me straight there and dropped me. I thanked him and made my way up to the house.

The usual inquisitive bunch had collected. The police had already put their cordon up and I could see both plainclothes and uniformed policemen moving around the house. Several constables had been posted along the cordon. I wanted to get to the house and talk to the investigators. I spotted Bodén among them.

I took out my old blue pass issued by the police in Stockholm and marched with an authoritative air up to the youngest and obviously most timid of the constables. I showed him the pass with its impressive text: "This card is valid for the years 1972 and 1973 (to the extent mentioned in the minutes of March 7, 1951, Office of the Governor of Stockholm) and admits the bearer to area cordoned off by the police."

The constable glanced at the pass and then at me.

"Okay then, sir," he said politely.

The bluff had worked and I went on up the little slope to the house. I had almost reached it when Bodén caught sight of me.

"How the hell did you get in here?" he barked, voice and face dark with suppressed anger.

"On my police pass," I replied truthfully.

"May I see it?"

I showed him the pass.

"You know quite well this is not valid here," he said.

"But it did the trick," I replied.

He glared at me.

"Who let you in?"

"One of the guys down there."

"Which one?"

"Does it damn well matter?"

"Maybe not," he admitted. "What do you want?"

"To see if you've gotten anywhere."

"You'd better ask the homicide squad."

"I've already done so," I said.

"Well then, you've no business here," he said curtly.

"Is Norberg here?" I asked.

"What do you want him for?"

"To ask him something. But perhaps you know."

127

"What?"

"Well, I phoned the laboratory earlier today. They told me that all of Sam Boy's tests were negative."

"That's right."

"Then how do you explain the fire at the vet's?" I asked.

"We're beginning to wonder now if it *was* arson. We're not so sure any more. It might have been a tramp who was careless with matches."

"That's possible, of course. That's really all I wanted to find out."

Bodén gave me a searching look.

"Since I have you here," he said, "what did you do after you had been to see us last night?"

"Went to bed, of course."

"Alone?"

"Yes."

"So you've no alibi this time either," he said, and turned on his heel before I could think of anything to say.

Could it be that he really suspected me? In that case, what motive could I have? True, the fact that I had been seen with Ring and Stayovic *could* be taken to mean that I was mixed up in some shady business.

Deep in thought, I walked slowly back to the hotel. It was still raining persistently. The whole of the main street was empty. Not a soul in sight. I hardly noticed the car that passed me and stopped a few yards ahead of it. I caught sight of the Gothenburg number plate and for some reason a warning bell began to ring in my head. I started to run back the way I had come. But it was too late. One of Conny Eng's pals from the dance at Näs caught up with me and grabbed my raincoat. I managed to wriggle out of it but now the others were there. This time kicks were of no help. Two of the thugs held me and the third punched me in the stomach. I felt the sour vomit spurting out of my throat. I flung myself from side to side to avoid the blows but in the end it was impossible. Just as I lost consciousness, I thought I heard a voice I recognized.

Who was it? Wasn't it Norberg?

Then I blacked out.

128

Norberg

It *was* NORBERG who was my rescuer in need. When I came to—I worked it out later that I wasn't unconscious for more than a minute—he stood leaning over me. He looked very dramatic standing there with his big police pistol in one hand. He gazed after my assailants' car, which swiftly disappeared.

"We'll get them later," he said. "How do you feel?"

I cautiously moved my face muscles. My lips were bleeding but teeth and bones seemed to be whole. The three thugs had not had Eng's foresight to furnish themselves with brass knuckles.

"A bit dizzy."

He supported me and helped me into his car.

"Just a minute," he said.

Calmly and efficiently he spoke into the radio and gave a description of the three men, the number of the car, and the road they had taken.

"They won't get far," he said. "Shall we go to the doctor?"

"No thanks, there's no need," I said valiantly. "If you wouldn't mind taking me to the hotel, I'll be fine."

He did so and practically carried me up to my room. I went into the bathroom and pulled off my stained clothes. After a shower I began to feel a little better.

"There now," Norberg said. "You look more presentable. But you're going to have two lovely black eyes tomorrow."

"Yes, it feels like it," I said.

"You don't seem to be very popular with Gothenburg tourists in Årjäng," he grinned.

"No, it doesn't look like it," I admitted.

"Were they the same guys who were with Eng yesterday at Näs?"

I nodded. I didn't want to speak unless I had to; my lips were

129

sore and my mouth hurt when I moved it. But one thing I had to ask.

"Have you interrogated Eng?"

"Yes, we have."

"What does he say?"

"He sticks to his story that you knocked his glass over."

"But I didn't."

"No. The witnesses we have talked to confirm your account."

I changed my mind about not mentioning my suspicions of Stayovic. Anyway, why should I shield him?

"It may have been that bigshot gambler Stayovic who was behind it," I slurred.

And I told Norberg about our encounter at the Grand.

"The same thing occurred to us," Norberg said, with an inscrutable look on his face. "It wasn't so hard to draw that conclusion. But why should he want to beat you up?"

"I can't imagine. Possibly he thinks I'm too interested in his affairs."

"Possibly," Norberg said, sounding unconvinced.

"Have you checked up on Eng and his contacts in Gothenburg?"

"Naturally. There's no doubt whatever that he's closely connected with the gambling clubs. On the other hand, there's nothing to indicate that he was hired by Stayovic."

I got up and went into the bathroom. My split lips felt very sore indeed and I put some ointment on them. My head was also beginning to ache, so I took a couple of aspirins.

Then I bathed my face in cold water. When I straightened up, I found I was the focal point of a merry-go-round. Everything was spinning around me.

I had to grab the sink to regain my balance.

"You're as white as a sheet," Norberg said. "Lie down on the bed. Even a slight concussion is not to be trifled with."

"Bodén seems to think I murdered the Railroader and Shag," I muttered.

It was some seconds before he answered.

"That's not quite the way to put it," he said. "Let's just say that he doesn't altogether exclude you."

My lips tasted bitter when I moistened them with my tongue.

"Why should I kill them?"

"Let me put forward an entirely hypothetical argument. Remember that, before you get worked up. I've noticed you're pretty hot-tempered at times."

"All right," I mumbled.

"First of all, you know all the people concerned," he said. "That has surprised us a bit. Consequently, you may be more involved with one of them than you will admit. It's a fact that you were at the race track when Karlsson-Gren was murdered, and that it was you who found him. Hypothetically—I repeat that—you could have made the whole thing up."

"You mean that first I murdered him, and then was stupid enough to run and discover him as soon as possible?"

"It's conceivable that you could have done so in order to confuse the issue."

"What else?"

"Well, you yourself have said that you've been a gambler. You make out that you've given it up, but we still have only your own statements to go by."

"Anything more?"

"Yes. Bodén, and I too, for that matter, have a feeling that you know more than you will let on. We may be wrong and we may be right. If we're right, perhaps you think you're shielding someone, but it *may* also be your own skin you're trying to save."

"But I told you this about Stayovic."

"Yes, but only after you'd been attacked the second time."

"What else?"

I tried to sound sarcastic, but didn't succeed very well.

"Your cash assets, for instance. It may be, as you say, that you had a lucky break with a win, but there's nothing to prove that the money comes from there."

"Where does it come from then?"

"We don't know. And don't forget that this is all hypothetical."

"I wonder whether it really *is,*" I retorted.

"How long are you staying here in Årjäng?"

"I thought of going to Stockholm sometime next week."

"When?"

131

"On Wednesday, I think. We're going to start my horse at Solvalla on Thursday evening, so I expect we'll leave here on Wednesday."

"Is he as good as that?"

"So Janne says. Oh! That reminds me!"

I suddenly remembered that I had six unclaimed 50-kronor betting tickets in my pocket.

"What is it?" he asked.

"I put three hundred on Stylist today and I forgot to collect the money."

"I thought you'd given up gambling heavily."

"Three hundred isn't heavily," I protested feebly.

"It's quite enough, in my mind," he said.

"A really heavy gambler bets ten times as much," I said. "Stayovic, for instance, put three thousand on the horse that came second in Stylist's race."

"How do you know?"

"He told me."

"Oh, so you know him pretty well."

"I met him through Bengt Ring."

"You seem to see quite a lot of Ring," Norberg said.

"I work for a paper which expects me to write something readable about this murder. As a result, I have to hobnob with people I don't greatly care for."

"But perhaps you care for Anette Lindgren?"

The question came like a bolt from the blue. I tried to be angry but couldn't be bothered.

"Well, she's a nice girl," I said lamely.

"You're evidently not the only one who thinks so."

"Oh?"

"According to our information, she's having an affair with both Ring and her brother-in-law Jan," he went on.

"That's more than I know."

"I'm not so sure. We've even heard gossip to the effect that she has granted you her favors."

If only she had, I thought. I'd have nothing against an invitation from that quarter.

"Exactly as you say," I said, moistening my lips once more. "Gossip."

Norberg rubbed his chin.

"You must be tired and want to be left in peace," he said. "But may I touch on one other matter?"

I nodded. Anyhow, I couldn't prevent him. It was he who represented the law, not I.

"Håkan Lindgren was with you at Näs last evening, wasn't he?"

"Yes."

What was he after now?

"They say he got pretty drunk."

"He drank a lot, at any rate," I said guardedly.

"But he's said to have been stoned when he got home?"

"Yes, Anette and Janne said so. He had such a hangover today that he couldn't go to work."

"Precisely. He didn't go to work today. Have you any comment?"

"Only that it's unusual for Håkan to drink so heavily. Janne and Anette mentioned that, too. He can hold a great deal of liquor, as a rule."

The expression on Norberg's face was hard to make out, especially since he sat with his eyes closed, as usual.

"Exactly," he said.

Now I saw what he was after. Or thought I did.

"If you think he was faking, and then popped up lively as a cricket and murdered the Railroader, you're wrong," I said.

"I don't think anything, but it's certainly an interesting theory. You should be a cop."

He got slowly to his feet.

"Take it easy now," he said. "And remember, it's not good to drink alcohol after a bash on the head."

"Thanks for the advice."

He was right, of course, but the minute he had left my room I got out my bottle of whisky and took a good swig.

That did the trick and I fell asleep almost at once.

Saturday

I WOKE UP with a splitting headache. Everything was swimming in front of my eyes. Moreover, I was bruised and aching all over. I knew I was swollen because I could see parts of my face that I'd never even caught a glimpse of before.

Gently, gently I got up and painfully made my way to the bathroom, as stiff as a ninety-year-old.

I hated the thought, but at last I gathered my courage and looked at myself in the mirror. It was not an edifying sight. My whole face was swollen and bruised. My eyes were bloodshot and my lips were split.

I ordered breakfast. When the friendly chambermaid brought the tray, she stared at me as if I were Frankenstein's monster.

"I was in a brawl yesterday," I explained.

"So I see," she said and vanished.

It was all I could do to open my mouth and the coffee burned like fire when I put the cup to my lips. I have very few principles, I'm afraid, but one of them is always to eat a proper breakfast. So I forced down eggs, bread, cheese, marmalade, and coffee. After that ordeal I felt better, and the physical pain was also easing up.

I lay dozing until I knew that the Stockholm papers had come, including that wretched national edition that is ready-printed about nine o'clock the evening before.

I usually find it hard to make use of the service in hotels and restaurants. In this respect, I am a model guest. If I order beer and the waitress brings milk, I say thank you and drink it. I abandoned these principles now, and phoned down to the receptionist, asking him to send up the morning papers. They were ages in coming and I kept thinking that it would have been quicker if I had run to the newsstand myself.

I glanced through the papers and found, not at all to my

134

surprise, that my report about the Railroader's death fought a losing front page battle against the detailed descriptions of the sex murder in Stockholm.

If it was a sex murder. The victim was a call girl. With all the money they make nowadays the motive could just as well have been robbery, or even revenge on the part of the big silent men who fix up apartments and empty offices for this lucrative business.

Drugs, prostitution, gambling, and possibly also the motor trade, work hand in glove in Stockholm, which is really no better than the American cities in the area of organized crime. The police sometimes say as much, but then along come our do-gooders in their smart overcoats and expensive boutique skirts, objecting that you certainly can't combat crime with punishment and police methods. Then the police ask rather cautiously if organized crime is something that really can enrich life for the happy city dwellers.

Our do-gooders retort that organized crime doesn't exist in Sweden. It's merely an invention of the police and the crime reporters who are in league together; the object of all this is to get higher grants for the police force and to divert information from the real needs of the people.

The real needs of the people turn out to be bombastic tributes to local associations and "mass movements" in which the reformers themselves are often personally involved. These people are just as revolutionary as sports journalists are reactionary.

My reflections were interrupted by the telephone. I recognized the voice immediately.

"They've arrested Håkan," Anette sobbed.

"For the murders?"

"Yes. They came and got him just now."

"Are you quite sure he's suspected of murder?"

"Yes. It was somebody called Ivarsson and he said that Håkan was suspected of murder. Håkan, who wouldn't hurt a fly. He's innocent, you must see that."

"I didn't say he wasn't. Where are you, by the way?"

"Here at the hotel."

135

"Is Janne there?"

"No, you idiot!" she wailed. "Why should he be here? I want Håkan back."

"Calm down. I'll get dressed and come to you."

I put the phone down. My God, what next? I called the police station and asked for Norberg. No, he was busy. Bodén then? One moment, please. The moment turned out to be about three minutes, then I heard the woodsman Bodén at the other end of the line.

"It's Berger," I said. "I hear you've arrested a man who is suspected of having murdered Shag and the Railroader."

"We haven't arrested anyone," he replied in a voice as sour as vinegar. "The homicide squad has."

"On what grounds did they pull in Håkan Lindgren?"

"Damned if I know," he snapped.

"So you think he's innocent?"

"Devil take me, I never said that."

"No, but you think so. Because you're convinced *I'm* guilty."

"Who said so?"

"Nobody. I've just got that feeling. Is he being questioned now?"

"I don't know."

"I just wondered, because I'm going up now to talk to his wife."

"That doesn't surprise me," he said spitefully.

"If you were here I'd belt you," I hissed.

"Or break my leg or stick a pitchfork in me or bash me with an ax."

I fought to keep calm.

"So you do think I'm the murderer."

"Yes," he replied.

"What if I'm recording this on tape?" I said. "Then you'd be in a fix."

There was a long silence.

"I wouldn't put it past you to be so devious," he said. "But I expect you're bluffing as usual."

"But just supposing," I taunted him. "Just supposing, Bodén. What a stink I could make in the papers. 'Policeman accuses journalist of murder.' It wouldn't be very nice for you."

136

"Threats have no effect on me," he said rather lamely.

Was the air starting to go out of him?

"May I have a word with Norberg or Ivarsson?" I asked.

"They're busy."

"When will they be free?"

"In a couple of hours, maybe. After the first interrogation with Lindgren."

I wanted to give Bodén one last kick.

"What if he confesses?" I said. "Then I can start a libel action against you with this recording as basis."

"Tape recordings don't count as legal evidence," he retorted swiftly.

"No, but they can be pretty damaging."

He slammed the phone down.

And I felt ashamed of myself.

Laboriously, I got dressed. I stuck a couple of bandages around my eyes to conceal the worst bruises and dabbed some ointment on my lips, which were now really something to be proud of.

I shuffled upstairs and knocked on Anette's door. When she opened it she cried out at the sight of my handsome face.

"What have they done to you?"

Her sympathy was balm to my soul.

"It was those guys from Näs who got their own back," I informed her. "It's not as bad as it looks."

That reminded me that I'd forgotten to ask the police whether those thugs had been caught by now.

"What's worrying you?" she asked.

I had never realized that she had such blue eyes.

"Nothing," I lied.

She examined me closely. Her cool fingers brushed the swelling under the left eye.

"You should go to the doctor with that," she said. "And your lips are an awful sight."

"Oh, it's not so bad," I said bravely. "A bit sore, but I've put ointment on them."

We stood there so near to each other for a few seconds and then she took a few steps backwards and sat down on an armchair.

"What am I to do?" she asked.

"I'm afraid there's nothing to do but wait," I replied.

"But Kalle, you must see that Håkan would never kill anyone. It doesn't add up."

"No, it doesn't," I agreed.

She threw me a quick glance.

"What do you mean?"

I cleared my throat and braced myself.

"I could understand it if he went for Ring, or Janne, too, for that matter, but I can't possibly see what motive he would have for murdering the Railroader, let alone Shag."

"He's not jealous," she mumbled.

"How do you know?"

"We talked it all over last night. It was as you said. I can do what I like, as long as I come back to him."

"Are you sure he means what he says."

She looked angry.

"Oh yes, he does. He doesn't lie to me."

I smiled.

"How can you be sure?"

"When you live with someone you get to know him."

I shrugged. I was not convinced, having seen examples of people who had been married for twenty-five years without ever really knowing each other.

"Don't look so skeptical, Kalle. You're too cynical."

"Maybe I am."

"Just what do you think of me?" she asked suddenly.

Yes, what *did* I think of her? The only thing I knew with certainty was that she had a devastating sex appeal.

"I can't quite make you out," I admitted. "I find it hard to fit you into a pattern."

"I don't want to be fitted into a pattern," she said. "I've always been myself. When I was little my parents always thought I was peculiar. They still do. No one's going to order me about. What I do is my own business and no one else's."

"Why did you get married then?"

"I don't know. But I do love Håkan, even if you don't believe me."

"No, I don't believe you. You imagine you love him."

"Listen to Mr. Know-it-all," she snorted.

"If you love him, I don't understand how you can treat him as you do."

"What do you know about love?"

"Not much, I admit, but I think you're underrating his feelings if you can't see that you're hurting him."

Ugh, what a moralizer I was, while at the same time desiring her.

She looked down at the floor.

"This was not what we were going to talk about," she said.

"I've been in touch with the police. It's the homicide squad who are behind the arrest. The provincial police don't seem all that keen."

"Then perhaps they'll let him go?"

"It's possible, if they haven't enough reason to keep him. And I don't think they have, unless he's guilty, of course, and they can produce technical evidence."

"He's innocent, I told you," she harped.

"Do you know whom the Årjäng police suspect?"

"No, but I hope it's Bengt."

"When did you last have sex with him?"

She leapt up and slapped my face. It was horribly painful.

"It's none of your business," she sobbed.

Blasted girl. She swung from one extreme to the other. Again I felt ashamed.

"You're right. It's none of my business."

"Whom do they suspect?" she asked, blowing her nose in a tissue.

"Me," I said, staring at her to discover any reaction.

She began to laugh, and there was a note of hysteria in her voice.

"You! You're not serious."

Absurdly, I felt hurt by her laughter. Was it so unthinkable that I could be capable of murder?

I know my reaction was strange, but there it was. I felt she'd underrated me in some way. But I said:

"Yes, ridiculous, isn't it."

139

She gave me a long look, then put out her hand.
"Poor Kalle, you—a murderer," she purred.
And that was that.

Saturday Afternoon

I WAS STILL ACHING all over when I hobbled off to the police station on Saturday afternoon. During the brush with the three Gothenburgers or whoever they were, I had also sprained an ankle.

My old friend Johansson with the side whiskers was on duty.

"Is either Norberg or Bodén in?" I asked politely.

I received a blank look as an answer.

"Yes, I think so."

"Would you mind seeing if there's any chance of a word with either of them?"

He looked slightly jittery.

"I think they're busy, but I'll ask."

He pushed a lot of buttons on the intercom and at last found the right one.

"Mr. er . . . er . . . What's your name again?"

"Berger," I informed him.

"Mr. Berger is here and would like a word with either you or Bodén."

"Send him in," came a voice from the intercom.

"Will you step inside, please, the chief of police will see you," Johansson elaborated.

"Thank you very much."

I shuffled in to Norberg. He was alone. He studied my face for a moment.

"That doesn't look too good," he commented.

"It isn't, either."

"How can I be of help?"

140

The voice was so kind, so helpful, so ingratiating—and so cunning.

"I naturally want to know how the interrogation with Håkan Lindgren is going."

"And here I was thinking you wanted to know whether we'd caught that trio who beat you up yesterday."

"Have you?"

"Yes, they're here in the cells now."

"Did they say anything?"

"No, only that they were getting their own back for what you did to Conny Eng."

"That sounds plausible," I said.

"Yes, doesn't it?"

"Are you going to keep them?"

"Oh yes, I think so," he replied. "We can probably make it assault and battery. Besides, two of them are prisoners who haven't returned from leave."

"What about the third?"

"It will be his first trip, but certainly not his last. He's Conny's kid brother."

"That supports the revenge theory," I said.

"Undeniably."

"But as I said, I came here mainly to see how the interrogation with Håkan Lindgren is going."

"The homicide squad is dealing with that."

"But you've been in on it?"

"Off and on."

"And what do you think?"

"That he's not the right man."

He made a short pause.

"But you're not to write that, of course," he added. "At any rate, you mustn't quote me."

"So you don't think an arrest is likely?"

"I don't think so for a moment, but on the other hand, you never know what a guy like Ivarsson will get up to. He's crazy."

"Why did they pull in Håkan Lindgren?"

"It was your fault originally," he said, fixing me with a stare.

141

"Your hints about simulated drunkenness fell into good hands when I passed them on to Ivarsson."

"You don't seriously mean that that's all they have against him?"

"He has no alibi."

"A motive then? He must damn well have a motive for killing two people!"

He picked up a pen and juggled with it for a few seconds. Then he leaned back comfortably in the swivel chair, closing his eyes as he said:

"I'm going to confide in you again, and I know it's stupid because one should never trust a journalist."

"Any more than a cop," I retorted.

"Exactly. At any rate, for some time now, Håkan Lindgren seems to have been taking drugs."

"The syringe!" I exclaimed, without thinking.

He gave me a long, hard look.

"What do you mean by that?"

I groped frantically for a reasonable explanation. The best tactics were to stick to the truth as closely as possible.

"I saw a syringe in Lindgren's stable the other day. Before the results of Sam Boy's tests were known, I had a wild idea that . . . well, you know. But, now there may be another explanation."

"Where was the syringe lying?" he asked.

"In the harness room."

"Where did it come from?"

"Jan Lindgren said that the vet had left it behind when he gave the horses in the stable vitamin injections."

"Syringes are not required for all drugs," Norberg went on.

I had already thought of that.

"No, you're right, of course."

"But you're in luck," he said. "He was evidently strung out on drugs."

"That doesn't make him a murderer," I protested.

"No, but it may supply him with a motive."

"What motive?"

"It's possible that Karlsson-Gren and Svensson, who both had a reputation for snooping around, had found out that Lindgren

142

was on drugs. He then saw no other way of silencing them but to . . ."

"How did you find out he was on drugs?"

"It's too silly to be true. He had a syringe on him. And some ritalin pills as well."

"Naturally he doesn't say where he got the drugs?"

"No, they never do."

"How many pills were there?"

"A dozen or so."

"A petty drug offense," I declared. "Not much to base a prosecution on."

Norberg scratched his chin thoughtfully, at the same time leaning forward and finally opening his eyes.

"We've searched his room at the hotel and there's nothing there either."

I heaved a sigh of relief. What luck that Anette and I had gone down to my room and not remained in hers. It would have been very pretty if the police had caught us in that situation.

"His wife was not there," he said, staring at me.

"No, she was with me," I disclosed.

I had the satisfaction of seeing him thrown slightly off balance. I was delighted. It was the first time I had managed to shake him.

"Oh," was all he said.

"She was naturally very upset that the police had pulled in her husband and she wanted someone to talk to."

"Oh, I see. Had she anything to say?"

"She is quite convinced that her husband is innocent."

"Are you having an affair with her, too?"

The question was harsh and authoritative.

"No."

"I don't believe you."

"That's up to you. You can believe what you like."

"Bodén told me that you had had a dispute with him this morning."

"I wouldn't call it a dispute exactly. It annoyed me that he seems to be so dead sure I'm the murderer."

"You threatened him, didn't you?"

"By no means."

143

"Your word against his," he said.

"Exactly."

"*Do* you have a tape recorder with you?"

He was actually smiling now.

"No, of course not. I just lost my temper, and when I lose my temper, I tend to say things like that."

"You lose your temper rather easily, don't you?"

There he was again with his crafty questions.

"Oh, I don't know. Most of my acquaintances would probably say the opposite."

"Where is Jan Lindgren today? Do you know?"

"No. Up at the race track, I presume."

"We haven't gotten hold of him yet. We'd like to know if he knew that his brother was a junkie."

"I doubt it. Now that I think of it, there are trotting races at Örebro today. He's probably driving there now. But he'll probably be back this evening."

Norberg made a few rapid notes on the pad in front of him.

"But the stables should have been able to tell you that," I went on.

Norberg actually looked abashed.

"I must admit we haven't asked," he said.

"Where's Bodén then?"

Now he was really embarrassed.

"I think he's searching your room at the hotel," he said.

To my own surprise, I reacted by laughing.

"What's so funny about that?" he asked.

"Nothing. I'm just tired, and the whole thing is downright funny. But I can tell you he won't find anything of value."

"If he did, it would be Anette Lindgren," he said, with an unkind expression.

"No, she's gone up to the track. Who decided to search my room?"

"I did."

"Did the homicide squad second the decision?"

"Yes."

"Well anyway, I have something to write about for tomorrow," I said, getting to my feet.

Norberg sighed deeply and looked unhappy.

"Yes, you have indeed," he said.

Bodén and I

I WENT STRAIGHT to the hotel and up to my room. The reception clerk looked hard at me and seemed to want to say something, but I ignored him.

Bodén was in the act of searching around in my old toilet case when I entered. Two policemen were assisting him in his search of the room. I could plainly see him recoil when he saw me.

"Found anything?" I asked.

He didn't answer.

"I asked if you've found anything?"

"No tape recorder, at any rate."

"Oh, so that's why you're searching my room. I must say it's an unusual reason for such a measure."

That stung him. He set his jaw and went on carefully examining my toilet things.

"What are you looking for?"

"I'm not obliged to answer such questions," he declared.

"May I use the phone?"

"Of course you may. No one has said that you can't use the phone. We're here on a search and nothing else."

"Fine," I said.

I asked for a line, dialed and got through to the paper. I was connected with the editorial desk and identified myself.

"I've got a good thing here," I announced, and dictated the following despatch: "The paper's special correspondent at Årjäng was subjected, on Saturday, to a rigorous search of his hotel room. The action was directed by Inspector . . . What's your first name, Bodén?"

"Erik," he replied, glaring at me.

". . . was directed by Inspector Erik Bodén. The order was

issued by the chief of police, Sven Norberg. The explanation of this unusual measure is that the local police suspect that the paper's correspondent might have something to do with the two murders at Årjäng. The search appears all the more extraordinary since the homicide squad on Saturday seized a stableman who is suspected of the murders . . .

"That will do for now," I said to the girl who was taking down the message.

"That's going to look pretty tomorrow," I said to Bodén.

For the third time, I was assaulted. First Conny Eng's three buddies, then Anette's slap in the face that morning, and now Bodén's halfhearted punch on my chest.

He instantly regretted it.

"Forgive me. I lost control. But you're such a rat that it's beyond belief."

"Was there one lie in what I told the paper?" I asked.

He was breathing heavily and his lips moved, but he couldn't get a word out. The two constables gazed at us, fascinated. I didn't feel particularly proud of what I had done.

But I stood my ground.

"Did I say anything that wasn't true?" I asked again.

Bodén clenched his fists a couple of times and then relaxed. He hurled my toilet case at the wall.

"No!" he shouted. "No! No! No!"

"Well then," I said. "Why get so angry that you feel you must hit me? You saw what happened, didn't you?"

I said this to the two constables. They looked first at me, then at Bodén, and finally at one another.

"No," one of them said. "We didn't see anything."

"You goddam idiots!" Bodén roared. "You damn well saw that I struck him. It's your blasted duty to tell the truth if he should report me."

"I've no intention of doing so," I said.

If only all cops were as honest and conscientious as Bodén! What a police force we would have!

They left the room. Naturally they didn't find anything. Then, I phoned the paper and asked them to withdraw the news item about the search of my room.

"Did they really make a search?" the assistant editor asked.

"Yes."

"Then, of course, we'll publish it."

"But I feel rather sorry for these cops who are involved."

"We can't consider that."

"But I may lose a couple of good contacts."

"No," he said, after a moment's thought. "We'll publish it."

I hadn't expected anything else.

Håkan

LATE THAT EVENING they let Håkan go. So late that I barely got the news through in time for the last edition. When he was set free he was, as far as I knew, no longer suspected of murder. On the other hand, he might be charged with a drug offense, but this wouldn't involve more than a fine.

Taking drugs is nothing unusual in Swedish horse racing, but it has mostly been a case of jockeys who have dieted drastically and, in one way or another, have had to compensate for the persistent pangs of hunger. It's madness when someone with a frame that is meant to carry one hundred and thirty pounds diets until he weighs only a hundred and ten. He may feel in need of a little consolation, and since there are a lot of calories in alcohol, drugs often take over.

"I get by with a little help from my friends," as the Beatles sang years ago.

When, in addition, the jockeys have to swallow diuretic pills prescribed by unsuspecting doctors, it can be understood that there's a big turnover in the profession.

In trotting there is not the same problem. A couple of our star drivers are anything but undernourished, but they do all right. Of course, they'd do even better if they were smaller—the sulky is lighter to pull.

I stood ready to receive Håkan when they released him. I had been sitting there like a vulture for several hours, waiting.

He seemed tired and edgy when he came out. He was pale under his tan and he kept rubbing his eyes.

"Hi," I greeted him. "Glad they've let you out."

"Hi," he said, looking bewildered. "Are you waiting for me?"

"Yes, I wanted to see what sort of time you've had."

"Pretty lousy. I don't like being locked up."

He spoke slowly, as if every word had to be squeezed out.

"Shall we go to the hotel?"

"Is Anette there?"

"I presume so."

As we reached the hotel I had a pang of conscience which was so brief that I had a guilty conscience about my reaction. Here was a man whose wife I had made love to while he was locked up wrongly suspected of murder. Yet I didn't feel particularly shamefaced. Odd.

"They thought I'd killed them," he said as we settled into a couple of armchairs near the reception desk.

I had steered him there in order to have him to myself for a while before Anette appeared on the scene.

"But I haven't murdered anyone," he went on.

The bewilderment was still in his voice. He obviously found it very hard to concentrate. He kept intertwining his fingers into an intricate pattern.

"No, I'm sure you haven't," I said. "But what reason did they give for your arrest?"

"They said I was pretending to be drunk the night before last—it *was* the night before last, wasn't it? I'm having an awful time remembering things."

"And were you pretending?"

"No, I *was* drunk. Really stoned. All I know is that I fell into bed and went out like a light."

"Was Anette with you?"

He looked at me with red-rimmed, despairing eyes.

"I can't remember," he said quietly. "I can't remember. I can't remember a goddam thing!"

It went against the grain, but I felt I ought to ask him about

148

drugs. It was chiefly the syringe that interested me. I felt rather guilty on that point. But how was I to tackle the subject? Well, I could blame the police and my work.

"I was talking to the police earlier today about you," I began. "They said you were also suspected of possessing drugs . . ."

I let the rest ebb out with a vague sort of tact.

Håkan sat there pulling at his fingers. Now and then he put his knuckles to his eyes.

"I did have some ritalin on me," he mumbled. His words were scarcely audible.

"Have you been taking them for long?"

"Off and on during the last year. I can stop whenever I like."

That's what they all say, I thought. They can all stop whenever they like, but mighty few do.

I must step carefully now. Not get carried away. Rub him the right way. Be sympathetic.

"Why did you start?"

"I don't know."

The reply came quickly. A little too quickly.

"Are you quite sure?"

He leaned his head back and began to yawn over and over again. It infected me and I began to yawn too.

"Anette," he said at length.

"But you told me the other evening that you didn't care if she had others as long as she came back to you."

"I only said that. Of course I care."

The voice was steadier now.

"She told me everything yesterday," he went on. "She even told me things I didn't know about."

What things, I was about to ask, but checked myself. There was a limit to my poking about in his private life. It wasn't essential for me to be more of a bastard than I had already been.

"Where did you get it?" I asked quickly.

"That's what they wanted to know too," he replied.

"And what did you say?"

"I get it from several quarters. Here and there. We're often in Gothenburg. You can get it in Karlstad too."

"But not here in Årjäng?"

149

"I've never bought any here."

"I'm not at home in junk circles, but I've heard that one usually sticks to the same pusher. But you evidently haven't?"

"No, I've bought it from a lot of different ones."

"How do you contact them?"

"Easy. You just stand and wait and along comes a pusher."

"But do you really have time to contact pushers when you're in Gothenburg? You don't ever leave the race track, do you?"

"The pushers can come to the track, can't they?"

"Does Anette know you're on drugs?"

He frowned, thinking hard.

"I'm damned if I know. Sometimes I suspect she's found out, but I'm not sure."

"So you have secrets from her, too?"

No reply. What was he to say anyway? The comment was quite unnecessary.

"Did the police ask anything about a syringe?"

He shook his head like a boxer who is groggy and waits for the referee to get to nine.

"My memory's so bad just now," he said. "But I've an idea someone asked me something about a syringe in our stable."

"Exactly," I confirmed. "Just after Sam Boy dashed against the wall, I found a blue syringe in the harness room. In the cupboard. I took charge of it. Was it yours?"

He sighed heavily.

"I'm sorry, Kalle, but I don't know. It may have been mine, but I can't guarantee it."

"Do you often use those nonreturnable syringes?"

"Yes."

"But they're only sold on a doctor's prescription. How do you get hold of them?"

"I'd rather not say. It's of no importance in this connection."

"Then it doesn't matter if you tell me."

He blinked hard several times.

"I know someone who can get hold of syringes."

Who could that be? A nurse, a vet? There were numerous possibilities. And it's well known that junkies have a curious

150

knack of getting everything they need to feed the ravenous beast inside them.

Should I ask him anything more? Perhaps about his relations with Bengt Ring.

"Does he sell dope?" he asked in genuine astonishment. "I didn't know that."

"No, it was just an idea I had. By the way, did you think Sam Boy was doped?"

He made no reply, but sat there self-absorbed. I repeated the question.

"No," he replied. "I didn't think it was doping. There was something else wrong. I'm inclined to think he was stung by something. It's the only explanation I can find."

"Then why was the vet's barn burned down?"

"How should I know?"

I didn't ask him any more. I left him sitting in the armchair and went upstairs. When I looked back he was making an effort to get to his feet. That was the last I saw of him.

Next morning he had vanished without a trace.

Sunday

IT WAS NORBERG who told me of his disappearance. About ten thirty on Sunday morning I was just getting ready to go up to the track and watch the Big Heat Race when the large chief of police called me up.

"Good morning," he greeted me. "How do you feel today?"

He didn't sound angry. Had he, perhaps, not read the paper and my nasty little report about the search of my room?

"Good morning," I said. "How are you?"

"Not so bad, considering. We've been faced with a little problem that we think you might be able to help us with."

"By all means, if it doesn't take too long."

151

"Would you mind coming over to my office?"

A few minutes later, I was again sitting opposite Norberg, who as usual was seconded by Bodén. A couple of newspapers lay on the desk. So he *had* read what I had written.

"Håkan Lindgren was released yesterday evening," he said.

"Yes, I know."

"You came and got him, didn't you?"

"Got him is hardly the way to put it. I wanted to talk to him. Pure journalistic curiosity."

"Then you two sat for a while talking in the hotel lobby?"

What was he getting at?

"That's right."

"Then you parted?"

"That's right, too."

"You went up to your room and Lindgren stayed there. Is that correct, too?"

"Whether he stayed there or not I don't know. When I last saw him he was just standing up."

He nodded and bit his underlip with huge yellow tusks.

"Håkan Lindgren has disappeared," he informed me. "Vanished into thin air."

"Who reported it?"

"No one really. We called up the hotel because we wanted him to sign the interrogation report. We spoke to his wife and she was thunderstruck. She didn't even know he had been set free. Then we spoke to the night porter who had seen you both sitting in the lobby."

"Isn't he at the race track?"

"We've had a car up there, and he hasn't been seen."

"There's probably a very simple explanation," I said lamely.

Nobody spoke for a few seconds. Bodén sat doodling.

"How was he when you talked to him?" he asked.

"Tired and edgy. He had great difficulty in concentrating."

"What did you talk about?"

I gave them a short account of our conversation. Selected parts, that is. I didn't want to reveal quite everything to the two energetic policemen.

Bodén drew a square, which he then began extending into a

cube. He took great pains to see that the perspective was as true as possible. Evidently he wasn't satisfied, for he soon scratched the figure out with his ball-point pen.

"Did he seem depressed?"

It was Norberg who asked this time.

"No, I can't say that. But he didn't seem to be all there."

"No drugs all day," Norberg said.

I hadn't thought of that. Stupid of me. That was, of course, the explanation of Håkan's behavior. He needed a fix, quite simply. That's all there was to it.

"Now that you mention it, I realize that's what was wrong with him," I said.

"He didn't come out with anything new?"

"Not that I could tell."

"Of course, you don't know what he said to us."

"No, I don't," I agreed. "But it couldn't have been very much more than what he told me. Besides, he remembers so little of what happened on Thursday evening."

"It seems to be dangerous to talk to you."

It was again Bodén butting in, perhaps because he had succeeded with a new cube and had started work on a third. What an architect the world had lost in him.

"I don't understand what you mean," I said.

But I did.

"You talk to Shag and then the next time you go to talk to him he's been murdered."

"I didn't go to talk to him," I objected. "I went to get a light bulb. I thought I had told you that."

"Yes, so you have. But then you talk to Håkan Lindgren, and he just vanishes."

I made no comment. There wasn't much to say.

"Don't you think it's rather strange?" he went on.

"No, not in the least."

"Why do you think Håkan Lindgren disappeared then?" Norberg asked.

An idea struck me.

"Well, you took away his pills, so I suppose he's gone to Gothenburg or Karlstad to get some more."

With a sting of malicious pleasure, I saw Norberg glance at Bodén, who stared back at him and then at me. Apparently that explanation of Håkan Lindgren's mysterious absence hadn't occurred to them.

I reflected that it was very likely that Håkan had gone off to replenish his empty stock of ritalin. He had really been in a bad way.

Bodén, who had savagely destroyed a new geometrical figure, glared at me.

"I don't know anyone who is as quick at thinking up explanations as you are," he rapped out.

"Well, someone has to when you can't think them up yourselves," I retorted nastily.

Why did I always let Bodén get my goat? Silly, very silly of me.

Norberg held up his hand.

"Now then, you two, don't start again," he said sternly. "I can't think why you always fly at each other's throats."

We two culprits sat looking down at the desk in silence like chastised schoolboys.

"Hasn't Anette anything to suggest?"

"No, she seemed badly shaken when we spoke to her," Norberg replied.

"That's nothing unusual," I said. "It doesn't take much for her to turn on the waterworks."

Bodén looked as if he was about to say something, but he shut his mouth again. No doubt, it had been another jibe at me.

"Now that Håkan Lindgren has been set free, what line is your investigation taking?"

I tried not to smile when I saw that, once again, Bodén almost had to bite his tongue off in an effort to refrain from comment.

"We'll continue with inner and outer investigation," Norberg declared.

"Well, it would be funny if you didn't."

"Yes, wouldn't it?" Norberg agreed. "And what are you going to do now?"

"Go up to the race track, unless Bodén wants to keep me here suspected of murder and kidnapping."

Bodén crossed out a cube so viciously that the pen went right through the paper.

"You must watch your temper," I said to him, "or you'll get into trouble one of these days. I almost thought you were going to hit me."

Norberg pounded the desk with his first, scattering papers, pens, and clips.

"STOP IT, for Christ's sake!" he roared. "Enough of this stupid nonsense."

"I don't like being suspected of murder. Least of all, on such flimsy evidence as you've got."

"You're not suspected of anything," Norberg growled. "I admit we made a mistake when we searched your room yesterday."

"Do you also think it was a mistake?" I asked, turning to Bodén, who was again busy with his drawings.

To my astonishment he gave a broad smile.

"Yes, it was a mistake."

"What's so funny?" I asked.

"Nothing, nothing. I merely thought we behaved rather foolishly. Don't you think so too?"

I wondered whether this was the real reason for his sudden good humor, but on the other hand I couldn't prove the opposite. So I had to adapt my tone to his.

"Yes, indeed," I said. "We certainly don't behave sensibly when we meet."

"No," he smiled. "We don't."

"May I go now?"

"Sure," said Norberg.

"Maybe you'll drop in again sometime," my friend Bodén added with an even broader smile.

Conversation with Trainer

THINGS WERE NOT quite as usual in Lindgren's stable. Håkan was not there and Anette too was missing. I found Jan, however, who didn't seem his normal cheerful self.

"Like some coffee?" he said. "One of the boys has made it, so it's not awfully good."

"How did you get on at Örebro?"

"Oh, I could have done better. I had one win, but otherwise they galloped with me. I'm not driving very well just now."

"The nervous strain, perhaps?"

"Possibly. But what in the hell has gotten into Håkan?"

"They say he has disappeared."

"Not only that," Jan said, blowing on the coffee in the plastic mug. "He has gone off with all the money we had with us here at Årjäng."

"How much?"

"Not a terrible lot, but over four thousand."

This merely confirmed the theory that Håkan had gone off to buy drugs. He must have been very desperate to act as he did.

"Has Anette got the day off?"

"Yes, she didn't feel up to coming today."

Jan was right about the coffee. It tasted like dishwater.

"Yes, it's pretty foul," Lindgren said, having evidently noticed my wry face.

I considered whether or not to broach the subject of Håkan's drug addiction with his brother. Maybe it wasn't being loyal to Håkan, but it was necessary to try and clear the matter up.

"Have you talked to the police?" I began cautiously.

"Only briefly. Anything special you're thinking of?"

"Did you know that Håkan is hooked on drugs?"

Jan sipped his coffee and put a lump of sugar in his mouth before replying.

"No," he said. "I didn't know for sure, but I had my suspicions."

"Why?"

"He hasn't been himself the last few months. He has bungled things that he always used to be able to manage and he's been driving badly."

"There may have been other reasons?"

"Yes, I grant you, but I had a boy with me a couple of years

156

ago who had the same problem, and he behaved in much the same way as Håkan."

"Did you ever have it out with him?"

"No, never. You know how it is. It goes against the grain to discuss that sort of thing. I could never bring myself to speak to him about it, though I meant to several times."

"You've no idea where he gets the junk from?"

"No, it's easy enough, I imagine. We're often in Gothenburg and I wouldn't be surprised if you can get it in Karlstad and Örebro too."

"Do you think Anette knew that Håkan was on drugs?"

"You'd better ask her."

Rather a sore point about Anette, evidently. I could perhaps follow it up and see where it led, if it did lead anywhere. There was no telling.

"Anette seems to have had some sort of confessional talk with Håkan the other evening," I said.

Jan drank up his coffee. He was quite composed. There wasn't a sign of nervousness in the open, sun-tanned face.

"Oh, really?" was all he said.

I decided to pursue the matter.

"He told me himself. Anette told him that she's been going with you."

"Well, I'm not the only one," he said.

"But you have, haven't you?"

For the first time he looked irritated. Not much, but still.

"Yes, I have, I have," he said. "But that was long ago."

"How long ago?"

"Last winter."

"Håkan seemed to think it was still going on."

"Then he was wrong. What about yourself, come to that? Are you quite innocent where Anette is concerned?"

"Yes, indeed I am," I lied.

He gave me a look, but didn't say anything. Besides, I was his client who owned one of the most promising horses in the stable. You don't get on the wrong side of people like that if you are a sensible trainer. And Jan is.

He changed the subject.

157

"What do you say about going to Stockholm tomorrow?" he asked. "We can let Stylist try out the track a few days in advance. He's worth it."

I thought it over. It was okay with me. I was on vacation and all the editors in the world couldn't stop me from going to Stockholm.

"Yes, let's do that," I said.

"Fine. Anette has promised to come with us and look after him. He couldn't have a better keeper."

"Is she up to it?"

"Yes, I think so," he said. "As long as she rests today, she's sure to be in form again tomorrow."

I spent the rest of the day watching the trotters. The weather had cleared up, the air was fresh, and the track had dried out after the rain of the last few days.

My face was still an awful sight, but oddly enough you never meet so many cheerful people as when you have a black eye. They are all smiles. It's nice to give pleasure to others.

I must admit that little by little I had come to respect the police. In the afternoon, therefore, I called them up and asked to speak to Norberg or Bodén. After a few hitches I was put through to Norberg.

As a concession to my self-esteem, I did not begin with my real errand.

"I'm putting a little story together, and I wondered if you've found Håkan Lindgren yet?"

"No, we haven't."

"If he has left Årjäng, have you any theory as to how he got away?"

"No, we haven't. He evidently didn't go by train. He may have hitchhiked."

"Has a nationwide alarm gone out for him?"

"Not as far as I know."

"Who would know?"

"The head of the investigation division."

"Have you had time to check all the alibis for the Railroader's murder?"

"Yes. They're all as weak as yours. Anette Lindgren does

confirm her husband's alibi and thereby her own as well, but that hardly makes things better. The Rings were out on a spree, separately, but can't remember exactly with whom. Ring was with a girl he hadn't seen before, and his wife had picked up a man who was also a stranger."

"What morals!"

"Yes indeed. *I* never run across girls like that."

"What about Stayovic?"

"Actually we have no cause to take an interest in him, but if we're to believe the hotel staff, he was sleeping sweetly in his room."

"Oh, one more thing," I said.

I had now come to my real errand.

"What?"

"I was wondering if you had any objections to my going to Stockholm tomorrow? We're transporting my horse to Solvalla tomorrow instead of on Wednesday."

"Why on earth should we object to your going to Stockholm?"

He sounded so sincere and so surprised that I almost fell for it. But I had learned to suspect Norberg. He was far from being as harmless as he sounded.

"Your doings and remarks the last few days made me think you'd rather not let me out of your sight."

"It's enough if we have your phone number and address in Stockholm."

I gave them to him.

"You haven't found out anything more that we ought to know?" he asked.

"No, I can't say I have."

"Nothing that can simplify our search for Håkan Lindgren, for instance?"

"No, I've spoken to his brother, but he has no clues to offer, which is unfortunate because he's as anxious as anyone else for Håkan to turn up."

"If he does turn up." Norberg growled pessimistically. "What about his wife, has she said anything?"

"I don't know. I haven't seen her since Håkan disappeared."

"But perhaps you will see her later?" he asked in a voice of silk.

"Yes, if not later, then tomorrow—she's coming with us to Stockholm," I informed him.

"Well, well, fancy that."

"She's the best groom in the stable," I snapped, instantly aware that there was no need for me to bite his head off.

"I merely thought it odd that everyone concerned suddenly goes off to Stockholm," he said, quite unruffled.

"There's a perfectly good reason. And none of us is under suspicion, if I've understood you clearly."

"Oh, I imagine you have," he said, thus leaving me puzzled about what he really thought.

"Then perhaps I won't be seeing you again," I said. "In that case, I'll say goodbye. Pity we didn't meet under more pleasant circumstances. But perhaps we'll meet again sometime."

"Perhaps we will," he said.

I hoped he was wrong.

With Anette

I PHONED IN my last report to the paper and told them that I was now resuming my vacation.

"Well, the Karlstad correspondent can see to the rest of the story if there is anything more," they told me from the editorial desk.

Then I went back to the hotel. I had thought of having an early dinner, but the restaurant was crowded so I went up to my room instead, and packed my things. And, incidentally, had a couple of drinks.

Thus strengthened, I had mustered enough courage to call up Anette. The phone rang several times before she answered. She sounded as if she had just awakened.

"May I come up for a moment?" I asked.

"Yes, if you like," she replied.

I grabbed the bottle of whisky and went up to her room.

"Come in," she called, in answer to my knock on the door.

She was standing in the middle of the floor, looking as sleepy as she had sounded. Her clothing, or rather lack of it, was disturbing. She was wearing a very short bathrobe of terry cloth and it was impossible to decide whether she had anything on underneath it. It didn't look like it, but then some of the panties nowadays are microscopic.

"I was asleep," she said. "I took a sleeping pill and went out like a light. Who won the heat race?"

Crazy about horses, she was. Fancy asking who won the heat when so much else had happened. I told her that Sören had won with Noble Action.

"He's superb," she said. "How did we get on?"

"Janne had a win with Stuart."

She shrugged.

"That's nothing to write home about. Won't you sit down, by the way?"

I did so and she sat on the other chair, tucking her legs under her. It was still impossible to say anything definite about her clothing. But then, that wasn't why I had come.

"I'm sorry about this business with Håkan," I said.

She gave me a searching look but said nothing.

"Would you like a drink?" I asked.

"I don't mind if I do."

I got some glasses from the bathroom. When I got back, she had brought out a bottle of mineral water. I mixed a drink and handed it to her. I poured some out for myself, but abstained from the mineral water.

"What's your opinion?" I asked.

"Of what?"

"Håkan, of course."

"I expect he has tired of me. He was bound to, sooner or later."

"It didn't sound like it the other day. He'd put up with anything at all according to you."

"That was then."

"What has happened since?"

She shrugged again. The bathrobe slipped down over one shoulder.

161

"I don't know. But he has gone."

"He'll probably come back."

"Not to me anyway."

"Do you want him back?"

"I'm not sure."

"Perhaps you already know that he's been on drugs for some time. Didn't you ever notice?"

"I never noticed a thing," she replied. "It's a complete surprise to me."

"But surely you must have seen scars from the needles?"

"I very seldom saw him without clothes," she said frankly. "Not for a long time at any rate."

"Do you mean . . ."

"Exactly."

"Poor Håkan," I said.

"And poor me," she added.

"Was he at home the night the Railroader was murdered?" I asked.

Again that shrug. The bathrobe slipped down still further.

"I think so anyway," she said. "I fell asleep almost at once. I'm pretty sure I would have noticed if he had gotten up during the night. He got up early in the morning, but he always does because of the horses."

What was it again the police had said? The murder could have been committed during the night or possibly early in the morning.

"You once said you have plenty of money."

"Yes, we have."

"But where did the money come from? Do you know?"

She sighed heavily.

"No, Kalle, I've no idea. But he had money all right."

"Janne says that Håkan went off with several thousand."

"So I heard. I can't understand that either. What does he want with all that money?"

The question hung in the air, and I had no answer to give her.

"I'm glad you're coming with us to Stockholm," I said after a while.

"I don't want to stay here alone. It's better to work. I think so anyway."

"Where will you stay in Stockholm?"

"I've some relations who usually put me up the few times I'm there," she replied.

"You can stay with me if you like. I've plenty of room."

"We'll see," she said. "Do you think I'm awful?"

"No," I protested.

But what did I really think? Wasn't I, in fact, rather shocked at her behavior? But then, who was I to judge? I, of all people on earth? Leave that to others who perhaps had more call to do so.

"All the same, I'm afraid I worry you a bit," she went on.

She certainly did worry me, but perhaps not quite in the way she imagined. Not wanting to get involved in an argument, I refrained from comment.

"I'm pretty sure there's a moralist somewhere inside you."

"No, I'm hardly a moralist," I replied.

"Well, *I* think so anyway," she mumbled. "Is there anything left in the bottle you brought?"

There was, and I poured her another drink. A stiff one—and half of it was gone in one gulp.

"Don't do that, please," I begged. "It doesn't help at all."

"There you are! There he is again: the Moralist."

Silence. What was I to say anyway? Perhaps she was right after all. No, I wasn't a moralist. I was amoral, if anything. Up to a point, at least. But it is imperative for a journalist who wants to get moved up and is not yet well established. The end justifies the means, said the Jesuits. But their goal was great and noble—everlasting life for human souls, even if the path to it lay via the stake.

"What time are we leaving tomorrow?" I asked.

"About eight o'clock. Janne's taking his car and we'll hitch the trailer to it. Then we'll be there by evening without having to rush. He'll win, Kalle. I think you can rake in a nice tidy sum if you want to back him."

"I don't go in for betting so much now," I said.

"I wonder. You give me the impression of being a gambler. But I may be wrong, of course."

"Yes, you are."

She gave me a searching look. Then she took another gulp of her whisky and soda.

"I'd ask you to stay for a while," she said. "But the fact is I'm not in the mood. So much has happened and I need to sort myself out."

I wonder whether you ever will, I thought.

"Yes, I understand," I said. "I'll see you in the morning, then. Look after yourself. Things will work out all right somehow, you'll see."

She looked very skeptical.

"Maybe," she said. "Maybe."

Rather disappointed, I picked up my whisky bottle, which was almost empty by this time. As I closed the door I saw Anette take off her bathrobe and lie down on the bed again. The sight hardly eased my disappointment.

She had nothing on underneath.

Damn the girl.

A Happy Debtor

BOTTLE IN HAND, I went back to my room, looking, no doubt, like a rejected suitor in some abysmally bad old Swedish film.

In the corridor I ran into the secretary of the race track, Allan Berggren. The official with the shaky finances looked almost elated, and the eyes behind the thick spectacles were lively and bright.

"Hi, Kalle," he said. "You do look down in the dumps."

"But *you* certainly don't. Have you time to come in for a moment?"

"Well, I don't know . . ." he said doubtfully.

"I've a little whisky left and a couple of cans of beer," I said enticingly.

"Not at all bad, in view of the fact that the summer meeting is nearly over."

We went downstairs and installed ourselves in my room. I gave him what whisky was left and made do with the beer for myself.

"Just what the doctor ordered," he chirped.

Whatever had got into him? He, who was always correctness personified—when he wasn't borrowing money from successful trainers, of course.

Without the slightest prompting from me he explained his state of exaltation.

"I've just gone and paid back the money to Janne," he informed me with shining eyes. "Two thousand cold, so now I won't have that nightmare hanging over me any more."

"Congratulations," I said. "Where did the money come from? Did you borrow from someone else this time too?"

He looked almost affronted when he answered.

"No, you don't catch me doing a stupid thing like that again."

"But there are others to borrow from besides a trainer."

"Oh, is that what you meant. I misunderstood you. I thought you meant that I had approached some other trainer."

"But you've got some money at any rate?"

"It came like a gift from above," he beamed. "We've had some money tied up in my parents' estate and yesterday, along comes my brother and asks if he can buy me out. I agreed on the spot and he handed the cash over right away."

"Fantastic," I said.

"Yes, I can hardly believe it's true."

"How much did you get?"

"Three thousand, so I even paid Janne interest though he has never asked for it."

"Decent of you."

He stared at me to see if I was being sarcastic. I was, in fact, but I don't think it showed. At times I have a poker face.

Berggren sipped his whisky cautiously. He wasn't drinking at anything like the same rate he was while sitting with Lindgren, downing one drink after the other. Now, he was once more his old careful, rather sectarian self.

I had finished my can of beer and opened a new one. As usual, I pushed the tab down into the can. I always do. A strange habit I have.

"Janne tells me you're off to Stockholm tomorrow with your horse," Berggren said.

I nodded.

"Do you think you have a chance?"

"Janne seems to think so anyway."

"Well, when he did 26 on Friday on that sloppy track with that fault, he ought to be in the running."

"There's quite a difference in the competition at Solvalla," I reminded him.

"True, but Rodney's Pride isn't at all a bad horse."

"No," I said, "but Brogren gave the race away. He should have pulled away harder and Stylist would never have caught up. He hadn't much left in him at the post."

"Are you sure?"

"Yes. Janne said the horse was almost played out."

"Almost? That might mean anything."

"He was tired."

"Have you seen the starting list for Thursday?" he asked.

"Yes," I replied, "in the paper yesterday."

"Who do you think will put up the biggest fight?"

"That Wallner horse, I should think. He galloped at the finish last time, but otherwise he's had a record down toward 22."

"I've half a mind to put a small bet on Stylist," Berggren said.

"Is that allowed?" I asked.

"There's nothing to stop me from betting at other racecourses. At my own track, of course, I'm not allowed to."

"No, of course not."

"I hear that you've had big offers for the horse," he said after a short pause.

"Who said so?"

"Oh, I heard it on the grapevine. I don't remember who told me. One of the stablemen."

"If the subject crops up again, you can tell the person concerned that Stylist's not for sale."

"But if the price is right, you'll make a deal, surely?"

"I don't expect ever to be offered the right price," I retorted. "It's far too high."

"How high?"

"Why do you ask?"

166

His glasses glinted as he turned his face toward me. The blue eyes were as innocent as a child's.

"Sheer curiosity," he assured me. "I didn't mean to be pushing."

"You're not, by any chance, playing someone else's game, are you? Someone I've already refused?"

"Good heavens no. Who would that be?"

"Oh, there are one or two," I replied vaguely.

I was thinking of Ring, Bengtsson, and Stayovic. All three had appeared to be interested in buying Stylist, but it *could* be that one and the same prospective buyer was at the back of it—Stayovic.

"I'm not surprised he's coveted," Berggren said. "Naturally we'd like him to stay at the Värmland tracks. We need good, young horses. Have you never thought of putting him in training at Solvalla?"

There, he touched on rather a sore point. To tell the truth I had been in touch with Sören Nordin. But he had a long waiting list and we hadn't settled anything. And Sören knows his worth. He charges a lot for his services; he has every reason to do so. When the horses stand up to his rigorous training, he gets results.

"No," I replied to Berggren. "He'll be staying with Lindgren."

"I'm glad," he said.

"It's always nice to please other people," I said. "What do you think about the Railroader's murder?"

He seemed rather upset by the sudden change of subject.

"I haven't thought much about it. Haven't had time."

"That sounds funny to me," I said pointedly. "You knew each other pretty well. After all, you lived next door to each other as children and everything."

"All the same, I haven't had time to take much interest in his murder," he maintained.

Now you're lying, I thought. And the devil got into me.

"He knew that you had borrowed money from Lindgren," I said, fixing my eyes on him. "I had a feeling it was Shag who told him."

I made a calculated pause.

"They're both dead now," I added.

With one blow, I had shattered Berggren's great satisfaction at having paid off his debt to Lindgren. His shoulders drooped, and the eyes behind the thick lenses grew tired and confused.

"Surely you don't think that I . . ."

"No, but don't try to make me believe that you haven't thought about the murder."

"Well, yes, I *have* been puzzled over it," he confirmed. "Bjarne was a gambler on a large scale and the murder must tie up with it in some way. It's the only explanation I can think of."

"Did you know that he incurred heavy gambling debts in Gothenburg, or wherever it was?"

Berggren hesitated a few seconds but then seemed to brace himself. At the same time, he frowned and his tongue darted over his lips like that of a snake about to strike.

"Yes, I did hear rumors," he said.

"From whom?"

"Oh, you know how it is in this game. You meet so many people. And there's no getting away from the fact that trotting stands or falls by its gamblers. They're not all exactly angels."

"No, no, but who was it that said so?"

"I've got an idea it was Janne."

I thought back. Yes, Lindgren *had* said to me that he suspected the Railroader of having lost a lot of money.

"You don't know whom he owed money to?"

"No."

His reply seemed quite sincere.

"Well, I do," I said. "He gambled away a lot of money at a club owned by a Yugoslav called Stayovic. Ever heard of him?"

"No, never."

"He's a close friend of Bengt Ring's."

"Is he, now. That sounds interesting. As you may remember my saying to you, we've taken a look at Ring's affairs. Your information certainly confirms our suspicions."

"Well, I think you can be quite sure that Bengt Ring is mixed up in the gambling racket. In confidence, I can tell you that the police have established that Ring is as good as bankrupt. But that doesn't rule out the possibility that he has other hidden assets in gambling clubs, for instance. If he's thinking of changing his line of business, it might be profitable to liquidate his debts by going bankrupt in the publishing business."

"Very likely. I'm grateful to you, Kalle, for telling me this. We want to get at Ring."

"Why?"

He grew confused again.

"Er . . . well, because we suspect him of involvement with illegal gambling. It takes money away from us."

"Nothing else?"

"Hm, we've been wondering about all the horses he buys. We think he enters horses here that should never be allowed on the track."

"But surely you can put a ban on their starting?"

"Admittedly, but the matter is a little more complicated than that. He has his horses with Janne, who is such a good trainer that even the worst old nags win now and then. And then we can hardly intervene, especially bearing in mind what a star Lindgren made out of Sam Boy."

"Were you surprised when it turned out that Sam Boy was not doped?"

"Yes, I must admit I was. Shag's story about the syringe in the stable made me inclined to accept the doping theory."

"So you believed Shag?"

"Believed is perhaps going too far, but he did know a lot more than you might think."

"Yes, I know."

He gave me a long look and I had a feeling he wanted to say something more. I may have been wrong, for he said nothing for a while.

Then, quietly and with lowered eyes, he murmured:

"You won't write anything about my business with Janne?"

"No. I've finished reporting about the murders. The others can take over. I'm off on vacation."

"I assure you, I've had nothing to do with the murders," he said with a dignified expression.

"I believe you. Would you like some beer?"

169

"Yes, please."

I opened the next to the last can of beer and poured some out for him. He drank it, thanked me, and left the room.

When he had gone, I sat there alone and put on my thinking cap. After turning things over in my mind for a long time, I reached a decision.

Although I had said my farewells earlier in the day, I went to the police station. The indefatigable Norberg was there, and I was shown into his office.

"An unexpected visit, but all the more welcome," he said, beaming at me. "Sit down, sit down."

I sat down opposite him.

"There's something I'd like to tell you," I said.

"Do you mind if I call in a witness?" he asked.

I smiled.

"No, not at all."

He spoke into the intercom and a plainclothes policeman appeared within seconds. He gave me a stealthy look.

"My name's Karl Berger," I said to him.

"Mine's Bengtsson. I'm from the homicide squad."

"Pleased to meet you."

Norberg switched on the tape recorder and told this instrument the time, the place, and who I was.

Then it was my turn.

"I've found out something that might have some bearing on the murder investigation," I began.

"Splendid," he said with a broad smile.

"You probably know who Allan Berggren is?"

"Yes, he's the secretary of the race track. I've met him. What has he been up to?"

I told Norberg and the man from the homicide squad about Berggren's affairs with Lindgren. I also told them that the Railroader had ferreted out the whole thing, and that Berggren had now had a windfall and had paid the money back.

"Why haven't you told us this before?" Norberg asked.

"I didn't get the Railroader's information confirmed until this evening," I bluffed.

170

"But it was startling enough for you to have passed it on to us earlier."

"Maybe. But that's how it is."

"Why did you come to us now, then?"

"I began to puzzle over the money that Berggren paid back to Lindgren."

"Let me hear," he said, his eyes glittering.

"It's not really so strange," I said. "Håkan Lindgren took four thousand with him when he disappeared. Now Berggren suddenly turns up and repays a loan to Janne. You follow me?"

"But why should he come and tell you about it?"

"Perhaps he wanted to forestall the matter leaking out through Janne," I said. "And also, to make sure that I wouldn't write anything about it. I promised him, as a matter of fact."

"What?"

"Not to write about it. And I haven't either. I've a favor to ask. If it turns out that he told the truth about the money from his parents' estate, please don't let it come out, or he'll get the sack."

Norberg whistled a snatch of "Five Minutes More."

"No, no," he said. "We're the soul of discretion. Nothing else you wanted to say while you're at it?"

"No, that'll do for now," I replied.

I walked back to the hotel and went to bed.

The Journey

NEXT MORNING, I paid my exorbitant bill at the hotel. I always feel rather low when I part from so much money.

We drove up to the track and Janne fastened on the little horse van that he had borrowed from an amateur at the track.

Then Anette led Stylist out. He looked rather excited at the thought of the journey and almost trotted into the cramped box where he was to spend the next few hours.

"What about the sulky?" I asked.

"I've phoned Stockholm. We're to be in Sören Nordin's stable and can borrow things from him. Svenne—you know, the kid in the stable—has to drive down to Åby on Wednesday with a load, instead of Håkan, and he needs more sulkies than I do."

"You've worked with Sören, haven't you?"

"Yes, for over a year. He and Uno Swed taught me everything I know. They're great, each in his own way."

"Sören is a pretty tough guy, isn't he?"

"Yes, hard as nails, but what he doesn't know about horses and how to look after them isn't worth knowing."

"What about Uno?"

"He's rather a different type. What he taught me chiefly was to read propositions in the right way."

"What do you mean?"

"When you're a trainer at a provincial track, you must match the horses properly, if you're to make it pay. It means you must read the propositions so carefully that you can start the horses where they have the biggest chance of showing what they're made of."

"But doesn't that also mean, in addition to hard work, that you have to rely very much on your stablemen?"

"Exactly. I learned that, too. Without capable hands in the stable, you might as well pack it in. But I've been lucky mostly. Håkan is a real asset, and the same goes for Anette, of course. She'd be still more useful if I could get her to drive in races."

"Not on your life," said Anette.

"Scared?" I asked unthinkingly.

Her eyes flashed.

"Scared! Of course not."

Janne glanced at me and smiled.

"I'd never have dared to say that to her. But horse owners, of course, are able to take greater liberties than a poor employer."

She was still glaring at me.

"So you think I'm scared," she said fiercely. "Janne! How does one go about getting a license?"

"I'll fix it," he said.

Then he turned to me.

"To think, I hadn't hit on that trick before."

"It wasn't a trick," I protested.

We were ready to set off. Anette climbed into the back and I sat in front beside Janne. He fastened his safety belt and helped me with mine. I'm a complete fool when it comes to things like that. For instance, I'm always just as nervous and wet with perspiration before I get the hang of all the contraptions connected with safety belts in airplanes. A stewardess usually comes rushing to help me and that makes me still more nervous. Once I was out on an assignment in an army helicopter. I had to put on a peculiar sort of life vest. I immediately pulled the wrong cord and the entire vest inflated.

We took the pretty but bumpy road between Årjäng and Karlstad. One of the most beautiful views I know of is when the road narrows near Åsebyfors and the great wide lake of Järnsjön glitters down by Sandaholm, where there's a beach unequaled anywhere. When we were kids, we used to cycle there from Årjäng. I wonder if youngsters nowadays are up to it.

Anette sprawled drowsily on the back seat. I glanced at her occasionally and she still looked angry. Evidently I had hurt her feelings by suggesting that she was afraid to drive in a race.

On we went, at a steady, even rate. I don't know much about cars, but I did know that Janne was an excellent driver. Calm, self-possessed, always on the alert.

Now and then we rested and Anette had a look at Stylist, giving him water, checking the padded bandages around his legs, and so on.

I had been turning over in my mind what to do about having told the police about Berggren's affairs with Janne. I had better come out with it since Lindgren was sure to be questioned about the matter sooner or later.

"By the way, Janne," I said, "I had no alternative but to go to the police and tell them you had lent money to Berggren."

"Have you lent him money?" came from the back seat.

Lindgren said nothing but drove on calmly. We were some-where on one of the long straight stretches between Karlstad and Kristinehamn.

"I went because Berggren told me he had paid off the debt," I said.

"Yes, he brought the money yesterday. Said something about some estate or other."

"The money Håkan took," Anette said.

I half turned around. Her expression was not so angry now.

"Exactly," I said. "Just what I was thinking."

Janne shook his head.

"No, he's not such a rat."

"I don't think so either," I admitted. "But I couldn't keep quiet about it. The police promised to handle the matter discreetly."

"Well, my conscience is clear," he declared.

"But it might show you up in a bad light," Anette said anxiously.

"It happens to all trainers sooner or later," he said. "However careful and honest you are, someone always comes along and says you're up to no good. There isn't one trainer who isn't talked about. Sometimes, it's a matter of well-organized campaigns to give him a bad name. Owners or gamblers who lose money and turn nasty are quite likely to take it out on the trainer."

"But I've never heard anything about you except this loan to Berggren."

"No, but then you're not often in Värmland."

"*Are* there stories going around about you?"

"Not to my knowledge," he said, and there was a murmur of assent from the back seat.

"Do you know whether Berggren himself bets," I asked Lindgren.

"I don't think he's a big gambler, but I'm sure he takes a chance now and then."

"He seemed to me very interested in this trip of ours and in Stylist's chances," I said.

"Yes, I know he backed Sam Boy quite a lot when we were traveling about with him."

"How do you know?"

"He said so himself."

"Did Bengt Ring make a lot of money by betting on Sam Boy?"

174

"He must have. The minute I started training Sam Boy, I saw what could be gotten out of him, and of course, I told Ring."

"You took him carefully at first?"

He laughed.

"Well, naturally, I never drove him faster than was necessary to win; and when I didn't win, it was because Sammy was so lively that he galloped."

We reached Solvalla in the evening. I was tired and wanted to go home, so I let Jan drive me to the subway at Blackeberg. He and Anette went on to the stable.

I went straight to my apartment at Agnegatan. A pile of mail lay on the mat, but it yielded nothing of any importance. Mostly bills. No, there was actually a money order too.

That was lucky. It evened things out.

I went to bed early.

Alone.

With Kollin

MY CONTACT with the Criminal Investigations Division in Stockholm is its chief superintendent, Lars Kollin. In some ways he reminds me of Norberg. Both are expert at concealing their capabilities behind a well-camouflaged façade. While Norberg acts the part of a kind and harmless uncle, Kollin is just the opposite: boorish, brusque, always swearing, and very intelligent.

I live only a few blocks away from police headquarters, so I was soon there. Since I knew that Kollin was a very busy man, I had called earlier and made an appointment.

"Come at ten o'clock, if you're able to get up so goddam early," he growled.

At ten precisely I knocked at his secretary's door. The same old gorgon who had been there for years. She eyed me critically, and asked what I wanted.

"I've been promised an audience," I said. "Berger is the name."
She looked very suspicious, but did condescend to knock at his door and ask.

"Let him in, for Christ's sake," I heard from inside.

There he sat behind his desk. With his hair brushed straight back and his wide-awake eyes, he was just the same as ever, even to the checked jacket. Maybe he looked a little more tired than usual. It's not exactly a sinecure to be head of Stockholm's C.I.D.

Kollin has seen everything. Ill-treated wives, battered children, stinking corpses, and death and misery in all forms. I know that he never gets used to it. But people who don't know him are convinced that he is a blundering oaf. He does nothing to disillusion them. Sometimes he amuses himself by doing a takeoff on the "tough cop" in an American film. Gun in holster, he swears and blusters, and people think he *is* what he pretends to be. But he isn't at all, and he's never so pleased as when he really takes people in with his acting.

"What goddam mess are you mixed up in now?" were his first words. "Come on, out with it!"

I told him in detail what had happened during my vacation. He listened attentively, now and then jotting down a note on the big pad on the desk.

"Oh, that goddam Ivarsson," he said. "He worked here with us at one time, and far be it from me to speak ill of him, but you won't find a bigger idiot anywhere. Norberg, I've spoken to on the phone, and by Christ, he sounds sensible enough."

It is said of Kollin that he finds it very difficult to say three sentences without resorting to at least one swearword. But it's not true. I have heard him talking to shocked and desperate people without swearing at all.

"Have you heard anything of Håkan Lindgren?" I asked.

"Only that a nationwide alarm was put out this morning."

"Do you know anything about Stayovic?"

"Are you here as a journalist?" he rapped out, taking off his glasses.

"No," I said truthfully. "I'm here as an interested party only."

"Milan is still in clover," he said. "Doing damn well. He has at least three clubs here in town and he runs them perfectly. Never

176

the slightest trouble, if you don't count such goddam trifles as suicide, embezzlement, and bankruptcy, of course. But he seems to avoid violence nowadays."

"So you don't think Eng was hired by him?"

"It's possible," he said, "but it implies two things."

"What are they?"

"He may be up to something that we don't know about, which, Christ knows, is likely enough considering our shortage of men."

"What else?" I asked, sensing the reply.

"That you have not been telling the truth when talking to me and other cops. And I wouldn't like to think that."

"I'm not keeping anything from you."

"I damn well hope not. I've practically had to vouch for you with Norberg. You seem to have driven them nearly frantic in the backwoods."

"If I did, it was quite unintentional."

For no reason I added:

"They've been pretty tough with me, too. Things have to be pretty serious before you search a journalist's room."

"Damn serious," he agreed.

"That sounds ambiguous."

"Think so?" he said. "I'm damned if I do. You mustn't be so touchy, Berger."

"One is apt to be touchy when suspected of double murder," I complained.

"Maybe triple murder, too."

"Yes, even that. Do you too think I'm mixed up in this? Nothing surprises me any longer."

"No, I don't," he said. "But I understand those guys who are not quite sure of you. May I ask what you're thinking of doing now?"

"I don't know."

"I can damn well tell you what you're not going to do."

"Oh?"

"And that is, rush off to brother Stayovic's gambling clubs this evening and raise Cain. It's not worth it. Let the police manage this from now on."

"Are you officially in on the investigation now?"

"Depends what you mean," he replied. "Since they've sent out this goddam stupid alarm for Lindgren, I suppose you could say that I'm vaguely connected with it."

"Am I being shadowed?"

"Why do you ask?"

"On my way here, I could have sworn there was an idiot in dungarees who started following me on the other side of the street."

"If so, those bastards from the homicide squad got the idea. It sounds just like them, in fact."

He was silent for a moment.

"Do you mean to say they had him dressed in dungarees?"

"Yes."

"They're crazy. Christ, those methods went out of fashion fifty years ago."

"Am I being shadowed?" I asked again.

"Not by us, anyway."

"Do you or don't you know whether I'm being watched?"

"You obstinate ass," he sighed. "Of course they're keeping an eye on you. Jesus, you surely understand that."

"So the C.I.D. is not behind it?"

"Christ, no. Do you really mean they had put dungarees on him?"

"Yes. Brand-new ones. Not a spot on them. He had a polo shirt on underneath, too."

"God save the King and the Royal Swedish Police Force," he proclaimed.

"Amen," I filled in.

"Hallelujah. Blessed are the poor in spirit, for theirs is the kingdom of heaven. With dedication to the homicide squad. I wonder what they will all do with themselves up there."

"You seem to be well versed in the Scriptures."

"I come from a very God-fearing home on the west coast," he informed me. "You've no idea how many times I've heard the Sermon on the Mount. I was sick and tired of it then, but actually it's damn fine."

"Do you ever go to trotting races yourself?"

"Yes, quite often, as a matter of fact."

He never ceased to astonish me.

"Do you bet too?"

"Oh yes, I turn in a ticket occasionally, but I've only had one win and then I got 656 kronor. You've had better luck, haven't you. It must have been a real jackpot you raked in."

"An old telephone number," I said.

"Which?"

"145 38," I replied.

He began to fidget with papers. Clearly the audience was at an end. I stood up.

"Are you going?"

"Yes, I'd better."

"Watch out for dungarees," he said. "And . . . Berger?"

"Yes, what is it?"

"You've given me an idea."

I left police headquarters in a thoughtful mood, puzzling as to what idea I could have put into Kollin's head.

I didn't even bother to check whether my shadow from the homicide squad was still on my heels. If he did come from there. I wasn't at all sure. He could just as well be one of Kollin's men.

I had thought of going out to Solvalla and watching the training, but it seemed too much of an effort. I phoned Janne instead.

"He's not here," said the stable voice, "but you can speak to the girl who's looking after the horse, if you like."

"All right."

After a minute or so I heard Anette's voice at the other end of the line. She really sounded pleased that it was me.

"I thought you were coming out today," she said.

"I thought so, too, but I've some things to see to. How is he going?"

"Fine, so far. Eats all he can get and seems happy enough."

"Where's Janne?"

"He went into town for a couple of hours. Had an appointment at a restaurant with a horse owner, I think."

"Any news of Håkan?"

"No, not a thing."

Her voice was completely neutral and I couldn't find a trace of any feeling in it. She seemed to have dismissed all thought of her husband, or else she was just acting like that to keep her spirits up.

"My offer to put you up still stands," I said.

"So I imagine," she said and hung up.

A Cry for Help

IN THE EVENING I went to the movies and saw a Western. It's great entertainment. If it's a real Western, of course. These new psychological, soul-searching films aren't Westerns at all, but a big let-down to the whole genre.

Afterwards I strolled around downtown for a while although it depresses me. At night the shopkeepers' paradise at Sergels Torg is quite dead, and has the appearance of some weird scene in a dream. All these shopwindows with hi-fi equipment, men's wear, correspondence courses, Soviet tourist publicity, sex paraphernalia along with black condoms . . . And no human beings anywhere. It's all rather frightening.

Should anyone get the absurd idea to take a walk from Sergels Torg down toward Gustav Adolfs Torg, he would find himself gazing down into the yawning abyss that was once a district of busy streets and now, thanks to the mania of municipal politicians, looks like the crater made by an atom bomb. Not a soul in that direction either. Dark condemned buildings, wailing drunks in search of a night's shelter, and one police car an hour.

Kungsgatan is a little better, for at least it still has a few restaurants and discothèques. But the sight of all the teen-agers, high on drugs, is not very uplifting.

Stockholm is not a lively city. It doesn't have a friendly atmosphere. It has a corroding effect on its inhabitants.

A couple of hard-core porno clubs in Klara Norra Kyrkogata were open. Prospective customers hovered around outside, trying to peer behind the gaudy decoration of the shopwindows to get a glimpse of the living-dead goods inside.

Live shows: girls, girls.

I hopped on a 52 bus and went home. I live in an apartment house that has been modernized by a gung-ho building contractor. The former tenants—pensioners and immigrants—could not, of course, afford the new rents, and people like me moved in.

The contractor was highly spoken of in the papers when he modernized the house. He left the old façade as it was, and painted it orange. "A welcome splash of color in what is otherwise a dreary street," one reporter wrote. But when you reach the front door all the old has vanished. The entrance is locked at seven in the evening so that no vagrants can get in. On my staircase, there are fifteen house telephones with nameplates and all. Prospective visitors have to do a voice test in order to gain entrance to this upper-bracket taxpayers' paradise. My friendly landlord in his camel-hair overcoat and faintly absurd checked cap has also installed an automatic elevator. It's an excellent contrivance, duly inspected and approved by an authorized elevator inspector. Two of the elevator walls have mirrors. This may seem superfluous, but the contractor explained the matter to me: "Service, you see, sir. In this way, the women tenants can inspect their backs too," he nudged me and winked, "when they take the elevator up in the evenings with their boyfriends." Those mirrors, no doubt, cost an extra couple of kronor in rent, but I expect they're worth it when the girls can look at their backs.

The apartments are full of practical things like teak, mosaic inlays, wall-to-wall carpeting, and to top it all, air conditioning. It's a "must" during hot summers, the building contractor said in his leaflet when he was advertising for tenants.

He found it pretty difficult to get people at first, but succeeded in the end by making the apartments cooperative and lending money to the tenants for the deposit. But he was only too glad to do it. He will have recovered his outlay several times over in a couple of years.

It seems one should be in the building trade.

I had only just gotten inside the door and put the coffee pot on the electric cooker with all its technical gadgets, when the phone rang. It was Bodén.

"Oh, so you're in now," he said.

"As you hear," I replied.

"I just wanted to tell you something that may interest you," he went on.

"Oh?"

"You told Norberg about Allan Berggren's transactions with Jan Lindgren. We've checked what Berggren said."

"Well?"

"It's all quite correct. He did get money from his brother last Saturday."

"That's fine," I said.

"Yes, at any rate, for Berggren. That clears him, doesn't it?"

"It should."

"Did you expect it?"

"Yes, I did, as a matter of fact," I replied.

My answer seemed to perplex him, since he was silent for some time.

"Are you still there?" I asked.

"Of course I am," he snapped.

"Are you responsible for my being shadowed here in Stockholm?" I asked abruptly.

"Shadowed?"

"People are trailing around after me all day long. First, an idiot in dungarees, then I spotted another guy helping him. They're standing outside, waiting for me."

"I know nothing whatever about it," he said.

"I believe you."

"What did you say?"

He didn't seem to believe his ears.

"I said I believe you."

"And I thought I'd heard wrong."

"You're so prejudiced where I'm concerned, Bodén. I am a law-abiding citizen who relies one hundred percent on the police and their ability to check crime."

"There, *now* I recognize you. You're only kidding us."

"I'm not at all," I protested.

182

"Oh yes, you are."

He sounded resigned.

"Do you still think I'm a murderer?"

"No," he replied curtly.

"Oh, you don't. Why?"

"Because my superiors have told me that you can't have murdered Shag and the Railroader."

"Good superiors you have."

"For the most part, anyway."

"This time, too?"

"I take it for granted."

He was not entirely convinced, but it was quite unnecessary to rile him any more. We politely took leave of each other.

My coffee maker began jumping about on the burner and I took it off. I waited until the coffee began to run down into the bottom part. Oddly enough, this always fascinates me. I don't quite understand the principle, but possibly it has something to do with heat and expansion.

I poured the steaming hot coffee into one of my big cups and treated myself to a brandy. Then I settled down with Payne's *The Rise and Fall of Stalin.* It's a period in modern history which never ceases to astonish me.

The house telephone buzzed and I went over to it.

"Yes?"

"It's me," Anette Lindgren said. "May I come up? If you want me to, that is."

Did I!

"Yes, do," I said, pressing the button to open the street door.

I was so eager that I went out onto the staircase and stood in front of the elevator like a faithful dog. She soon appeared, dressed in jeans and loose-fitting overblouse.

"My God, how pretty you are," I exclaimed.

"I'm too fat."

"Nonsense."

We went inside. She looked about her curiously and the intelligent eyes registered everything.

"What a lot of books you have," she said when she saw my bookshelves.

"I'm an intellectual snob."

"I wish I had time to read," she said.

She was calm, self-assured, and relaxed.

Which is more than I would have been if I'd had the same news as she now told me.

"Håkan called me up an hour ago," she said, looking as if she had remarked on the weather.

"*What* did you say?"

She smiled politely.

"You heard me. Håkan called me up an hour ago."

"Tell me more."

"I was still at the stables, seeing to your champion."

"You mean you stayed on at the stables until ten o'clock?"

"That's nothing unusual. I had a couple of the stableboys to keep me company."

As she said it she looked straight at me, a pack of imps dancing in her eyes. She knew quite well that she inflamed me with her hints.

"Well?"

"The phone rang and one of the boys answered. He said the call was for me. I recognized Håkan's voice at once, but he sounded a bit peculiar."

"What did he want?"

"He wanted to see you."

"Me? Why?"

"He said you could help him."

"How could I help him?" I said.

"That's what *I* asked him, but he wouldn't say how."

"Where and how are we to meet then?"

She gave me an address in Kungstensgatan just near Sveavägen.

"Is that all he said?"

"Yes, then he hung up."

"And you're sure it was Håkan?" I asked.

"Yes-es."

"You hesitate."

"Not at all, but as I said just now, he sounded a bit peculiar. Not that it's so strange under the circumstances."

"No, of course not. When are we to meet?"

"Any time tonight."

"It sounds crazy," I muttered.

"Yes, doesn't it."

I thought it over for a moment, then I called up the switchboard of my paper. I was in luck. The operator was one of the old guard and we were good friends.

"Oh, so you're in town on vacation?"

"Where else would I be? Do you have the Red Book handy?"

The Red Book is a telephone directory in reverse. It has the addresses and in this way you can check who lives there. That is, if they have telephones. I gave her the address I had gotten from Anette.

"Would you mind having a look who lives there?"

"Hang on a minute."

She was soon back.

"Have you a pen?"

She read out the names of a lot of private tenants and a couple of firms.

"Just a moment," I said to the operator.

"Did he say which floor?" I asked Anette.

"Yes, the ground floor. There wasn't much to choose from, he said."

"That's fine," I said to the operator. "I've got the information I want. Thanks a lot."

"Are you coming?" I asked Anette. "We're going to call on a firm called Bileco."

"What sort of firm is it?"

"One of the big gambling clubs in town," I replied.

The Gambling Club

IT DOESN'T TAKE LONG to get from Kungsholmen to Kungstensgatan. We walked to the subway at Fridhemsplan and took the train to Rådmansgatan. Then, we were soon there.

The house was one of many just like it in that part of Stockholm. An ugly apartment house built at the end of the 1930s.

Out on Sveavägen the traffic was streaming past, but on this street it was quiet.

The front of the building contained a tobacconist's with the usual display of girlie studies. There was also a drab little provision shop with Greek letters on the window, a ladies' hairdresser with pictures of the most curious hairdos, and of course, a sign saying Used Cars. There isn't one building in this district where they don't sell cars.

The front door, like the apartment house where I lived, had a row of buttons and a house telephone. Beside one of them were the printed letters BILECO.

At that moment a party of three turned up, two middle-aged men and a teen-age girl.

"Are you going in too?" one of the men asked, pressing the button three times.

"Yes, that was the idea," I said.

A click announced that the door was now open, and Anette and I followed the other three inside. They walked quickly to one of the doors on the ground floor with BILECO engraved on a large brass plate.

Another bell. Four rings this time. There was a peephole in the door. After half a minute or so, the door was opened and we went in.

It was like entering a new world. Thick carpets, a bowing cloakroom attendant, and a crowd of people. In the cloakroom was a taste of what lay in store: three one-armed bandits, each for a different-sized coin. The passage into the cloakroom was very narrow, not even wide enough for two people abreast. A precautionary measure, in case the police should unexpectedly take an interest in what went on behind BILECO's sign.

The obliging attendant took our coats. He looked critically for a moment at Anette's jeans, but he let them pass. Nowadays it's hard to be sure just where the money is.

"Good evening, sir. Good evening, madam," he said with a bow.

I had heard that soft accent somewhere before.

"This is a gambling club," Anette whispered in my ear.

"Evidently."

Out of sheer curiosity I put a krona into the slot of the nearest bandit. There was a rattle, bells rang, and lights blinked.

The attendant rushed up.

"Congratulations," he said, taking out a key.

He turned it, then pulled out a hundred-kronor bill from a drawer in his little table.

"You're in for a lucky evening, sir," he said.

Anette's eyes were shining and she also bribed the bandit with a krona. It rattled diffidently and nothing more happened.

"Unfair," she said.

From inside the apartment came a subdued hum, and as we moved inside, I could hear the muted voices of the croupiers.

The main room looked like a Las Vegas gambling casino in an old American film. The only difference was that people were not in evening dress.

I immediately noticed a handful of so-called celebrities scattered about at the tables. A roulette wheel had star billing in the place, but there were also poker tables of the kind I remembered from the fairs at Årjäng. But I suspected that the stakes here were considerably higher.

I looked around the room and at once spotted someone I had not expected to see—Bengt Ring. He was standing at the roulette table with a girl draped about him who was not Mia.

I nodded in his direction.

"Do you see?" I said to Anette.

She made a face.

"Do I!"

Ring had a large pile of chips in front of him. He looked more pleased with himself than I had ever seen him before.

"Did you know he was in town?" I asked.

"Didn't I tell you?" Anette said. "Oh yes, he was out at Solvalla today, watching Janne drive Stylist fast."

"How fast did he drive?"

187

"Only 28 over the distance, but there was lots in reserve. As you know, Stylist never exerts himself when he doesn't have to."

"Were there a lot of railbirds there?"

"Dozens, but Stylist is never impressive in training."

I glanced around, trying to spot Håkan Lindgren, but there was no sign of him. I was not surprised. There was something fishy about that telephone call to Anette.

"There's no Håkan here," I said. "Shall we go?"

"No, wait a while."

"All right."

I was uneasy. I had a feeling I was on hostile ground, and that is never healthy. My suspicions had been aroused the minute Anette mentioned the address in Kungstensgatan. I recalled having once visited a gambling club in that neighborhood, but the actual address had slipped my mind. But I did remember that it said BILECO on the door, and that's why I checked with the Red Book.

We stood in the middle of the floor, rather at a loss. A girl dressed in a kind of Playboy costume glided up with a tray.

"Would you care for a drink?" she said.

I took a whisky and Anette a concoction with gin.

"Is it still on the house?" I asked the girl.

But it was an entirely different voice which answered.

"But of course, Mr. Berger. How nice that you have found your way here."

It was my old friend Milan Stayovic who stood there in a midnight-blue tuxedo. His smile was so friendly.

"I thought you said you were in the publishing business?" I said.

"Did I? Well, there's nothing like a little variation. Any luck so far this evening?"

"Yes, I won a hundred kronor on one of the slot machines."

He looked quite distressed.

"Jackpot," he said. "I didn't think it was possible. I must get the boys to have a look at that machine."

And he laughed so that his gold crowns gleamed in the soft lighting.

"Do you know Håkan Lindgren?" I asked him.

"No, but I know that he is married to the charming lady in your company," he replied gallantly.

"We were informed that he would be here."

"He has been missing for a few days, hasn't he?"

"Yes," I confirmed.

"I don't understand why he should be here. But I see that our friend Ring is also honoring us this evening, and he should know whether Mr. Lindgren has been here."

We went over to the roulette table. There was still a large pile of chips in front of Ring. He didn't notice our arrival. His eyes were riveted on the little ball dancing around. When it at last came to rest, the croupier pushed over still more chips to Ring.

Stayovic tapped him on the shoulder. Ring swung around and saw us. He didn't seem particularly surprised.

"Well," he said, "look who's here?"

He nodded down at the fair creature who was clinging to his arm. Her eyes looked at the pile of chips gloatingly.

"This is Chris," he said, introducing her. "Say hello to Mr. Berger, Chris. You're in the entertainment business so you should keep on good terms with the press."

"How do you do," the girl said politely, still feasting her eyes on the chips.

"Chris has the night off. Otherwise, she works hard at the Funny Girl Sex Club. Don't you, Chris?"

"Sure, Benke. I have three live shows every night."

"Together with a guy called Alex," Ring filled in. "The variation isn't invented that they don't know."

"Very interesting," Stayovic said. "But it wasn't to hear about her career that Mr. Berger came along. He wonders whether you have seen Håkan Lindgren here this evening?"

"Håkan? No, I haven't. Was he to be here?"

"So I was told," I replied. "Do you often come here?"

"Oh, now and then."

"Have you ever seen Håkan here?"

Ring glanced quickly at Anette.

"He has been here a couple of times," he said. "Last winter, I think. It was in connection with Sam Boy's races at Solvalla, if I remember rightly."

189

"Do you believe that?" I asked Anette.

She nodded in confirmation.

"It's quite possible," she said. "The more I get to know about Håkan, the less he resembles the guy I knew. But he hasn't been here this evening?"

Ring shook his head energetically.

"Aren't you going to cash them in?" Chris asked.

"When I'm fifteen thousand ahead and winning every time? I'd be crazy."

Stayovic gave a little malicious smile. The conversation was beginning to bore him. Then he turned to me. His brown eyes sized me up. They had an almost hypnotic quality. I felt ill at ease. My anxiety didn't lessen when he said, "I'd like a word with you in private."

What was I to do? I was in enemy territory and my chances of escape were nil.

"Why, sure," I said.

"If Mrs. Lindgren doesn't want to wait here, she can sit in another room."

"Yes, please," she said.

We went into another part of the large apartment. First we came to a small room with a couple of easy chairs.

"Perhaps you wouldn't mind waiting here," Stayovic said to Anette. "We won't be more than five minutes."

You can get beaten up in five minutes, I thought as I followed him.

The next room was evidently Stayovic's office. Very simple and unpretentious. A hefty young thug stood lounging in a corner with his hands in his pants pockets. I felt a tingling in my testicles and in the pit of my stomach at the sight of him. The man looked inquiringly at Stayovic. I tensed my body. At this point, I couldn't produce a drop of saliva to moisten my lips.

"Go out for a while, will you," Stayovic said to the man, who left the room quickly. He moved with a supple rhythm. Like a cat.

"Who was that?"

"My helper," Stayovic said with a smile.

I could just imagine what that hood usually helped with.

190

Stayovic looked at me again. I may have been mistaken, but I fancied I now saw a gleam of amusement in his eyes.

"You had me rather worried at Årjäng," he said. "I didn't care for your insinuations about being beaten up."

Automatically I put my hand to my face. The purple bruises were still very tender.

"So I looked into the matter," he went on. "I was interested, as a matter of fact, because Conny Eng did actually work for one of my, er, business friends in Gothenburg. But I think Conny is losing his grip. He used to be very good at his job. Now he'd be easy game for anybody. Drinks, probably. Now Stanko doesn't. He's the guy who was in here just now. He's in very good shape. I think he'll be Swedish middleweight champion this year."

I listened without interrupting him.

"I've gone into the matter. If Conny was doing someone's dirty work, he certainly wasn't hired by us."

I passed my hand again across my face.

"I believe you," I said.

He was pleasantly surprised.

"How nice that we understand each other again," he said in his gentle voice. "I wouldn't like to get on the wrong side of the Swedish press. That wouldn't be good public relations. And your horse is still not for sale?"

"No, not for money," I said.

He laughed boisterously. I left him to his mirth and went out to Anette. I wanted to get away as soon as possible.

"Come on, let's go," I said.

I asked the attendant to phone for a cab.

"It'll be here in a minute," he said, "but it will stop on the other side of the street. It would be just as well if you waited for it there."

"I understand."

We did as he said. After five minutes a taxi came, and we drove home to my place.

Anette stayed the night.

I was almost happy.

The Phone Call

THE NEXT MORNING Anette went off to Solvalla at the crack of dawn. I told myself I ought to go with her, but didn't manage to carry out my good intentions.

I stayed in bed until about eight o'clock, then I got up and had breakfast. There was some bacon left in the refrigerator and this, together with a couple of fried eggs, set me up for the day. Coffee, too, of course.

Then I had a shower and shaved, not an entirely painless process, as the bruises on my face had to be negotiated with care. But it didn't hurt as much as before.

I thought over what Stayovic had told me, and was convinced that he had told the truth. Was the explanation so simple that Eng was merely out to pick a quarrel? It was possible. And it wasn't so strange that his pals had retaliated. The more I thought of it, the more probable it seemed.

Then I phoned police headquarters and asked to speak to Kollin.

I was put through to his gorgon. No, the inspector was engaged and was not to be disturbed. In my most servile tones I begged her at least to inform Kollin who was calling. But she wouldn't relent.

"I did actually have some important information about a murder he's investigating," I said, piling it on.

"Then why didn't you say so?" she snapped. "We'd have been spared all this."

"Kollin here."

"It's Berger."

"What's so goddam urgent now?"

I told him of my doings the night before, especially mentioning my conversation with Stayovic.

"We already know you were there."

Yes, of course. That hadn't occurred to me. My shadow had naturally followed me to Kungstensgatan.

"Is it a fancy club?"

"Yes, pretty rich."

"I must make a raid there some time. And this guy Ring is also in town, you say?"

"Yes."

"It's damn nice of you to look after Håkan Lindgren's wife," he went on.

"Shut up."

He gave a coarse laugh.

"Is she hot stuff?"

To prevent a flow of abuse, I decided to shut up myself.

"So, you don't think that goddam rogue Stayovic has anything to do with the beating up?"

"No, I don't think he has."

"Then whom do you suspect?"

I put forward my theory about Eng's pugnacity.

"It's possible," he agreed. "I didn't understand either why Stayovic should go for you. They're always so goddam scared of the press, those guys."

"Just what he said."

"What are you going to do now?"

"I thought I'd go out to Solvalla. So you can tell the guy who is waiting, and he can go on ahead."

"Have I said *we* are shadowing you?"

"No, you haven't, but I take it for granted since you're so well informed."

I had just finished dressing when the phone rang. My first thought was not to answer it, but at last I did pick up the receiver. I heard the click that tells you that the call is being made from a public phone.

"Berger."

There was silence for a few moments and then, "Hi, Kalle. It's Håkan."

Yes, it sounded like him.

"Hi. Where are you?"

"I'm in Stockholm."

He spoke slowly, with abnormally long pauses between the words.

"I want to talk to you," he went on.

"Why?"

"I need help."

"Go to the police," I suggested.

"No, I don't want to. I'm scared they'll lock me up again. I couldn't stand it."

"Why must you talk to me?"

"Perhaps you can help me."

"Well, what is it?"

"I can't tell you over the phone. Can't we meet instead?"

He gave me an address.

"Where's that?"

"At Aspudden. I'm staying there."

"Was it you who called up Anette yesterday?"

"Yes."

"Then why didn't you come?"

"I was outside BILECO, but I saw that you were being shadowed when you came. So I cleared off."

"I'll be there in a couple of hours," I said.

"Can't you come at once?"

He sounded frightened and upset.

"No, I can't manage it before. Take it easy now. Everything will be all right, you'll see."

"Do you think so?"

"Yes."

He hung up and I sat down and began to think. First of all, was it really Håkan who had called up? Yes, I was pretty sure of that. I recognized the Värmland dialect. And secondly, should I go and see him, or should I call up the police?

It was a difficult decision, but at last I made up my mind to go out to Aspudden. But if there was to be any point in the trip, I must shake off the plainclothesman who was sure to be standing outside waiting for me.

I spotted him almost the moment I came out into the street. He was no longer disguised as a workman. No, this time he was a

194

large man in a sport jacket and black police pants. Typical cop shoes completed his smart outfit.

He was very easy to get rid of. I had only to change trains quickly at Odenplan. Now it was time to start looking around for number two; I was convinced that the cunning Kollin wanted me to notice the first.

I jumped off again at St. Eriksplan and began to stroll up and down the platform. Several trains came and went, but I waited. At last I had spotted him. A portly man of about fifty in a well-cut suit and with an umbrella hanging elegantly over one arm.

When the next downtown train came I took it, and got off at the central station. I went up to the snack bar in the main hall and had a beer.

The man with the umbrella stood at the foot of the stairs waiting. I let him do so for half an hour. With great satisfaction I noted that he had to keep shifting his weight from one leg to the other. It wouldn't hurt him to make some extra effort to earn his pay as a detective sergeant. Eventually I went down into the subway again. This time I got into a train going north. I stood in the first car.

With his umbrella swinging gracefully, my shadow stepped in and stood in the second car. Just as the doors were closing, I squeezed out and had the satisfaction of seeing the umbrella man trying in vain to do the same as his car passed me.

I was sorely tempted to poke out my tongue at him, but I restrained myself. There was, of course, a risk that Kollin had put a third man on my tracks, but I doubted that he had enough people to spare in vacation time.

At any rate, I went back to the central station and stood at the taxi stand. There were plenty of taxis, so I soon got one. I gave the driver the address at Aspudden, told him I was in a hurry, and off we went. Small technical inventions for traffic such as red lights and lanes didn't seem to bother him in the least. There are one or two drivers like that in Stockholm Taxi, and unfortunately their number is increasing. I'm always scared when I take a taxi anyway, and this idiot frightened the daylights out of me. He put me down at the right address and I paid him.

"Well, here's your goddam junkie's pad," he said, gunning off. Oho, so that's how it was.

Håkan had said that the name on the door was Nilsson. The apartment house was semi-old and dilapidated. Most of the names on the directory were foreign, but there was also a Nilsson. It was on the third floor. There was no elevator. I met an elderly woman on the stairs. She glared at me. I raised my hat politely and she looked astounded.

I was slightly out of breath when I got to the third floor and stood outside the door. I rang the bell, but nothing happened. I rang again but still nothing happened.

Then I pressed down the handle and tried the door. It was open.

I went in.

A few minutes later I called Kollin from a phone booth just outside. It must have been from there that Håkan had called me.

One Less

IT WAS EASIER to get through to Kollin this time. The gorgon put me on to him at once without any argument. I could imagine the reason.

"It's Berger," I said.

"You, is it, you bastard? What do you want?"

He didn't sound too happy. And he wouldn't be any happier when the conversation was over.

"Are you angry because I shook off the portly gent with the umbrella?"

"It was goddam unnecessary. Don't you understand we're keeping an eye on you for your own sake so that you won't get into trouble? You've done so twice already."

"Thanks for your concern. But as a matter of fact, I've gone and done it again."

"Hang on a minute," he said.

He was soon back.

"What do you mean?"

"There's no need for you to trace the call," I said.

I told him where I was.

"Well, what sort of trouble are you in?"

"It's not so much me as Håkan Lindgren," I said. "He's dead."

"I'll come right away. And stay where you are. Remember, for Christ's sake, or I'll wring your neck."

They were at the apartment in less than no time. First a patrol car. I went up to the two men in it.

"I'm Berger," I said. "Shall we go up, or do we wait for Kollin?"

"He said we were to wait," one of the constables said. "There's a junkie's pad in this house."

"So I've heard," I said.

Kollin arrived a few minutes later in a private car. He was accompanied by three other men with grave faces. People began to gather around us.

"Going to do something about it, at last, are you?" a white-haired man said. "About time too. The junkies have been in and out of here for months now."

"Come on," Kollin said.

We trudged up the stairs. If anything, it was farther this time.

"Here it is," I said. "It's open."

We went into the apartment, which was in a mess and indescribably dirty. Empty bottles, filthy, torn blankets, mattresses on the floor.

"Where is he?" Kollin asked.

"In the bathroom."

He pushed the door open with the point of his shoe and went in. I didn't need to follow him since I had already been in. Håkan Lindgren was hanging from the radiator. Apparently he had made a noose from some old electric cord, put it around his neck, and then leaned forward.

Kollin came out again quickly.

"Why did you come here?"

"He called me up and asked me to come."

"Why didn't you tell us?"

"He asked me not to. He was afraid of being locked up again. He said he couldn't stand it."

"Could he stand it now?"

Kollin's voice was full of suppressed rage.

"No," I said quietly.

"Was he hanging like this when you found him?"

"Yes. The door was open and I had a look around the apartment and only then did it occur to me to look in the bathroom too."

"And then you went out and called me up?"

"Yes."

"No one else here when you came?"

"No. Is it usual for them to hang themselves like that?"

"It happens."

The apartment was filling up now. The forensic technicians were setting up their apparatus, and the coroner was in the bathroom.

After a while he poked his head out.

"He hasn't been dead long," he said. "An hour at the most."

"Why didn't you cut him down?" Kollin asked.

"I saw that he was dead."

"Have you seen dead people before?"

"Many times. And when I saw that he was dead I didn't want to touch anything."

"What consideration for the police!" he exclaimed.

"Keep your temper now," I said. "I only wanted to help Håkan."

"*You* did! When you've had his wife with you all night."

"That's nothing to do with it. I can still have wanted to help Håkan."

"All right, all right," he said. "But you're damn well coming with us."

"Am I suspected of anything?"

"NO!" he roared. "But I've damn well got to get your story down in black and white, don't I?"

"Yes," I replied meekly.

"Can you cope with this for now?" Kollin asked one of the grave and silent men who had come with him.

"Sure."

The doctor came out of the bathroom, swinging a stethoscope around, around. He scratched his nose.

"It looks like suicide all right," he said. "But he must have been determined to take his life. What strength of mind to squat there and then throw yourself forward. Jesus!"

"Are you coming?" Kollin said to me.

"Yes."

As we were about to leave the apartment, he spoke to one of the lab men.

"You haven't found a farewell letter anywhere? They nearly always write one."

"No," replied the hefty, fair-haired technician whom I recognized from earlier cases. "But he took a fix before he did it. We've found a syringe out here."

"What color was it?" I asked.

He looked first at me and then at Kollin.

"The ordinary blue nonreturnable type," he said. "Why do you ask?"

I explained that I had found a similar syringe in Lindgren's stable.

"Oh, I see," he said, without showing the slightest interest.

I followed Kollin down the stairs in silence. Inquisitive people were standing on the staircase and outside the street door. We got into the car. Kollin drove. He seemed to have calmed down somewhat. I sat beside him and didn't utter a word during the drive from Aspudden to police headquarters at Kungsholmen. Not until we entered his office did he break his silence.

"Will you tell his wife?"

"Yes, of course."

"And his brother too?"

"Yes."

A new silence.

"Can't you see you're putting yourself in a damn bad light? Supposing it turns out not to be suicide, then you'll be the first to fall under suspicion."

"But it was suicide, wasn't it?"

199

"Yes, it seems like it, but you never know. I'm never damn well sure of anything before I know for certain."

"You said yesterday that I'd given you an idea."

"Did I?"

"Come off it. How has it worked out?"

"Time will show. Today, I think."

He wouldn't say any more. Then, I had to go out to a detective sergeant and give my account of how I had gone out to Aspudden and found Håkan Lindgren. Just before we had finished, Kollin looked in.

"Don't forget you've promised to notify his wife and his brother," he said.

No, I certainly hadn't forgotten.

"By the way," he said, "what you said about that phone number seems to be correct."

"What phone number?"

"The one you kept as a standing bet. I've checked up and it's correct."

"Of course it's correct."

I couldn't make out what he was driving at.

"I still bet on that number for sentimental reasons."

"What was it again?"

I couldn't help smiling.

"145 38," I said. "Had you forgotten?"

"No, but I wanted to see if you'd remembered it."

"You don't trust your fellow humans very much, do you?" I said.

"No, I'm afraid I don't."

"Getting back to Håkan, do you think he was the murderer and that that's why he committed suicide?"

"I don't know. It's possible, of course. Even probable."

"So, perhaps you regard the case as cleared up now?"

"That's not for me to decide. It's up to the homicide squad. I've promised to call up Ivarsson."

"Is he still at Årjäng?"

"Yes. Sending men to all the houses as usual. It's a mania with him, that door-to-door campaign."

"Well, I'll be seeing you," I said.

"No doubt," he replied.

Then a quick smile flitted over the stern face.

"It was clever of you to spot Hansson. He's the best man I have at shadowing." ·

I mumbled something by way of answer.

"Presuming now that Håkan did commit suicide, we have only three suspects left," I said.

"Who?"

"Ring, Jan Lindgren, and Anette."

"Four," Kollin said.

"But I thought Berggren was cleared? He'd got money from his brother."

"You're so modest, Berger. You're forgetting yourself."

Condolence

I took a taxi from police headquarters out to Solvalla, not bothering to check whether I was still being shadowed. I took it for granted, however, that Kollin was keeping an even more wary eye than usual on my doings.

I found Anette by the exit from the stable area to the track. She was perched on the rail like a bird, with stablemen on either side of her. I'm sure they were more interested in her than in the horses on the track.

One of these horses was my Stylist, and Janne was in the sulky.

Anette caught sight of me, hopped down from the rail, and came over to me.

"Hi," she said. "Janne's going to drive 2,000 with him."

"Håkan's dead," I announced abruptly.

"I was expecting it. Did he commit suicide?"

"Yes."

"I thought that's how it would end."

"You don't look very upset."

She tossed her head, sending her hair flying.

"No," she said. "I stopped grieving for him a couple of days ago, when I found out that he was not the man I thought he was. If anything, it's a relief now that he's dead."

"I was the one who found him, in a junkie's pad at Aspudden."

"Nothing surprises me any more."

In the middle of this condolence conversation she pressed her stop watch, as Janne started off on his two laps. On his offside, he had one of Solvalla's established racing stars.

"Now let's see how he stands up to Zolimit," she said.

I shut my eyes. Was she really as unconcerned as she made out? At any rate, it was not for me to induce her to act the part of the mourning widow.

"They opened 24 the first 500," she said to me.

Soon afterwards, the two horses passed us. Stylist was slightly bigger than Zolimit, but both had the same low, supple gait.

"He's good, by Christ, that Värmlander," said one of the guys on the rail.

"That's what I told you," Anette snapped. "They steadied down now. The first lap wasn't any faster than 27."

When they came around the next time, they were still steady. But in the middle of the last curve, Sören suddenly accelerated and Zolimit flew past Stylist with three or four lengths to spare. One of the guys on the rail scoffed.

"What do you say now?" he asked Anette.

"You wait," she replied calmly.

On the way back to the stables, I saw that Sören and Janne sat talking to each other. The next horse was already waiting for Sören and he jumped out of one sulky into the other.

Janne caught sight of me.

"Here's the owner," he said, pointing to me.

"Hello there," Sören greeted me, putting out a strong hand. "Not a bad horse you have there. Pity I haven't got it in training."

That was an unusual compliment coming from Sören Nordin. "Not bad" is about the most he will give when praising a horse.

"Janne says he's not for sale and *that* I can understand. But if you change your mind, I can probably come up with a buyer."

"We'll see," I said.

I was worried in case Nordin might say something about our

contacts in connection with training. But either he was discreet or else he had forgotten all about it. He hadn't seen me at the time, we had talked on the phone.

Anette took charge of Stylist and I asked Janne to come with me. We sat down on a bench. He seemed to guess what was coming.

"You look strange," he said. "Is it something to do with Håkan?"

"Yes, he's dead. Suicide."

I told him what had happened.

"Maybe it's just as well. He'd have ended up a wreck in any case. I want to remember him as he was a couple of years ago."

Håkan's death certainly didn't arouse any great grief in the next of kin. A thought struck me.

"Can you drive tomorrow?" I asked.

He gave me a look which implied that I understood very little of the realities of life and death.

"Why shouldn't I? My keeping out of the sulky won't bring him back to life."

He paused.

"Do the police think it was Håkan who killed Shag and the Railroader?"

"It's possible they do, but it's up to the homicide squad to decide."

"I see. Can I give you a lift into town? I'm going in to buy some clothes and one or two things."

"Thanks," I said.

As we drove out of the stable area, we met Bengt Ring and his new girl. Evidently he still had some money left from his winnings at BILECO.

"Serve him right that he didn't see Stylist's work," Janne said.

"Oh, word will get about."

He eyed me narrowly.

"I never spare horses in training in order to improve the odds," he said.

"I know that."

When I got home, I tried to reach Kollin on the phone, but it was impossible. According to the gorgon, he had gone out.

203

I asked to speak to someone else who was working on the investigation of Håkan Lindgren's suicide. At last I was put through to a detective inspector who said that his name was Tingvald Dudderud. With a name like that perhaps you can't help being a policeman. I told him who I was and I could tell from his voice how uncertain and cautious he became.

"I was only wondering whether it has been established that Lindgren committed suicide?" I asked.

"The pathologist is inclined to think so," Dudderud said.

"So, it's not certain?"

"No, but we're working according to the suicide theory."

"Nothing more to indicate that Lindgren is guilty of the murders in Värmland?"

"No."

"Has the press taken an interest in Lindgren's suicide?"

"Only the central news agency, which had been tipped off by all those amateurs who sit with the police radio switched on the whole time."

"Well?"

"We said that it looked like suicide and they backed out at once."

Dudderud sounded self-satisfied. He had tricked the press and it's not often the police succeed in doing that. I had one of my absurd attacks of wanting to protest.

"Then all you have to do is wait until my paper comes out tomorrow," I said.

"Are you really going to write about this?"

"Why, of course," I lied. "I'm onto a good thing."

"It depends how you look at it," Dudderud said thoughtfully. "I can never bring myself to think that suicide is a good thing."

I was about to say that Håkan's brother thought so, but held my tongue.

"No, you're right, of course," I said with lamblike meekness.

My reply put him off in the middle of his moral indignation over the vulture instincts of journalists.

"No, I feel that one should respect death in that case," Dudderud said.

204

"What's Kollin up to anyway? Is he out buying a car or has he gone to a porno shop?"

Tingvald Dudderud sounded really shocked.

"Now look here," he said sternly. "Inspector Kollin has gone to the Swedish Trotting Association for a conference."

"Well, I'll be damned," I said without thinking.

Kollin Again

I WAS HAVING DINNER when Kollin called up.

"Hi, there," he greeted me. "How are things?"

"Fine."

He sounded elated.

"I thought of going to Solvalla tomorrow. Can we meet there?"

"Sure," I said. "I'll probably be up in the press tower."

"See you there then."

"You sound very cheerful."

"Do you think so?"

"What did you do at the Trotting Association?"

"Checked something."

"How did it go?"

"Well. Damn well."

"Have you found out something?"

"Yes."

Then, of course, I tried to pump him, but failed.

"I can tell you more tomorrow," he said.

Tomorrow.

Thursday

Thursday came.

At midday it started to rain. It poured. The track would be heavy going by the evening. I called up Janne.

"How do you think he'll make out in this weather?"

"He's not at his best on a heavy track, but he won at Årjäng when it was also muddy."

"Shall I back him, do you think?"

"Heavily?"

"Depends on what you say, and on the odds."

"Pile it on," Janne said. "If nothing foreseen happens, he'll win. I've had people here today offering almost any price for him after his work yesterday."

"Do you still think I shouldn't sell?"

"If you get over a hundred thousand, then grab it. Any horse can break down. It's not so easy to scrape so much money together on the track."

"It could mean that you won't keep him for training."

"I know."

"I'll think it over."

Sam Boy

I went out to Solvalla early that evening. First, I took a turn down to the stables and found Stylist his usual indolent self.

It was still raining hard. Coming down in buckets. I heard on the radio that it was already approaching a record for Stockholm.

No Swedish sports crowd is more expert than that at Solvalla.

206

Trotting fans who go there are far above their ice hockey and football colleagues at Johanneshov and Råsunda. There are very seldom any public protests at Solvalla, despite all the money at stake. When people do react, there's a reason for it.

Foreign drivers who come to Solvalla are always impressed by the expertise of the spectators. Ask Johannes Frömming, Gerhard Krüger, or the French ace drivers. I once asked Hans Frömming about this. He agreed that the Solvalla crowds were in a class by themselves. "Here I can come second with a favorite and still be applauded when I drive back to the stable," the little German said. "That doesn't happen anywhere else I've driven."

It was so gray and murky that the lights were on, although it was in the middle of the summer. The spectators sought shelter from the rain in the new glass-enclosed grandstand, the restaurants, and any other place where they could keep dry.

At the stables I ran into Ring. The girl Chris was still with him.

"How are things?" he asked.

"Fine. Where's Mia?"

"In Karlstad with her mother; she'll be along in a few days. Is your horse going to win today?"

"He might," I replied.

"They say he went like a train yesterday?"

"Yes, he showed his paces very well. Did you hear that Håkan Lindgren is dead?"

"Yes, someone said so."

"Aren't you surprised?"

"I couldn't care less, to be honest. I mind my own business and let others mind theirs."

"Do you write about the entertainment business?" the girl asked.

"No, I'm afraid I don't. But I can mention you if I'm talking to the entertainment editor."

Her face lit up as if she had received a present.

"Oh, aren't you sweet!" she exclaimed. "If you want to see me sometime, you know where I work."

Ring swallowed a couple of times.

"Chris has one big talent," he said. "And she exploits it for all she's worth in every position."

"Why shouldn't she?"

"Why shouldn't she, is right!"

I left them and climbed the stairs to the press tower. It was only five thirty, but Kollin was already there, waiting. He was dressed in a light summer suit and looked like anything but a policeman. The wide-awake eyes studied me. He held a program in his hand and was writing out a ticket.

"Well, can I take your horse as a sure thing?"

"Yes, you can."

"Is he so goddam good?"

"Yes, he is."

He marked down his crosses after careful thought.

"How many columns are you betting?"

"Sixteen," he said.

"You're a real gambler."

"If you've nothing of the gambler in you, you'll never be a really good cop."

"And you're a good cop?"

"Sure," he said in a disarmingly matter-of-course tone. "I'm a damned good cop."

"What modesty," I said sarcastically.

"Why should I be modest over something I know is true?" he retorted. "I have my failings, God knows, but no one can say I'm not a damn good cop."

"So you've solved this riddle now, have you?"

"Not the ticket, but if you mean the murders, I do know the answer."

I stared at him as he drew another cross on the coupon.

I noticed what long fingers he had. He filled in the number of columns and the date and looked up.

"I thought Sam Boy was too good to be true," he said.

I said nothing, but let him go on.

"Sam Boy was a ringer," he disclosed. "I suppose you know what a ringer is?"

I did know. A ringer is a horse with false registration papers. I nodded to let Kollin know I was with him.

"As I said, I thought Sam Boy was too good to be true, especially as Ring usually buys old nags to be able to write them

208

off in his tax returns. Luckily, they still had the blood specimens at the laboratory and could run a test to establish parentage."

"And it didn't fit?"

"No. Whoever the father of Sam Boy is, it's not Prince Sam. He's not to blame. It's by no means the first time that horses were exchanged like that."

No, it has happened several times. The most advanced experiment in that line was carried out by a couple of farmers from Dalsland when they exchanged their nags for considerably faster Norwegian horses. They got away with it for a long time—they were very cunning—and made a lot of money before being finally found out.

"Well, who staged it?" I asked. "Was it Ring?"

"Think hard now, Berger. Is he really the most likely one? No, the guy we're going to nab the minute he has driven your goddam horse is, of course, Jan Lindgren."

Janne

"WERE YOU REALLY as surprised as you seem?" Kollin asked. "I can't think that."

"I've had my suspicions about him," I said, "but I couldn't think of a motive."

"I see."

"Have you a lot of men here this evening?"

"Yes, we've placed them here and there," he replied. "We want to avoid a lot of fuss, so we're letting him drive."

I put on my raincoat and Kollin did the same.

"I'll just hand in my ticket," I said.

"So will I."

We went down and had our coupons stamped. I had put together a coupon with ninety-six columns and Stylist a certainty.

There were no spectators yet. Only a few genuine fanatics stood leaning on the rail, mostly kids and teen-agers.

We made our way up to the press tower again. Kollin was completely relaxed. Calm and confident.

"But surely you must have a bit more than that before you can arrest him," I said.

"Not much more than circumstantial evidence so far, but we'll fix that. It can't be anyone else. Oh, one thing. Do you remember that he gave you a lift from the race track at Årjäng to Bjarne Svensson's home?"

"Yes."

"You said he drove straight there. As far as we can find out, he had never been there before. So, how was it he drove straight there without asking you the way?"

I said nothing.

"And he was certainly very smart after Karlsson-Gren's murder," Kollin went on. "He drove out to exercise a tender-footed horse on the forest roads, didn't he?"

"Yes."

"Lindgren, who was always so particular about his appearance, drove in shabby old coveralls. You remember that too."

Indeed I did.

"Well, we think he had his bloodstained clothes on under the coveralls. During the training drive, he hid the clothes somewhere. But we'll find them, don't you worry."

"Håkan must have been in on it," I said.

He nodded.

"Presumably. But his nerves couldn't stand the strain."

We were sitting by ourselves up in the press tower. The atmosphere was unreal. Trotting journalists whom I knew walked past but none had any idea what we were talking about.

"You'll have the scoop on all this to yourself," Kollin said.

"I don't care. I like Lindgren a lot."

"So you didn't think him capable of this? Wanting to make money out of a ringer? We think he exchanged the horses when one of his fast horses suddenly became ill a couple of years ago. It was a bay rather like Sam Boy. It was sent to the glue factory, but it was Sam Boy who ran in the race. The blood tests don't exclude that possibility."

"Shag must have found out and told the Railroader," I said.

"Very likely, but all that will come out at the interrogation."

"Don't you think he suspects anything? He's not dumb."

"No, he's not dumb, but he hasn't a chance to get away."

Stylist was to run in the first race. The horses filed past. Lindgren looked just as usual. He made a trial start with Stylist, who caught on at once. He seemed spry.

The favorite in the race was the Wallner horse, a small stallion who made a good impression in a couple of quick trial starts. The indicator showed that both he and Stylist hovered around 2.50. Evidently, the word had gotten out about Stylist's quick work.

For that matter, a couple of the countless tips papers had noticed Stylist during training and had hoisted a warning flag.

But in a second trial start Stylist broke into a long, angry gallop. What was the cause of that? He didn't usually behave like that. The gallop immediately affected the indicator. The odds on Wallner's horse dropped to two and for Stylist rose to 3.25.

"Why is he galloping?" Kollin asked.

"We want to push the odds up," I said.

I stood up to leave and place my bet. Kollin came with me, obviously not wanting to lose sight of me. I put 500 on Stylist to win. Actually, I should have put on a lot more, but I didn't dare to bet so heavily these days.

When we got back to the press tower Anette was waiting for us.

"I was here anyway placing a bet, so I came up," she said to me.

"May I introduce Detective Inspector Lars Kollin from the Stockholm police. This is Mrs. Anette Lindgren."

She looked hard at us.

"Something's wrong," she said.

"What would that be?" Kollin asked gently. "Nothing is wrong. Everything is as it should be. Berger and I are old acquaintances. I came out because his horse is racing."

"You can stay here during the race, can't you?" I asked.

"If you like."

She was still rather suspicious.

There were fourteen horses in the race. On the 20-volt there were four, with Stylist on the outside. Wallner had the seventh track on the first volt and took the lead at once.

Janne was in no hurry. He dropped behind one of the other horses in the volt and stayed there quietly during the first lap. In the straight he made a spurt and Stylist strode majestically past some competitors toward the lead in the third pair on the outside.

When there were 700 left Lindgren began to drive. My giant found it rather heavy going in the mud, but coming down the straight he did struggle up alongside Wallner's Amery.

"He's tired," I said to Anette.

"Don't worry. He'll win," she said confidently. "Janne has some in reserve. Trust me."

It was neck and neck between the two all the way down the straight. The drivers rocked and jolted, but neither of them used the whip. I watched them through the field glasses and fifty yards before the finish, I saw Lindgren look about him. At the last moment he put the whip to Stylist's rump and the rascal shook himself and gained a yard or so. Then Amery seemed to catch up and I wasn't sure of the outcome.

"Stylist won," Anette said. "I looked at the sulky wheels. But my goodness, Janne was slack. And why does he keep looking around him like that?"

"We're waiting for the photo finish," the loudspeaker announced. "But the place horses are known." And the voice read them out.

Janne climbed down from the sulky and went and stood beside Stylist while he waited for the result of the photo finish. Now and then he stroked the horse over the muzzle.

The loudspeaker again:

"The winner is number 12—Stylist."

"There, you see," said Anette with a note of triumph in her voice. "But why doesn't he drive up?"

No, Janne certainly wasn't in any hurry for the post parade. He seemed to be having trouble with the reins.

And then I realized what was going to happen.

In the field glasses, I saw Janne make the reins fast on Stylist's back. Then he glanced around him quickly a couple of times and suddenly leaped over the fence. As he raced across the empty space by the entrance, he pulled off his driving colors.

A few seconds later he had vanished like a ghost in the rain.

212

Kollin watched the scene without looking too worried.

"He won't get far," he said. "I have men outside every entrance. I expect they've caught him already."

The Confession

KOLLIN TURNED OUT to be right on every point.

Lindgren was seized by three detectives who were standing on guard outside the entrance. He put up a halfhearted resistance but, on the whole, he seemed relieved it was all over. He was allowed to rest overnight, but in the car on the way to police headquarters he confessed that he had murdered Shag and the Railroader.

When he had had a good sleep in one of the cells, he went on with his confession. The record of the interrogation cleared up a number of points.

"What was your motive?"

"Money, of course."

"Were you in financial difficulty?"

"Not at all, but the more you have the more you want."

"Did your brother know that Sam Boy was a ringer?"

"Not at first, but he soon found out. He had an astonishing knack of recognizing horses. I trained Sammy."

"When you say Sammy, you mean the horse whose real name was Juniper?"

"Yes. I trained him at home on the farm, but as soon as I took him in to the track, Håkan recognized him."

"And then you bet on Sam Boy?"

"Yes, we could decide ourselves when he was to win."

"No one else was informed about the horse's real identity? The owner for instance?"

"Ring? No, he didn't know anything. He can hardly see the difference between a mare and a stallion."

"Let's go on to Sam Boy's death on the race track; had you doped him?"

"No, why should I? He was a splendid source of income."

"And your brother didn't fix his death either?"

"No, he didn't. I can't prove anything, of course, but I imagine that Sammy was stung by a gadfly and dashed into the wall in sheer panic."

"Then the vet's barn burned down. Had you anything to do with that?"

"Yes, I set fire to it."

"Why? The horse wasn't doped, you said just now."

"I was afraid his identity might be discovered. I realized that there was a possibility of being found out, that way."

"As you may remember, Mr. Berger was beaten up twice during his stay at Årjäng. Were you, by any chance, behind that too?"

"Yes, I fixed it with Conny. I knew him through Ring. But that was only the first time. The second was the guys' own idea."

"We come now to your brother's suicide. For I take it that it *was* suicide?"

"It must have been. At any rate I had nothing to do with that. Håkan was at the end of his rope. He couldn't go on. His nerves were never very strong, anyway. He got jittery very easily. I think that's why he couldn't keep going as a trainer. Too much stress for him. And the way Anette ran after other men didn't help matters."

"Yourself, for instance."

"For instance, yes."

"She didn't know about Sam Boy?"

"No."

"How did you find out that Karlsson-Gren knew that Sam Boy was a ringer?"

"He told me the same day the horse died."

"Did he try to blackmail you?"

"No, not at all, but I was certain that he wouldn't be able to keep his mouth shut for long."

"What about Svensson?"

"That was proof that Shag couldn't keep his mouth shut. He

had blabbed to the Railroader, and then when Shag died . . ."

"Yes?"

"Well, then the Railroader came to me."

"And wanted money to keep quiet?"

"Exactly."

"And so he died, too?"

"Well, what was I to do?"

Yes, what was he to do? And what would I have done in his shoes?

I don't know.

End and Beginning

I GOT A GOOD STORY that Thursday evening at Solvalla. Praise from the editor, too, and that never does any harm. You always have to see that you're noticed by the big chiefs. The worst thing possible is to be forgotten.

Next day it was decided that the head stableman in Lindgren's stable, for the time being, was to manage the flourishing concern that the Lindgren brothers had left. Soon the horses would be dispersed to different trainers, and in a few years the whole thing would be forgotten.

Stylist remained in Stockholm, and I managed to talk Sören Nordin into taking charge of his training.

Anette also remained in Stockholm. With me.

I lived in the best of worlds.

"Are you going to keep on with trotting?" I asked her.

"I don't know. Maybe I'll get a job with a trainer here in town. There are so many to choose from."

"So you haven't tired of trotting?"

"No, why should I have?"

Her surprise seemed sincere. I made the reflection that there might be several reasons for her to give up trotting, which had robbed her of so much the last few days.

"It's no good crying over spilled milk," she said.

I agreed with her.

"All the same, I'm finding it hard to get over Håkan's suicide," I said.

"Yes, of course," she admitted. "But Håkan was at the end of his rope."

The same words that I was to read a few days later in Kollin's interrogation report of Janne. His sister-in-law was equally convinced that Håkan was done for.

She had a dreamy look in her eyes as she sat in my best easy chair with her arms around her drawn-up knees. She seemed extraordinarily content with life. No sudden fits of weeping any more.

"Do you think you can cope with me?" she asked.

I smiled. Arrogantly, I hoped.

"I'm sure I can."

"Maybe."

And without looking at me she added, "I wonder whether Håkan and Janne ever suspected that I knew that Sam was a ringer. As credulous as children, both of them. A good thing to have the money anyway."

As credulous as children!

And what was I? At any rate, I wasn't arrogant any longer. I already hated her slightly and wanted to get rid of her. When she tricked them so thoroughly, she was not likely to behave any differently toward me.

But I would find a way out all right. I usually do. As when Håkan went to pieces with drugs and I let him commit suicide just to have Anette to myself.

"You and I can have a good time now that we're rid of them both," she said.

There was only one way to be rid of *her*. I must watch my step and not make any mistake.

"This is only the beginning for us," she went on dreamily.

The beginning of the end for you, Anette.